CALIBAN'S COLT

Nelson Nye

WESTERNS

First published 1950
by Dorchester Publishing Co., Inc
of New York City

This hardback edition 1991
by Chivers Press
by arrangement with
Dorchester Publishing Co., Inc

ISBN 0 86220 989 7

British Library Cataloguing in Publication Data

Nye, Nelson
  Caliban's colt.
  I. Title
  813.52

ISBN 0–86220–989–7

The characters, places, incidents and situations in
this book are imaginary and have no relation to any
person, place or actual happening

Printed and bound in Great Britain by
Redwood Press Limited, Melksham, Wiltshire

CALIBAN'S COLT

CALIBAN'S COLT

For years the feud had been festering like an open wound. On one side was Starl Crefts, the most vicious man in the territory. He was eating up land like a starving wolf, and no one stood in his way.

Against him was young Danny Brockett, inexperienced and untried, but unbending in his determination. He swore he'd leave his bones bleaching in the sun before he'd let any man push him off his ranch.

But he needed more than guts. He needed the wild stallion they called Caliban's colt. Bred to be the finest stud in Arizona, Caliban's colt was now an outlaw, feared and despised, hunted and shot at . . . like Danny himself. Together they had about as much chance against Crefts as spit on a griddle, but they'd rather die than live as cowards . . .

Also available from Gunsmoke

NEW BOSS AT WAGONWHEEL

THE DAUNSY LOOK which had fallen over young Dan Brockett's features since the death of his father two weeks before appeared to be somewhat lifted as he stepped out of the Wagonwheel ranch house and let the warped screen door slam behind him. It was not a cheerful look he flung over the patched and sagging fences, the ramshackle barn and the whoppyjawed corrals, but it was a less morose look than his face had been accustomed to wearing and Wishbone Reilly, soaking up sun on the bunkhouse bench, knocked out his pipe and growled a greeting. "World must be treatin' you better this mornin'."

"Where's the boys?" Danny asked, looking around him curiously.

"I got 'em to workin' that south fence ag'in. You jest can't git wire t' stay on them posts—you know how them blasted steeples pops out! What you got on your mind, young feller?"

Danny said: "You remember this place ten years ago?"

The foreman grinned. "When your Dad an' me had jest got back from the war? *Do* I—Golly!" The old man's eyes brightened up like gold eagles. "This here," Wishbone said, "was a *real spread* in them days—greatest hoss-raisin' outfit in all Arizony! Wagonwheel on a hoss meant the top o' the market. Why, folks used t' come here from——"

"What made them quit?"

All the fire went out of old Wishbone's eyes. He seemed to wizzle and shrink like all the breath was wrung out of him. And that remembered grayness crossed his cheeks and deepened the lines around his eyes and mouth. It was astonishing how a man so robust could suddenly appear so frail and frozen.

It was a phenomenon Danny had witnessed before.

For the long last ten of his eighteen years—for almost as long as Reilly'd been foreman—Dan could remember these same dire shifts and changes, stretching back through the years in ever more closely recurring attacks to that black and blustery wind-riven night when Starl Crefts and his men had come rampaging into the Wagonwheel yard and driven off ten of his Dad's best saddlers.

Danny never had been able to get the straight of that business. It was never discussed—or not to his knowing—was never fetched spang into the open and threshed out once and for all and forgotten. The events of that night had been wiped off the books, like the horses Starl Crefts and his men had gone off with—indeed, right many a time Danny'd caught himself wondering if that whole nightmare sequence were not just something choused up out of dreams.

But he knew better than that.

It had happened, all right. Too many things had been changed by that night, too many things dated back to it. Before it this ranch had been a real place, a tophand concern that was the envy of many. And this house, now fallen on evil days, had been the home of gracious living, of sunlight and laughter, the secure abode of trust and confidence. Its spacious rooms had been friendly with people, its stables filled with sleek horses, its yard with the excitement of many comings and goings.

All that was changed.

In a twinkling, it seemed, the whole world had turned over, thrown off its axis by the Spanish-American War. His Dad's sickness—result of injuries sustained at San Juan Hill or perhaps during some of the jungle fighting—had gradually worsened until, wasting away, he had taken to his bed in a shaking fever. Danny's mother had died and everything connected with the running of the ranch had been turned over to this strangely changed Wishbone who never again had laughed from that night.

But that night of Crefts' visit wasn't mentioned. It had been sponged away like spilled milk from a floor—a skeleton carefully locked in a cupboard, strangled and consigned to the dark corners of men's minds, sealed by silence but not forgotten.

Something of this thinking was in Danny's voice when he asked again with a suggestion of impatience: "What made them quit?"

3

"Well, you know how it is," Wishbone sighed, getting hold of himself. "People move away . . . git into other businesses—nothin' ever stays the same in this world. A man ups and changes jest like fads and fashions does. One minute you're up and the next you're plumb outen it."

He put his pipe in his pocket, wiped his hands on his trousers. He shifted his look to the tumbledown corrals where the horse he generally used when he found need of one stood on three legs and dozed in the sun. A fly droned past and he said more purposefully, "I expect I'd better git——"

"Just a minute," Danny broke in. "I'm not through talkin'. I'd like to understand better what's happened to this place. You tell me ten years ago our stuff was in demand; now we can't hardly even *give* a horse away— what's the matter with them, anyhow? I've been lookin' them over. Some of our horses look to be right good ones."

"Oh, they're good enough, I reckon—if you kin find someone t' buy 'em."

"What'd you get for that bunch you took to Tucson three months ago?"

"Them yearlin's? Round twenty-five apiece."

"What did we used to get for our yearlin's?"

"Times change," Wishbone said as though he were tired of the subject. "What a man gits today ain't no indication of what he'll git ten years from now."

"But we got a deal more than twenty-five apiece, didn't we?"

4

"If I remember correckly, we got aroun' three hundred. But, like I said, we didn't hev no trouble gittin' rid o' colts then. Our big problem in them days was tryin' t' hold out a few."

"That," Danny said, "is what I'd like to find out about—about how come this change. About how come they've all taken to buyin' their horses elsewhere."

Wishbone looked at his hands without comment.

"I been goin' through the books," Danny told him. "Ten years ago we had fifty-eight head in our colt crop. Last year we had twelve. This year nine——"

"It was your Dad's idee that we had ort t' cut down. After all, where's the sense raisin' colts you can't sell? It costs money t' raise stock in this country . . . we ain't had a real rain in the las' three year. When you got t' feed stock out, you got t' git good prices, if you're a-goin' t' break even. Your Dad knowed——"

"I'm not arguin' that. I'm not even complainin' about the shape of our stuff. I know a horse can't be expected to look like much when he's turned out on the desert eight months out of the year. What I can't seem to get through my head," Danny growled, "is why this whole country stopped *buyin'* horses from us."

Wishbone stirred and looked off toward the corrals with the air of a man kept away from his work.

It riled Danny up in a way. Wishbone had been bossing this outfit for going on ten years and no one had ever had to tie him up to keep the old codger from overworking himself. About the hardest chore Wishbone put in time at was sitting around wishing that things would get better.

Not that Danny didn't like old Wishbone. He was the salt of the earth and, in his Army days, had been known as one of the best dang hoof-shapers in Roosevelt's cavalry. But every time Danny looked around and saw the sad plight of this once great ranch, it made him ache to see how the outfit was being let go to ruin. Wishing, no doubt, was all right in its place but what this spread needed was a little elbow grease and he proposed to see that it got some.

"You can start right now to pullin' down those corrals," he told his Dad's foreman in the crisp business tone used by J. Cornelius Herald, the Squawberry Flats banker. "Long as this place looks the wreck it does now, a man can't much blame folks for not comin' round here. We'll rebuild those corrals for a starter. Then we'll get at that barn and——"

"Great sakes!" Wishbone gaped, with his jaw hanging down like a blacksmith's apron. "What in the world are you figgerin' t' do that fer?"

"I'd like to look at this ranch like it was ten years ago."

Wishbone peered at the determined look of him, stared a long while and then slowly shook his head. "Well, you won't never do it—never in this world," he said with conviction. "You might jest as well try t' move the Cobble Mountains. Dawgone!" he groaned, shaking his head again. "Don't you know it would take a young fortune t' put this place back in shape? An' where would be the sense in it?"

"As for that," Danny said, "we will cross that bridge when we come to it."

"Eh? Come to it? Sufferin' snakes! We won't never git within spittin' distance of it—'twould take twice the men you got on your payroll t' even make a dent in the work thet's piled up here. I done what I could but it takes cash in hand t' run a spread big as this one. You can't git blood out of a rutabaker, boy!"

He blew out his cheeks and snorted. But gradually his features settled into their accustomed creases and he shook his head sadly as he looked Danny over. "You show a fine, healthy spirit, which is a good thing t' see in a boy o' your age—puts me in mind of your Daddy, how he used t' tie into things. But there's no sense battin' your head ag'in' a wall. There's things in this world that a man jest can't tangle with . . . and this here ranch is one of 'em."

Danny smiled. "A man can try, I guess, can't he?"

A forlorn kind of pity peered from Wishbone's eyes. "You don't understand, boy. There's times I don't rightly understand myself, but I can tell you this: There ain't no amount o' work goin' t' put this ranch back into operation."

"Why not?" Danny asked, for he was never the one to be licked before he started. "How come there ain't?"

"Because—" Wishbone said: "Jest because, by godfreys!"

"Because ain't no reason. It took more than 'because' to put the skids under this place."

"Aye," Wishbone growled. "An' more'll be brought, you kin lay t' that! You jest lift up one finger t' better this spread——"

He broke off and peered around, looking over his shoulder.

"Yeah?" Danny scoffed. "And then what'll happen?"

Wishbone turned a frozen face with his eyes white-ringed like a stallion bronc's. "Don't do it, boy—don't you do it!"

That gray look was back in the lines of his cheeks and the rasp of his voice was like an old frog's croak.

It came over Danny suddenly that this was fright which he saw in the foreman's features, and he looked over his shoulder with his own breath quickening. What could there be to scare Wishbone like that in merely the thought of trying to rebuild Wagonwheel?

With his mind pawing over the likeliest answers, he looked a long while at his Dad's old friend, but he did not arrive at any helpful conclusions.

Wishbone *was* scared, and it wasn't just the prospect of work that uneased him. Of that much Danny felt certain. But what there could be about the idea of rebuilding Wagonwheel to throw the old man into such a gray sweat was a bit more than Danny could get his teeth into.

Nor could he figure out why Wishbone's look should unsettle him, yet it did. It juned up a queer, prickly feeling inside him, like the feeling he'd had that time the horse threw him among the rocks of the creek winding through the south pasture. A kind of foreboding, a presentiment of disaster.

But he shook it off, even managed a parched grin. He took a deep breath and said earnestly, "It's time this ranch got a new lease on life. If it raised the best horses ten years ago, it can do it again. Get your sleeves rolled up and——"

"Good for you!" a voice cried, and they both whirled about to see Paula Herald, the tomboyish daughter of J. Cornelius, thrusting a leg through a hole in the fence.

FREE ADVICE FROM A LAWYER

THEY WATCHED her wriggle through and come on across the yard at a stride more natural in a boy than in a girl. But that was just like her. Everything she did she seemed to do at a swagger. She could fork any horse and never pull leather; she could shinny up a pole. She knew about guns and could shoot about as good as Dode Forney, the sheriff. She could wrestle like a boy and was no more scared to do it. "Wild as Paula Herald" was a saying in that country.

" 'Lo, Snooper," Danny grunted.

She looked thoughtful this morning and only stuck out her tongue as a matter of habit. Stuffing the tail of her shirt in her Levis, she said to Danny soberly, "I hope you meant that."

"About fixin' up the ranch? 'Course I meant it—why wouldn't I? Don't you reckon the place could stand it?"

"Yeah, but . . . " She considered him a moment, blue eyes weighing him with an unaccustomed earnestness.

"You'll be boss of this place now. What are you going to do with it?"

"Fix it up like I told you."

"And then what?"

Danny threw her a frown. "Try to run it, of course. Try to make it pay out."

"Yeah, but how?"

Danny studied her. He couldn't think what she was getting at, nor why she should suddenly appear so serious. He saw her look over at the tumbledown barn, the whoppyjawed posts of the sagging corral.

He said, "Ten years ago this here was a ranch, and a good one. When my Dad was up and about, the Wagonwheel brand on a horse stood for something. It was full guarantee you were feastin' your eyes on a real *runnin' horse*—as good a sprinter as could be found in the country."

Then he added a little defiantly: "I been figgerin' to make it mean that again."

"Good for you!" cried Snooper. "That's just what I was hoping you would tell that old gander!"

Then the intense look of her toned down and softened. She said, "But can you do it?"

Wishbone snorted. " 'Course he can't do it—he's jest whistlin' at the moon! It's all well an' good fer a feller t' ack like he could whip his weight in wildcats, but any dang kid in three-cornered pants would savvy it'd take a mort of cash t' put this spread where it was ten year ago. Where's he t' git it? Pick it off the bushes?"

Danny met Paula's look and didn't speak for a moment. Her father was a banker and if he wanted to be right neighborly, he could loan Danny enough to get the place put back in shape. The place was still worth more than that much money; but there was no answering light in the look Paula gave him.

"Well, I'll get it," Danny said. "You just leave it to me."

But he couldn't quite choke back the sigh that came out as his glance, following Paula's, saw everywhere the signs of neglect and shiftlessness that marked this for a "haywire" outfit. Who would loan money on a spread in this shape? Some rancher, maybe, who knew the Wagonwheel's background, but never a banker.

There was no use fooling himself about that.

Everything was against it—even his size. For he was not a rawboned, husky young giant, like so many of the ranchers' sons in this region. His father, Duke Brockett, had fit into this country, one hundred and eighty-six pounds of pure man who could break down a door with one blow of his fist when he'd gone with a grin to join the Rough Riders.

But that grin and this run-down ranch, to all intents and purposes, were all that his Dad had bequeathed to young Danny. In size and appearance he took more after his Maw, a frail Southern woman who had died before her time.

Even in his boots he could barely hit the mark at five foot two and, although he ate like a horse, the best he could do on the scales was 120—and he wouldn't weigh that when he was stripped down. No one ever called him "Dan," for that was a man's name; he was just "that

Brockett boy" to the folks who did business around Squawberry Flats.

He might as well try to fly as to try to borrow money.
And, if his size weren't enough, his age would have licked
him. Age and size together gave him no chance at all and,
deep in his bones, Danny mighty well knew it. Old Wishbone was right, he was whistling at the moon.

He shrugged and grinned ruefully as he met Paula's
glance.

"Anyway," he said, "if hard work counts for anythin',
I'll manage *some* way to get the place fixed up. I've got
good health and I ain't afraid of work."

Paula said impulsively: "*I* believe in you, Danny—and
I'll help you!"

Wishbone sniffed. "Talk's cheap," he said, "but it takes
hard cash t' git anyplace in this country——"

"I've got a crew," Danny said. "We got everything we
need right here on the place. We can pull enough planks
off those sheds to fix the barn. The corrals are like the
fences. Most of the timber's good, all they need is rebuilding. With you and me and the crew all workin'——"

"I expect," sighed Wishbone tiredly, "it's time you was
told a few hunks of the truth. This spread ain't made
expenses in the last eight years; it taken all your Daddy
saved jest t' keep it goin'. The crew ain't had a payday in
goin' on three months. Curley's got a wife—he can't keep
workin' fer nothin'. Tol' me jest this mornin' he'll be
pullin' out tonight. Limpy's got a chanct t' git put on at
the B Bar. Duckfoot—Cripes, the smartest thing you could

do with this place would be t' onload it onto the highest bidder—an' I mean *now!*"

He slogged off his hat and bitterly cuffed the bunkhouse wall. He clamped on the hat again, glowering, and screwed up his face and spat. He did everything Paula could think of except meet Danny's look.

"I know you been countin' big on gittin' this spread built up ag'in—I've seen it workin' in you like yeast in a barrel o' moonshine beer. Gosh knows I hate t' talk this way but whatever you do'll be wasted. You might jest as well pour sand down a rat hole!"

A choking silence gripped the yard.

"But," breathed Paula dismally, "if he could manage to fix it up a little——"

"Looks won't be makin' no difference. He'll git one price an' one price only."

Something passed between them and the girl's eyes darkened but Danny was too lost in his thoughts to notice.

He said stubbornly: "It made money once——"

"Aye. Duke Brockett had a way with him an' he had strength besides."

Old Wishbone's voice trailed off and quit. His eyes and thoughts went far away.

Danny kicked at a horse apple.

The old man's eyes came back and he sighed as though all the weight of the world were on him. "I reckon I shouldn't never of come here."

Paula said: "Well—" and shut her mouth.

Wishbone put a wrinkled hand on Danny's shoulder. "You got a mort o' spunk fer a lad your size. But as your

14

Daddy's ol' friend, I'd be a ingrate an' worse if I encouraged you in tryin' t' patch up this place. A man can't fight ag'in' fate, Danny."

"What's fate got to do with it?" Danny growled. He shook off Wishbone's hand and started for the toolshed.

"Where you off to?"

"I'm goin' for a crowbar and get to work."

"Fetch me one, too!" Paula called out after him.

Wishbone shook his head and said nothing.

But when Danny came back with the pair of bars Wishbone said, "I'll take the big one."

"Thought you didn't want any part of this business?" Paula said.

"It's still Danny's ranch an' tearin' down corrals ain't no work fer a girl——"

"Girl yourself!" Paula scoffed. "Don't you worry about *me!* Is there another of those bars in the toolshed, Danny?"

"You hold the posts while we pry them loose. I guess we better take the stud corral first."

They followed Wishbone over, never noticing the dust coming up the road. They watched Wishbone try a post with his hand and saw that it was all he could do to budge it. "Kinda solid," he said. "If they're all like this, we'll hev our work cut out. Whereabouts you wantin' t' start on it, Danny?"

"Might's well start at the gate and work round. Reckon we'll need a pick?"

Wishbone scowled sourly. "More like we need our heads examined. Here—lemme try this gatepost. Ugh!"

He threw a glance at Paula. "Hop over t' thet shed an' fetch me the pick-axe."

She was off like a shot and pretty soon she was back with it.

Wishbone hefted it and spit on his hands.

"Wait a minute," Danny said. "Let me sink a few holes around it first with this bar. . . . You reckon these posts is in solid caliche?"

"Of course," Paula ventured, "you wouldn't *have* to move the posts. Couldn't you just refasten the poles across them?"

Wishbone scowled. Danny felt a little chagrined himself. That was always the trouble with having Snooper around you. She was a great hand for making suggestions and, too frequently, they were good ones.

"We could try it, I guess," he said somewhat testily, and threw down his bar. "Take the other end, Wishbone, and see if you can get that balin' wire unsnaggled."

They had all been so busy not a one of them had noticed the roan horse and buggy now pulled up beside the ranch house door. Nor did they see the well-fed and frock-coated figure that, with a reefed umbrella, was getting out of the vehicle as though a scorpion had crawled up his pantsleg. But all heard the man's clomping boots and irate shout.

"I'll thank ye to leave that corral fence alone!"

Wishbone dropped his pick.

"Lawyer Teel!" gasped Paula, and Danny gaped at him in dismay.

Folks would rather see buzzards roosting clean across

their rooftops than to see Moses Teel coming in at the gate.

By conservative estimate he had dispossessed more hard-up people than the British had driven out of Nova Scotia. He wore mutton-chop whiskers and spectacles with a black ribbon and the only beaver hat seen in Folderall County. Across his ample and rumbling paunch he packed a gold watch chain that looked like a cable and he never appeared in public without his folded-up umbrella.

But for all of these foibles and his fussbudgety ways, he had seldom been known to inspire much laughter. Folderall folks didn't laugh at vermin and he was generally regarded as being three degrees lower than the belly of a snake.

He was lawsuit man for the country's biggest mogul, grasping Starl Crefts. He was the thumbscrew used by Crefts' Clover Cross Land and Cattle Company for liquidating anything which stood in its way. He was a sanctimonious rascal, and everybody knew it.

He hadn't come into the yard twenty paces when Poncho, the black shepherd, woke up and came out of the shade of a greasewood in a barking rush that stopped Teel in midstride. With a white-cheeked snarl the man flung up his umbrella and only then did Danny, reminded of common courtesy, call the dog off.

"Cur like that can get a man in trouble," the lawyer growled, still glowering.

Poncho was no cur but Danny let the matter pass. "He doesn't act like that often. It must have been the loud way you were talking. Would you care to sit on the porch

17

where it's cooler?" he asked politely, but Moses Teel ignored him, running his jaundiced eyes over the place.

Danny could not think what had fetched the man here, but a mounting dread came to cramp and quiver his stomach as the attorney waddled up to them and severely inspected the poles of the corral across the tops of his steel-rimmed cheaters.

Paula's eyes were big around as saucers and she instinctively shrank away as Teel's uncharitable gaze passed over her and came intolerantly to rest upon the worried face of Danny.

"I take it you're the Brockett boy," Teel said.

Danny nodded.

"Then I expect you're the fellow I've come out here to see."

Moses Teel took off his spectacles and polished them with great care. Putting them back on his nose, he skewered old Wishbone with a testy glance. "What's this fellow hanging round here for?"

Danny said, "That's Wishbone Reilly—he's the foreman of this ranch."

"You don't have to tell me," the lawyer said in the grating tones of a gate hinge skrieking. "I know all about him." He brought his glance back to Danny. "I don't wonder I find the place so poorly. Way it stands right now, we'd be lucky to get ten cents on the dollar."

"*We!*" Danny gasped, suddenly finding his voice. "Where do *you* come in on it? If you came out here to talk me into sellin' this ranch, you've just wasted your time."

"Indeed," said the lawyer, pursing up his lips. "I'm relieved to hear you say so. I had hardly expected you to have the cash——"

"Cash?" Danny stared at him blankly. "Cash? You been touched by the sun?" he demanded with a scowl. "What cash are you talkin' about?"

The lawyer looked about with a lofty contempt. "A stableyard hardly seems quite the place to transact business——"

"Looks kind of like you've got tangled up somewhere. I've no business to transact——"

"Quite right," Teel said. "I thank you for reminding me." And he turned his uncharitable look on Wishbone. "The boy's entirely right, for a child has no business. When Duke Brockett's will was probated you were named as this boy's guardian, Reilly."

He looked his disapproval, sniffed and said in a righteous manner: "Under the terms of the will the estate was left in trust to him, you to be its manager until such time as he should come of age. The whole thing was—shall we say 'unorthodox'? My client, of course, should have presented his claim before the will was probated. Against my advice, he chose to wait, however. He took a natural Christian viewpoint, not wishing to involve the boy in a maze of litigation."

He paused to adjust his spectacles and looked at Wishbone sharply. "As man to man, Mr. Reilly, I naturally supposed the lad would wish to sell the place and reimburse my client——"

"Reimburse 'im fer what?" asked Wishbone.

"When a man borrows money doesn't he usually pay it back?"

"Danny ain't borried nothin'," Wishbone said uneasily.

"Danny, no. But the sins of the fathers . . ." Moses Teel spread his hands. "My client, Mr. Crefts——"

"So that's it!" Wishbone growled, starting forward. But a look from the lawyer stopped him dead in his tracks.

"As I was saying," Teel resumed, "my client, Mr. Crefts, holds a mortgage on this place——"

"I don't believe it!" Danny cried.

"What you believe, or do not believe, is not very likely to butter any parsnips." The lawyer sniffed. "You may take my word for it Crefts holds a mortgage. This mortgage secures a short-term note given by your father——"

"You'll have the devil of a time ever proving that, Mister!"

Moses Teel curled his lips in a gold-toothed smile. "You'll have the devil of a time ever proving any different. That mortgage right now is in the Squawberry Flats bank."

"I don't care," Danny choked. "My father never signed it!"

"Your father may not have mentioned it but his signature is certainly on that mortgage. Suppose you let me finish. Duke Brockett was hard up. He wrote Mr. Crefts, acknowledging this condition, and asked for a loan of four thousand dollars. With this money, your father proposed to put the property in shape, hoping to sell it.

"While Mr. Crefts, himself, had no use for this property and was not particularly anxious to lend such a sum of

20

money on it, he foolishly allowed sentiment to becloud his business judgment. Your father was a neighbor and a sick man, besides. Since he had only asked to borrow on a short-term note, and was securing the note by a mortgage on the property which the money was to put into salable shape, Mr. Crefts' Christian conscience bade him lend your dad the money. I drew up the note myself—and the mortgage as well—and mailed them to your father for his signature.

"The day before his unfortunate demise, this man Reilly fetched them in to me, took the money in cash and——"

"That's a dadburned lie!" Wishbone's eyes were wild with fury.

The lawyer looked him over.

"Do you deny that you rode in——"

" 'Course I don't deny it! I rode in, all right, but not t' fetch no mortgage—an' I never lugged off no four thousand dollars!"

"You'd better figure out a smoother story than that." Teel smiled like the cat with a mouthful of goldfish. "If you go into court with that sort of tale, it will look pretty bad for a man with your record when we bring in our witnesses and pass around the receipt you signed when you got the money."

DANNY BURNS HIS BRIDGES

THE SILENCE bulked like clabber.

A queer look was working over Wishbone's cheeks and his long-fingered hands splayed out like talons that hungered to reach for the lawyer's fat throat.

But Teel's gold-capped fangs flashed another smug grin and then he fixed a dire look on Danny.

"I suppose you know a son is held accountable for his father's debts? The best thing for you to do is to sell this place and repay that money while you've still got a chance to come out with something."

Danny had been too dazed really to comprehend the full significance of Lawyer Teel's words. But now the implications were sinking their barbed points into him and he stood rooted in consternation, gaping at the man through the dusty rubble of his toppled and collapsing world.

Through that clamor Paula's small voice asked, "How much could he hope to get for this ranch?"

"Not very durn much, the shape it's in now. But enough, anyway, to——"

"But that's ridiculous!" Paula snapped. "This ranch was——"

"*Was* is right," pronounced Moses Teel with a contemptuous sniff. "Right now it isn't hardly worth——"

"And is that why Starl Crefts sunk four thousand dollars in it?"

The lawyer's shape stiffened and he looked at her balefully. "Don't you think, my dear, you'd better leave men's affairs to those that are most concerned in them? I feel quite sure your father——"

"When I tell my father——"

"Your father," Teel purred, "will hardly care to be told his daughter's been hobnobbing around with——"

Paula's lips suddenly fluttered. "All right," she said queerly. "All right—I'll keep still." And she went over, very meekly, to the bench and dropped down.

If Danny'd held any hope he'd wake out of this nightmare, he lost it right then. Seeing the wind taken out of Snooper's sails like that was enough to have impressed a more stubborn soul than Danny's. He turned away from Paula, his head veering slowly as though it were being pulled about against his will.

Moses Teel smiled sourly, and all the implications of what he'd said to Wishbone came clamoring back into Danny's thoughts. But he clenched his fists as he saw the lawyer grin.

"Aside from selling this place, is there anything else I can do . . . ?"

"You've got to pay off that note no matter what you do—that is, of course, if you want to keep this ranch. Your father borrowed that money to fix the place up. It's doubtful if he could have sold to any profit, even had the money been used as expected. As the place stands right now you'd probably just about clear enough to pay off the note."

"But you'd advise me to sell?"

"I don't see any other way you'd ever get it paid."

Teel took off his spectacles, idly twirled them on their ribbon. Then he brought them to his mouth and puffed a couple of times on them before, very carefully, he put them back on. He said: "The terms on which this money was borrowed call for a payment of four hundred dollars on the first of each of the next five months. On the first of the sixth month the balance—a matter of two thousand dollars—must be paid. Should any one of these payments fail to be forthcoming at the specified time, I will be forced to have the sheriff close you out to protect my client."

Danny stared at him blindly. His stricken eyes clung desperately to Teel's face but all he could see was that terrible debt. Four hundred dollars a month! And on the sixth month two thousand! What in the world could his Dad have been thinking of? Why, this was monstrous—incredible!

And yet . . . there'd been nothing impracticable about Duke Brockett. He'd come into this country at about Danny's own age and had started out with nothing but his two bare hands. Nothing but his hands and a lot of stubborn courage.

24

Danny clenched his teeth. He had that much himself—but his father hadn't been faced with having to pay out in cash money. . . .

He looked to Wishbone for guidance, but the old man wouldn't lift his eyes off his boots. His brief surge of spirit seemed to have withered at the root.

Danny took a deep breath and tried to pull himself together.

Poncho trotted over and looked up at him inquiringly and Danny, fighting hard to keep back the unmanly tears, blindly rubbed the dog's head where it pressed against his thigh.

"Ain't that kinda rough?" he said when he dared trust his voice.

The lawyer shrugged. "No rougher'n most. When a man comes to earning his bread and butter, sentiment is best left out of the deal. I'll grant it does seem unfortunate your father had to die without taking you into his confidence—but that's the way things go in this world, nobody ever thinks of dying. I expect things look pretty dark to you, but this whole thing, my boy, may well turn out to be the best thing for you. The Lord giveth and He taketh away," Teel intoned piously. "Who are we to question God's works?"

And he looked around him benignly. "Anyway," he said, getting back to the subject, "the money was borrowed and, if you aim to keep this place, you will have to pay it back."

In a choking voice and with his fists clenched tight,

Danny said: "Could—could you manage to extend that time a little?"

"I'd be most happy to, my boy, but the choice is not mine. I advised Mr. Crefts against making this loan. I pointed out its condition, the extreme unlikelihood of digging up a buyer who would take it at a figure insuring any profit. But Mr. Crefts was adamant. His old friend was hard put and needed succor. It was his plain Christian duty, Mr. Crefts informed me, to loan your Dad that money."

"It seems strange," Danny said in a baffled tone of voice, "Dad never said anything to me about it. What did he do with the money?"

"It doesn't seem," Teel said, "as though he wasted very much of it trying to fix this place up." He glanced about him disparagingly and shot a dark look at the Wagon-wheel foreman. "If Duke didn't get the money, you'd better talk to Reilly. He asked for it in cash and we've got his signed receipt."

Wishbone looked as though he were sick to his stomach.

Teel addressed himself to Danny. "If you decide to sell out, I'll see what I can do about digging you up a buyer——"

"Don't bother," Danny growled. "I've got no idea of sellin'."

"You haven't got much choice."

"What I've got's still mine, though."

Teel snorted. "Look at this thing sensibly. I should think you'd want to get all you can out of it. Probably wouldn't be much, but I always say half a loaf's better than no loaf at all. You think it over."

And, with a curt, sneering nod, he turned on his heel and started for the buggy.

With his mind a chaos of surging thoughts, Danny watched him go. His knees were shaking and his insides felt like a wrung-out rag. A kind of desperation appeared to take him by the throat as he watched Crefts' lawsuit man carefully stowing his umbrella underneath the seat.

The buggy groaned to his weight.

"Don't bother," Danny choked, "to fetch anyone out here. My dad worked hard to make a ranch of this place and he and my mom're both buried on it. Long as I've got——"

"It's no skin off *my* nose what you do," Teel grunted. "First time you lapse a payment I'll be out with the sheriff and take the place over—chew that up with your porridge."

"Then you better come armed!" Danny flung at him.

4

PAULA TAKES A HAND

"GOOD FOR YOU!" Paula cried. "I was itching to tell the old goon as much myself—but, just the same, you shouldn't have done it," she sighed, frowning after the dust of the lawyer. "What if he tells around town that you threatened him? You know how thick he and Crefts are with the sheriff—suppose they put you under a peace bond or something?"

"I don't care." Danny scowled. "It's time someone told that old walloper somethin'! Him and Starl Crefts! They just about figure they *own* this country—and maybe they do, but they don't own *me!*"

"Boy talk," Wishbone said, looking hopeless.

"It's more than talk," Danny flared. "I *mean* it! They may put me off this ranch but they're sure goin' to know they've done a day's work!"

"Just the same," Paula said, looking worried, "I wish you hadn't talked that way, Danny. Forewarned's forearmed. I wouldn't put *any*thing past that lawyer—nor Starl Crefts, neither. They'll find some way——"

But Danny wasn't listening. He was recalling some things and his eyes were on Wishbone in a way the old foreman found it hard to take.

He rasped his hands along his pants. He edged a glance at the corrals and swallowed without comfort. "Guess there ain't much use pullin' them down now . . ."

He let his voice trail off and kind of sagged at the shoulders. "No sense fixin' things up fer Crefts an' thet lawyer——"

"I want to know," Danny said, "what you meant awhile back when you allowed I would never get this place put in shape again—when you said I might as well try to move the Cobble Mountains."

"I kinda felt this comin' on," Wishbone said, eyeing his boots.

"Yeah—for ten years, I reckon." Danny's face turned grim. "I'm recallin' you said you ought never to have come here. I'm recallin' a lot of things. It looks to me, Wishbone, like you've known a heap more than you've been lettin' on—and the same goes for you, Snooper."

Paula lifted her chin. "It wasn't my place to tell you things about this outfit." She flung the red hair back out of her eyes. "Why don't you ask Wishbone?"

"I'm *askin'* Wishbone."

The old man looked as though he were ready to eat worms. "I—I done all I could t' make it up t' your Daddy—I told him Starl Crefts wouldn't never let it drop. That man kin hate like a Injun. He don't never fergit. He's——"

"Riddles!" Danny scowled. "I'm not askin' for riddles! I want to know what's been goin' on around here. All

29

that gab about Christian duty! I haven't forgot how Crefts came here one night and went stormin' off with half our best saddlers and no one liftin' a hand against him. I aim to get to the bottom of this business and there's no use you standin' there shiverin' and shakin'. Why didn't you tell me Dad was borrowin' money?"

"He wa'n't borryin' no money——"

Danny looked at him grimly. "What did you do with the money Crefts gave you?"

"He never give me no money."

Danny stood a long moment without saying anything. "Well, what about the mortgage? Did Dad sign that note?"

Wishbone grimaced. "There wasn't no note an' there never was no mortgage."

Paula's head flew up and flung back her hair.

Her eyes looked enormous but Danny wasn't noticing; all his mind was taken up with what Wishbone had told him. "No mortgage?" His mouth fell open. His eyes bugged out like knots on a stick. "Do you stand there and tell me there wasn't any *mortgage?*"

"It wa'n't no mortgage I fetched into town. Nor it wa'n't no dadgummed note, by godfreys."

"What *did* you take in? What'd you go to town for?"

"I took a note from your daddy—a letter, that's what. Crefts wrote Duke a offer—wanted t' buy up this place. Offered fifteen thousan' for it, cash in hand. Made Duke s' mad he like t' clumb outa bed. When I got him cooled down t' where he could jest about see straight, he had me t' fetch him ink an' a paper. Then I propped him up an' he wrote that letter tellin' 'em where t' head in at."

"And that's all you went to town for—to mail it?"

Wishbone nodded. "Aye, that's what I went fer. But not t' mail it. You know how Duke got—keyed up fer fair. I knew soon's I seen what he wrote in that letter it wouldn't be put into no dang mail. He wanted them wallopers t' *git* it. Right now. An' they did. They was both there, waitin' in the Pinto Bar's back room, an' I put that letter right in Starl Crefts' fist. 'There's Duke's answer,' I says, an' turned around an' walked out."

Danny looked at him blankly. "You—you're sure that's all it was—just a letter?"

"I ort t' know," Wishbone growled. "I stood right there by his bed whilst he wrote it. An' I was right there watchin' whilst he stuffed it in the envelope an' licked it shut."

"And there wasn't any note or any mortgage?"

"How many times I got t' tell you?"

"What'd you give him a receipt for?"

"I never give him no receipt."

"Then Teel was lying," Paula breathed.

"What's the odds?" Wishbone said drearily. "Things bein' like they are, what difference does it make?"

"If he lied about that, he probably lied all the way. If he hasn't any note——"

"He's got a note, all right. Make no mistake about that—an' don't never doubt he's got a mortgage, neither. You can't beat a stacked deck an' that's the on'y kind Crefts uses."

Danny stood there a moment, letting it soak in. "But if Dad's signature's been faked——"

"Prove it! Yer daddy laid in his bed fer nigh onto ten year; what business there was I handled it fer him. There ain't a man in this country would know ol' Duke's writin' enough t' git up in a court of law an' say so."

Danny took a turn around while he thought about that. He looked at Paula, then at Wishbone. "Well, but . . . Even if we can't rightly prove they faked Dad's signature, it seems to me they overplayed their hand when they claim you signed a receipt for that money. All you got to do is get up——"

Paula shook her head.

"Well, I don't see why not. He can deny the whole business!"

"He could if everything was the way you think it is. But it's not," Paula said, tossing her hair back impatiently. "You've been trying to solve a puzzle without having all the pieces. Look around at this ranch. Remember how it was before your dad took sick? Just think back a little. Didn't Starl Crefts come in here and drive off some horses? Did your father try to stop him? Did he ever make a move to try to get those horses back?"

"What do you know about that?"

Paula said: "I'm just trying to show you that you can't put out a fire with a mouthful of wind. It's plain Starl Crefts intends to get this ranch. I don't see how you're going to stop him. When he makes up his mind he's got to have a thing, he gets it."

"But all Wishbone has to do," Danny said, "is to

deny he got that money. He can deny ever signin' that paper——"

"He can deny it, all right, but that won't change a thing."

"I'd like to know why not——"

"Tell him, Wishbone."

Wishbone did not look very happy.

"Tell him," Paula insisted. "It's his right to know. Tell him about that colt."

5

VITAL INFORMATION

FOR A LONG, still moment Wishbone stood without moving while the gray look clawed at his cheeks again and all the wrinkles of his sagging face appeared to writhe and twist like smoky heat. But he didn't go into his shivering and shaking. He didn't appear to be doing very much of anything until he raised one of his uncalloused hands and scrubbed the back of it across his jowls.

He sighed, shook his head and cleared his throat like a grampus.

"What colt?" Danny asked.

Wishbone puffed out his cheeks but Paula's look wouldn't let the old man leave it there. He squirmed around in his clothes but the look kept right after him and he finally said like a man who has chewed up a wormy apple, "That dang yeller foal the ol' she-devil dropped——"

"You mean Caliban's colt?"

"Aye," Wishbone nodded, "though they be callin' him different since he's got himself growed."

Danny's mind went back through the visions evoked by the old man's words to the gaunt claybank mare, Caliban, with the clubbed front hoof who had once been the pride of his Dad's stock of horses. She had never been much for looks with her dropped-down belly and bony head. "Cantankerous" the boys had called her and even Duke had conceded she had a pretty robust temper.

Danny remembered his dad's pride the day he'd fetched her home. "Best dang mare in a thousand miles," he'd told them. He'd gone clean to Gonzales, Texas, to get her, and folks had reckoned he'd been clear out of his head to give five hundred dollars for a mare well into her twenties and who didn't much look like she'd even get through the winter.

But Duke had just grinned. Back in Texas, he'd told Danny, she'd had quite a reputation. She was by War Dance, a son of Lexington, and out of a daughter of Old Billy and, up to half a mile, had defeated the best horse stock of Texas.

Duke had bred her to his great roping horse, Barlow, a son of Barney Owens out of a sister of Lock's Rondo, and the following spring Caliban had found them a little yellow horse colt with white mane and tail. He had a bald face, Danny recalled, but he had shaped up pretty well, though old Caliban had died before she'd gotten him fully weaned.

"I thought we sold that colt," Danny said.

"Aye, we sold him right enough—an' fer a pretty penny, too. Your daddy sold him to Starl Crefts fer nigh onto a thousand dollars afore he was six months old."

35

He sleeved his face and stood there a moment staring down at the dog.

"Well?" Danny growled when it looked as though the old man had said all he aimed to. "What about him? What's the colt got to do with it?"

Wishbone roved a faded glance across the hills and, pulling off his hat, beat the dust on his leg and then squatted down to pull a sandburr out of the paw Poncho lifted, meanwhile snatching a covert glance at Paula.

But there wasn't very much Snooper ever missed and the look she threw back at him was bright and disdainful. "All this fiddling around won't help it. Tell him."

Wishbone laboriously got up off his bootheels. "An' t' think," he said sadly, "I should hev t' take such sass off a chit of a girl thet's hardly dry behind the ears—me thet was onct the pride of the cavalry. Why, ol' Teddy said hisself I was the best hoof shaper——"

Paula said impatiently: "Go ahead and tell him!"

"Where I made my mistake I shouldn't never of come here. All I know is blacksmithin', but account of my experience in workin' with horses, I let Duke talk me into takin' on this job——"

"Nobody's going to break down and cry, so quit feeling sorry for yourself and get it over. It's your fault much as it is anyone's that this Wagonwheel Ranch isn't what it used to be—yours an' that colt's. Go on now and tell him before I do it myself."

Wishbone's wrinkled cheeks sagged and he shook his head glumly. "I'll take what blame is due me—but it's a long ways from bein' all my fault. This thing goes back

36

to before I ever come here—back even before thet colt was ever borned. It goes back to your Daddy's horse-huntin' days . . . clean back t' Kaintucky where he came onto yer maw whilst he was huntin' him a stud thet would put the ol' run in them hosses he was raisin'. Right there's where it goes to, an' him marryin' yer maw was the start of it."

They both looked at him blankly, and Wishbone said, "Didn't you know Starl Crefts was sweet on her, too? Wal, he was. Many's the time Duke has tol' me how they got their start in this country. Crefts come from Tennessee with a little jag of hosses, an' both him an' yer daddy was runnin'-hoss men. An' each of 'em was bound his stock would be the finest."

The Wagonwheel foreman scowled and said abruptly, "Havin' interests in common, they got along pretty good until Duke's stock of hosses commenced t' show a little edge. On the surface they stayed friendly, an' then one spring Crefts come back with a stallion which he said was a son of the great Imported Leamington. Said he'd got him in Kaintucky, at some little town called Springfield, an' tol' Duke all about some gal he had met there.

"The nex' time he went back Duke went along with him. Duke had been figgerin' t' go back anyways, not havin' at that time jest the kinda stud he wanted. So Crefts says, on account of the Injuns, it would be a heap smarter if they went back together—an' that was what they done."

He lifted up a hand to swipe at a fly. Then he rummaged through his pockets and got out his pipe and stood a while holding it, peering off across the desert with a far-away look.

"Yeah? Then what?" Danny demanded impatiently.

"Yer Daddy fell in love with this gal Crefts had told about."

Old Wishbone filled his pipe, making quite a business of it, plainly thinking back to the things Danny's dad had told him.

"Gee!" Danny cried. "Was that Mom? Did he marry her?"

"Yep." Wishbone sighed. "Crefts had started home with a little bunch of mares—prob'ly hadn't no notion of the way the wind was blowin'. 'Course, there rightly ain't no tellin' how much Belle thought of Crefts. Thing is, she married yer father an' he fetched her here t' Wagon-wheel."

He dug a match from his pocket and tapped Danny with it. "Right there, I figger, was the start of this business—the beginnin' of the downfall of Wagonwheel."

He lit his pipe and scowled out over the brassy waste where the road Teel had taken rambled off through the heat toward town.

Poncho, the black Australian shepherd, got up off his haunches and came over and thrust his cold nose into the hollow of Danny's hand. But, for once, Danny had no word for him. He was too taken up with the old man's story, with the pictures that story had uncovered and the light it had spilled across hitherto untracked places.

"But the colt—I still don't see how Caliban's yellow colt

could have had anything to do with it. I can see how Crefts might have been upset a little——"

"Upset!" Wishbone's eyes rolled around in his head. "Upset ain't no dang name fer it! Even in them days he wasn't no man t' yell boo at. Alls he had t' do was crook his littlest finger an' forty men woulda jumped to his biddin'. It's a wonder t' me he didn't tear the place apart! But that wasn't all——"

"It wasn't all by a long shot," Paula declared.

"Of course," Wishbone growled, "Duke had the right to marry anyone he pleased, but it wasn't to be thought Crefts could be crossed up like that an' take it. Addin' insult t' injury, Duke hadn't been back with his bride but two weeks when, right under Crefts' nose, he bids in the hoss Crefts had plumb set his heart on."

"Barlow?" Danny whispered.

Wishbone nodded. "Barlow. They'll tell you Crefts near went crazy. He stayed in the Pinto Bar five days an' nothin' ever passed his lips but whisky. Half this country stayed plumb away from town an' no man dast open his mouth t' him until one night Duke walked in with a grin an' tapped Crefts on the shoulder. 'I hear you been passin' some remarks about me.'

"You could of heard a fly crossin' that room about then. The crowd stood around like chunks of wood. It looked like Crefts' eyes would roll off his cheeks. Then he grabbed out his gun an' Duke slapped it away. Crefts fell outen his chair an' lay whimperin' on the floor like a kicked cur dog right in front of all them people. It was a terrible sight."

Snooper's voice asked tightly, "Then what happened?"

"There didn't nothin' happen. But you kin bet Starl Crefts ain't never fergot—nor he ain't fergot how Duke dragged him out an' flung him into his saddle an' paid the swamper's kid four bits t' see 'im home. Nope—he ain't never fergot. An' he won't never rest till ever' last thing Duke stood fer has been wiped off the face of this earth."

In spite of himself, Danny shivered. In this new light the task that faced him seemed well nigh insurmountable.

"But the colt," he asked—"what has Caliban's colt got to do with it?"

Wishbone sighed. "I reckon you've heard tell of Pale-face?"

"You mean that wild yellow stallion?"

"Aye, thet dang yeller devil that's been stealin' all the best mares outen this country— Aye, that's the one. That's Caliban's colt."

Danny stared at him, astounded. "But I thought you said——"

"Yes," Paula smiled. "Crefts bought him, but . . ."

The old man knocked out his pipe. "Snooper's right. It's time you were told. With all his hate an' stored-up devilment, Starl Crefts," he said, "knowed better than t' monkey with Duke. He quit comin' to the ranch, sold off the bulk of his high-priced hosses an' went in fer raisin' cattle. This was a great cattle country in them days, with grass standin' up t' the belly of a hoss. The war come along—I reckon Crefts seen it comin'. He didn't volunteer like your daddy done. He stayed right here an' made money—a good pile of it. When ol' Duke come back—

when he was invalided home—Starl Crefts was the brass-collar dog in this country an' yer daddy wasn't nothin' but a busted-down soldier."

"But he still had Wagonwheel——"

"Aye," Wishbone nodded. "He still had the ranch. Your maw had done pretty well, managed t' hold it together an' hang onto the market. It was her what got that smart idea of holdin' auctions. Ever' fall folks would come here from all over t' bid in the cream of the Wagonwheel yearlin's.

"When ol' Duke got so's he could git around ag'in, he went off an' come back with that dun mare, Caliban. That Squawberry Flats crowd, I guess they thought he had gone soft in the head—but Duke knowed hosses. He'd fergot more about 'em than most folks ever learn. As I said, he bred the dun t' Barlow an' the follerin' spring she found him this yeller studhoss, Paleface."

Old Wishbone's eyes lighted up at the memory. "He was the best lookin' colt ever seen in this country—good all over an' strong an' deep-chested. Looked like he would be a boss hoss anywhere you put him, but he showed from the first he was the kind you'd hev t' handle with a pair of kid gloves. Smart! A heap too smart t' stand fer any abuse. It was right then yer Daddy got took down bad with the shakin' fever an' yer maw sent fer me."

"You mean," Paula asked, "right after Caliban's colt was foaled?"

"Aye," Wishbone scowled, "that was when he got worse. He'd be up a few days an' then down twice as many—there was lots of the boys got took that way later, long after the jungle fightin' was over. I reckon it finished off a heap more than the Spanishers. Anyways," he sighed, "that's when yer maw up an' sent fer me."

"And how was Dad when you got here?"

"He looked t' be better. He was up an' around again, layin' out the work an' doin' hisself near as much as three men. He was figgerin' on buyin' him one of them pumps an' puttin' in a big tank north of that shoulder—figgered t' sow that whole south pasture in hay.

" 'Course he never did do it. He never got at it. Them shakes an' the fever finally put him t' bed. Time Caliban's colt got t' be a short yearlin', Duke knowed he had done his last day's work.

"He called me into the house one day—yer maw was there with him. All eyes, she was, lookin' white an' scairt. 'Shaper,' he says—that bein' what they had called me in the Islands. 'Shaper,' Duke says, 'I reckon I've about reached the end of my string. Someone's got t' help Belle look after this place. I wish you'd stay on a spell an' take over.'

"I told him I wasn't cut out t' be runnin' no ranch—but you know how he was. Had it all fixed up in his mind I would do it, an' nothin' I said never made no difference. 'Belle can't do it alone. An' I sure can't. It needs a man on the job an' I ain't half a man now.'

"I give him all the argyments I could think of but he was bound an' determined I was goin' t' boss this ranch. Didn't make no difference if I didn't know sic 'em—I was the only man in the country he could trust."

Wishbone grimaced. "Them's his very words. He

would of been a heap smarter to of sold out right then, for if the's anythin' Crefts knows how t' git the most outa, it's another man's shortcomin's."

He lapsed into silence, deviled with his thoughts.

"The colt," Paula reminded him. "Now tell him about that bald-faced colt."

"Yeah . . . yeah, the colt," Wishbone whispered in a kind of shuddery way; and seemed to settle deeper into the run-over heels of his brush-clawed boots.

He suddenly met Danny's gaze with a straight, hard look. "I told Duke plain I wasn't cut out t' be ramroddin' Wagonwheel, but he kep' insistin' an' I expect his confidence—misplaced though it was—done considerable t' soften me into finally agreein'. Most folks has weaknesses, if a man would dig t' find 'em. Ol' Duke only had a couple, bein' long on trust an' short on temper—one was all Crefts needed.

"All this time he had waited like a spider, watchin' an' listenin' like a pussyfootin' cat. Ol' Duke, I reckon, had plumb fergot about Crefts, an' I hadn't heard then about their trouble over Belle, or about how yer Daddy had bought ol' Barlow or give that swamper's kid four-bits t' pack Crefts home. Even if I'd heard, I never would of suspicioned how a spite that old would ever come t' touch me."

The hand that held his pipe commenced to shake as with an ague.

"Never onct, since the night Duke paid thet kid to take him home, did Starl Crefts open his mouth ag'in' your father. Sly that devil was and mighty smooth t' hide his

43

thinkin'. But the spleen was workin' in him an' then, one day, he came over here.

"I was out in the barn lot, shapin' hoofs fer shoein'. All the colts of that year's foal crop was standin' on the stake line. Of a sudden I knowed I wasn't alone an', turnin' round, I seen him. He was settin' there on his big black horse with his wolf's eyes fixed on thet bald-faced colt.

"Fer mebbe five minutes he never opened his mouth. Then he says in that raspery voice of his, 'What critter's this?' and I tells him. 'Fer sale?' he asks. I allows as how he'd better see Duke, an' off he goes to the house without answerin'.

"That evenin' your daddy called me into his office. He had got himself up an' was settin' at his desk. Like he pointed out, we didn't hev no trainer that could do the colt justice. If he'd been able t' git about himself, he coulda made a real horse out o' Caliban's colt. Starl Crefts, he said, had offered nine hundred an' sixty-eight dollars fer him. He wanted t' know what I thought of it. I told him he'd better take it, an' that's what he done.

"We never heard nothin' more about the colt except that everyone around town said he was shapin' up fine t' hev the build of a outstandin' rope horse an' that, quick as he had growed enough, Crefts was figgerin' t' put him in trainin'. He had a top-hand roper at his place called Shag Kelley an' when Duke heard that Shag would probably break the colt he was fit t' be tied. 'That heavy-handed bronc stomper'll make a outlaw out of him—plumb spoil him for sure!' Duke ranted. Gosh, but he was mad. 'You git over there,' he says, 'an' tell Starl Crefts I'm buyin' that colt back!' "

"And did you do it?" Danny cried.

"I went over there, yeah. Starl Crefts jest laffed at me. All his hands was standin' round an' they laffed with him. Then, sudden, he quit cacklin'. 'You go tell that high-an'-mighty walloper you work for that he ain't runnin' things 'round here no more—not any. I'm the one that calls the tunes now, an' if I take a fancy t' hamstring that colt, I'll hamstring him.. If I feel like pullin' the frogs off his hoofs, I'll do that, too. Now git offa my land an' don't come back here *never!*' "

"GOSH!" Danny groaned. "What did Duke say to that?"

"Alls I told him was thet Crefts wouldn't sell. I'd been afraid fer his life to of told him any more. At that, I thought he'd plumb burst his buttons. He got so juned up it put him flat on his back fer the next two weeks."

Wishbone scrubbed a hand across his jowls in that odd way he had when he was feeling extra poorly. "T' make it short, Crefts wasn't up t' startin' nothin' with Duke, but he wa'n't no more afraid of me than a sparrer. I'd got into the habit of goin' up t' town fer the mail on Thursdays—rain or shine, I never missed. I'd got t' sorta timin' myself. So many minutes t' the Elk Creek crossin', so many more t' the buffalo flats. I'd got it down t' where I was hittin' it right on the dot—a hour an' forty minutes t' where the road goes through them eighty acres o' boulders thet divides Crefts' summer range away from his winter. You'll recall thet place, I reckon?"

Paula cried scornfully, "As if he didn't pass it every day of the seven winters he went into town to school!"

Wishbone ignored her as he would a bothersome fly. "You remember how thet land lays? How them ol'-time floods dug down through that holler t' tear out them rocks an' how, t' the north of 'em, the ground pushes up through them foothills in thet tangle of scrub pine an' oak brush? Well, Crefts remembered it, too, I figger, an' laid all his plans accordin'.

"Mebbe he had somebody out t' spot me—I dunno how he worked it. Alls I know is, when I reached them rocks they looked jest the same as they allus look, forsaken an' lonesome as a hoot-owl. I'd got pretty near halfway through 'em when, alls to onct, I heard the dangdest, kickin'est, hoss-squealin' racket—like the devil an' all his helpers was emigratin' on cartwheels.

"I done jest what you or any other feller would of. I dug in my spurs an' headed fer the racket—it come from in back o' them two biggest buttes. When I'd come almost up on 'em, a flash o' color lit outa them rocks, goin' hellity-larrup spang across the road, an' into the rocks on the other side an' on up through 'em, headin' fer the brush, an' me spurrin' after it an' pilin' on the timber.

"I knowed what it was quick's I seen the yeller hide of it—Caliban's colt! I was on a pretty good hoss that day, but I couldn't git close enough t' dab my rope on 'im; an' the further we went, the more ground he put between us."

Excitement blazed in Danny's eyes. "What'd you do?"

"I took down my rope. But when I could of made my throw he kept duckin' an' twistin' round them rocks an' I never had no chanct. It was even worse when he got into thet brush. I don't know what I figgered t' do—or even why I went after him; but I could see he was gittin' away. That was when I woke up to the fact thet I was bein' follered.

"I hauled my hoss up pronto. There was a bunch of guys boilin' outa them rocks, yellin' like Comanches an' three or four of 'em firin'. It was the firin' stopped me. I didn't see much sense gittin' salivated over somethin' I couldn't make heads nor tails of. I set there an' waited with my hands up where they could see 'em."

Wishbone scowled at the remembrance. "It was Coffin Creek Charlie an' a bunch of Clover Cross riders. They was in a sod-pawin' mood an' no mistake. Charlie come up with his hoss on its haunches. 'Put a rope on 'im!' he says, an' they done it. I didn't hev no gun on me an' ever' time I tried t' git a word in, I would find Charlie's fist cuttin' off my talk. He musta hit me a dozen times on thet ride 'fore I had the sense t' keep my mouth shut."

"Where'd they take you?"

"They talked like, at first, they was figgerin' t' string me up; but Charlie was roddin' the deal an' allowed he'd git Crefts' say on the business. 'We kin allus hang 'im,' Charlie says, 'an' there's bigger trees growin' right at the ranch.' An' thet's where they took me, t' Crefts' headquarters at the Clover Cross.

" 'We caught this waddy rustlin' off with thet colt you bought from the Wagonwheel,' Charlie says to Crefts, an' nothin' I said made a dang bit of difference. Charlie claimed they'd been combin' the rocks fer strays, had heard this racket an', slippin' up, had seen me hazin' thet colt fer the hills. He claimed they'd yelled fer me t' stop, but that I'd took out all the harder an' that, if they hadn't started shootin', I'd of had the colt clean outa the county.

" 'Where's the colt?' Crefts asks, an' they tells him the colt had got clean away in thet clutter of gulches an' canyons that zigzags off through the Cobble Mountains."

"What'd they do then?" Danny asked, eyes popping.

"They fetched me home t' the Wagonwheel. It was late when we got there, well after midnight; but they got Duke up with their swearin' an' shoutin'. 'This skunk,' says Crefts in that gratin' voice, 'was caught tryin' t' run off Caliban's colt. I got five eye-witnesses thet seen him doin' it. When my men tore loose with their rifles he quit, but that colt's clean gone off in them mountains.'

"He didn't give Duke no chanct t' say nothin'. He'd got it figgered right down t' a gnat's eye whisker. He knew Duke wouldn't throw me over an' he knew Duke couldn't never prove he was lyin'. 'We oughta strung him up—an' it ain't too late yet!' he says. 'You know how this country feels about rustlers. Trouble is with me, I'm too chicken-hearted; when I call a man *friend* I try t' live up to it. But that's all past. I've got my belly full of *your* kinda friendship. If you want that dang colt, you kin go out an' hunt him; I'm takin' my pick of ten head of your horse stock an' if I miss anythin' else, I'll come back for the rest of 'em!' "

And that was the story. That was how the best horse spread in five hundred miles had been reduced to the status of a "haywire" outfit. Greed and spite and trickery, and the natural inclination of people to believe the worst.

"Now you've got it," declaimed Snooper. "Now you can see——"

Danny said, "I don't blame Wishbone," and the old foreman's look was grateful. He'd been caught like a rat in a trap, condemned by appearances and by the stacked deck of lies passed around by Crefts' crew. A man can't fight whispers. And that was the measure of Starl Crefts' cunning. He made no public charge against Wishbone, had done nothing the Wagonwheel boss could hit back at. Danny's father's old friend was just a pawn in Crefts' game, a tool to be used and to be used again.

Danny saw it all, now. Having heard the old man's story, it was not hard to see the steps Crefts had taken to bring ruin to Wagonwheel. In a country where a man's means of getting around—indeed, as often as not his very means of survival—depended on a horse, a horse thief pretty generally was regarded as being about the lowest form of life imaginable. And it had not been so very long ago when such a man would have been shot wherever taken, or hanged from the nearest tree.

But Wishbone, of course, had never stood in danger of death. He was Starl Crefts' golden goose, the means of Crefts' revenge; a tool contrived and sharpened to ruin Duke Brockett's credit and spell the end of Wagonwheel.

But what to do about it?

Danny clenched his fists but there was, as Wishbone had found out before him, nothing to strike at, nothing a man could get his teeth into. It was like being a fly in a cobweb. He might wriggle and writhe and groan in his anguish but the gossamer strands of Crefts' duplicity held him as surely as bands of iron.

It was no trouble at all to understand Wishbone now. Small wonder he'd quit laughing, that he'd seemed so sort of slack and shiftless. Naturally he'd feel Danny's hope of rebuilding Wagonwheel futile!

But there *must* be some way—there *had* to be.

Danny could not face the thought of losing Wagonwheel. Somewhere there must be a way to beat Crefts. Feverishly his mind ran through the possibilities, and he had to admit that there did not look to be much hope.

But he would not give up; he would never give up until the last breath of life had left his body. That was the way he felt about Wagonwheel. Love of the place was in his blood, in the very marrow of his bones, and he could not abandon hope until every chance—even the most unlikely— had been exhausted.

But there'd be no way past the forged note or that mortgage. Danny was convinced of that as soon as he had heard Wishbone's story; that part of Crefts' plan was foolproof. Danny would certainly have to pay off that mortgage or Crefts, through Teel, would take the place over.

And there was no use in looking to Wishbone for help.

The old man, of course, was innocent of the whispered things that were told of him. Duke Brockett had given proof of that by keeping him on, even though by so doing he had strengthened Crefts' hand and given weight to the calumny which linked his brand with thievery. Duke had seen right away what was back of this business, but that hadn't taken the curse off Wishbone. The people in this country considered the old man a horse thief lucky to be alive, and it was the weight of this conviction which had taken the heart out of Wishbone.

Wagonwheel's foreman was a beaten man and would certainly never be anything else so long as the past hung over him.

Long after Paula had gone and the crew had come in and eaten, Danny sat alone atop Bald Knob, a lonely butte two miles north of the house, trying to think his way out of this mess. But the more he thought, the more certain it seemed that Starl Crefts would do just as he aimed to do and take Wagonwheel away from them.

There was just one chance that he could see to beat Crefts. He would have to get that money. Four hundred a month for the next five months, and two thousand dollars on the sixth month! He just *had* to do it. There was no other way to save Wagonwheel.

As Danny finally headed for home, he considered this carefully and, when he came into the yard, there was Huron Jones, stout friend and chum of Danny's school days.

Huron was so big it took an out-sized horse to pack him. Fat-cheeked and freckled, he was the butt of more good-natured jokes than any other two fellows in that Squaw-berry Flats country. But he never showed any resentment and got along fine with everyone. His folks had died when he was just a little shaver and he'd been brought up by Tom Lark of the Turkey Track, a two-bit spread that ranched back in the hills. Danny hadn't seen much of

Huron since school days; Huron was working for Tom now and a cowpuncher's work didn't leave much time for visiting.

Huron's freckled face grinned. "What you lookin' so down about?"

Danny waved the question aside. "How come you to be darkenin' my doorpost?"

"Oh, Tom's expectin' one of them buyers to come out an' look over his cattle—some fella from Tucson. I'm supposed t' pick him up at the Flats an' see that he don't get lost gettin' out there. But no kiddin', Danny, you look all swelled up like a poisoned pup. What's eatin' you?"

"I got troubles," Danny growled, and told him all about it.

Huron whistled. "Goin' to put you right out in the snow, eh? I always figured Starl Crefts was low down enough t' carry sheep dip. What you goin' t' do? If they can make that signature stick, they've got you."

Danny sighed. "I don't guess there's much doubt but that they can make it stick. Like Wishbone said, if I was to take it into court, it don't look reasonable in the face of Starl Crefts' influence that anyone would dare say it ain't Dad's signature. You know how much my testimony'd count for. An' the way they've got things rigged against Wishbone, his word wouldn't be worth the breath he'd waste to give it. The only way I can see, I've just got to pay off that mortgage."

"But how *can* you?"

"I'll find a way," Danny muttered.

"Well, I hope so," Huron said. "Short of stickin' up the

Squawberry Flats bank, though, I sure don't see how you're ever goin' to do it."

Danny had spent more time on Bald Knob than he'd figured on and was surprised now to realize that the day was about gone. Already the bunkhouse lamp had been lit and Danny, happening just then to glance in that direction, noticed Wishbone, with his head stuck out of a window, peering across the yard in their direction. "That you, Danny?"

"Yeah—me and Huron."

"Well, you better come over here," Wishbone grunted, and something in his manner—perhaps the odd way he said it—sent a drumbeat of warning across the cold tightness of Danny's thoughts. Huron, too, must have felt it, for Danny caught the quick lift of his friend's questioning glance.

"There's somethin' wrong," Huron said. "It's too quiet around here."

It did seem strangely still, sure enough. Danny threw a disturbed look in the direction of the corrals, but the gloom was much too thick to see if anything were penned there.

"Horses wouldn't be sleepin' this early," Huron said. "Funny we don't hear no sound from your crew—I don't believe they've come in. It just ain't natural for men to be——"

"Come on," Danny said and, with Huron following, he crossed to the bunkhouse.

Wishbone met them at the door, the lamplight showing

the dull glumness of his face as he stepped back to let them enter.

"You know I told you this mornin' Curley'd be leavin'—Well, he's gone. The whole crowd's gone—Limpy, Duckfoot—ever' last one of 'em. I wouldn't never of believed it!"

It was plain enough that he was speaking the truth. There wasn't a blanket on the bunks. The row of pegs along the wall showed neither coat, vest nor hat. There wasn't a warbag left in the place. Even the greasy deck of dog-eared cards was gone from the table.

The crew was one of the things Danny had thought about during those hours he had spent on Bald Knob. He'd been shocked when Wishbone had told him how the men hadn't been paid in going on three months. But he had aimed to make it up to them; even though he couldn't afford to keep them on any longer, he had meant to pay them every nickel they had coming. It was a jolt to find they had walked out on him with never a one of them waiting to say goodbye.

Their going brought home to him even more grimly than Teel's ultimatum the overwhelming odds Crefts had stacked against him.

The numbness of despair laid its crushing weight upon him and it was all he could do to keep back the tears.

He couldn't look at Wishbone or at Huron either. Blindly he stared at that row of empty pegs.

Wishbone sighed. "I kin understand Curley. quittin', but the rest of 'em . . . I wouldn't of been surprised even t' see Limpy goin', knowin' he'd been offered a chance on the B Bar—but the whole push an' caboodle of 'em! Where'll they go? Why didn't they wait till you got here before they pulled out? There ain't one amongst 'em that ain't worked fer Wagonwheel six year or better——"

"It's Crefts," Huron said, and the old foreman nodded. "He's bribed them or scared them into pullin' their freight."

7

PALEFACE

DANNY had gone to bed more whipped out and hopeless than he ever believed it was possible to be. For hours he'd lain tossing and twisting in the black shadows of his room before God's mercy had prevailed to give him sleep. Even Huron Jones, stout friend though he was, had told Danny plainly he was whipped before he started, but Danny wouldn't give up.

"Where's the sense beatin' your head against a rock?" Huron growled. "You got no more chance gettin' hold of all that money than I got of . . . of . . . Gosh, you won't get no farther'n I could throw a post hole. My boss, himself, couldn't raise that much cash! An' even if you got it, Crefts would find some way of doin' you out of it—he ain't got no more scruples than a hydrophoby skunk. You got to realize that feller won't stop at nothin'. If it was me—an' I tell you this frankly—I'd take what I could get an' sell out right now."

Danny reckoned Huron was very probably right; but

Huron wasn't him, and the Brocketts weren't the sell-out kind. He might lose the place, but it wouldn't be for lack of doing all he could to save it. So long as he had one horse to eat its grass, he would never holler calf rope, never knuckle under or permit Crefts' Clover Cross to annex one loved acre.

Again and again his mind explored the angles, pawed over the possibilities, ever and always arriving at the inevitable conclusion that there was just one way to hold it. He could remain as boss of Wagonwheel only if he could manage to pay Crefts off, to meet the condition set forth in Crefts' forged note.

It was not a cheerful concept but it was the one he bedded down with. He wasn't entirely ignorant of the ways men sometimes took to pile them up a stake quickly; to his credit it may be said that he considered these but briefly, discarding them, not through fear, but because, in his upbringing, they would not be counted honorable.

He was up the following morning a considerable while before daylight, working swiftly and efficiently, getting a pack together, cleaning and oiling his rifle, moving about with barefooted stealth, careful lest he wake Wishbone. The low-turned lamp and the early hour gave an eerie feel to the business and his shadow, cast on the walls and ceiling, assumed monstrous diabolical shapes as it crouched and flung itself around the room.

He had two good reasons for not waking Wishbone. On the kind of trip Danny had in mind the old man's company augured little in the way of help and might well doom the effort to failure. Even more important, in

Danny's mind, was the need for not leaving Wagonwheel deserted because, once Crefts understood that he was determined to fight for it, there was nothing you would put past the man.

So Danny propped up a note on the table for Wishbone: *Stick close to the house and keep your eyes peeled. I'll be back when you see me. Don't worry.*

What Danny had in mind was to try and sell a few horses; enough, anyway, to take care of the next two months' installments on that note. That would give him time for a breather, time to look around for some more practical means of freeing Wagonwheel from Crefts' clutches.

This stock was good—even Crefts admitted that Duke knew horses; and Danny hated the thought of having to part with any of them. Duke's love of good horseflesh was strong in Danny and he wanted, like his dad, to breed the best available. It was no easy choice to decide which ones to part with.

The younger stock, of course, might be more readily salable, but the older horses would fetch the most money, the four- five- and six-year-olds. By the same token, these latter, being mature and in some cases broken horses, were apt to benefit his own breeding program when, and if, he could lift that mortgage.

The pride of Duke's stud, of course, was old Barlow—now in his twenties—the father of Caliban's colt. Long known as an outstanding roping horse, and as a sire of top rope horses and of speed as well, Barlow obviously would bring the most money; he might even bring as much as five hundred dollars—but Danny couldn't bear the thought of parting with Barlow.

It was not much easier to stomach the thought of selling broodmares, yet it was twenty of these that Danny finally decided on. His study of the ranch accounts had shown him the brand supposedly carried a total of thirty-eight matrons, of which seventeen were still in their prime.

He had to do considerable riding to locate the ones he wanted, eventually settling on seven of the best, filling out with five fillies and eight aged mares. Surely a band such as this should bring at least eight hundred dollars.

By the time he had his stock cut out it was well past noon and he was feeling hot and hungry, but he knew he must push on. Who could say when Teel, or some other of Starl Crefts' hirelings, might not take it into his head to visit Wagonwheel? The sooner he was back, the better.

He encountered a little trouble persuading Poncho to go home. The dog had worked hard all morning and couldn't see why he shouldn't go along with the band. But in the end, reluctantly, the dog turned back.

Danny felt pretty mean, seeing the look in Poncho's eyes as he sat with lolling tongue, watching them out of sight.

Danny's little band of mares was fresh and restive and he was anxious to get them strung out along the trail where there would be less likelihood of them trying to bolt or scatter. He decided to lunch later, when they should be well into the comparative coolness of the foothills and the miles put behind them should have welded his charges into a single, adhesive, more easily controlled unit.

Not that he felt any real premonition of trouble. Rattler, the bay gelding he was riding, was a thoroughly reliable animal, and one with a lot of experience. He knew when to dart forward, when to cut around. He had what the boys called "cow savvy" and plenty of good common horse sense to go with it.

Danny figured on taking this band up to Tucson, feeling that he would get a better price there than at Tubac, Elgin or Benson. He wasn't going there because it was farther away. He had no intention of sailing under false colors. He meant to offer these horses under the brand plainly visible upon their left shoulders. Probably some of those folks up in Tucson would have heard the dark whispers Crefts had circulated, but that couldn't be helped. Some of them, like enough, might try to use it as a reason for hammering the price down, but that couldn't be helped, either. He'd be up against that deal, no matter where he took his horses.

The afternoon wore on. Danny stayed his hunger with a cold snack munched from his saddlebags as he rode.

Poor old Wishbone! He had sure had a time of it. Small wonder he'd quit laughing, living all these years under the stigma of being thought a bought-off rustler. That wouldn't be pleasant or easy for any man. It must have been a terrible thing for a smith who had once been the best hoofshaper in Teddy Roosevelt's cavalry.

He had done the old man a considerable injustice in thinking of him all these years as a lazy, shiftless, don't-give-a-dang fellow, an inadequate putterer whose careless indifference had let a great ranch go to pieces. Now that

61

he'd heard the old man's story, what had happened to Wagonwheel was more understandable. It never occurred to him to doubt Wishbone's story. Crefts had maneuvered him into a corner and he hadn't had the wits to find his way out. If Duke hadn't been flat down on his back, Crefts would never have been able to get away with it— probably never would have tried it. But he'd gauged Duke's friend correctly. For Wishbone the sky had fallen; he simply couldn't look beyond the jaws of the trap.

But Crefts wasn't dealing with a Wishbone now. He would find Danny built of a different fiber. The Brocketts weren't the kind to take a licking lying down.

By mid-afternoon Danny had made fifteen miles. No remarkable distance for the time consumed, but he was satisfied. When you drove horses to a market, the best way to do it was by easy stages; twenty miles a day was plenty. Many a time he had heard Duke say that, to a buyer, fat was the prettiest color, and he needed every cent he could get for these horses.

The higher ramparts of the Cobbles were commencing to turn blue. There was good graze down in this hollow— exceptionally good, considering the long drought—and Danny was content to let the horses browse a little. He could easily make another five miles before nightfall. From the other times he'd been over this trail, made and used by the burros of Mexican wood-choppers, he remembered an ideal spot for making camp.

The place he had in mind was a little box canyon. Perhaps half a mile in length, it cut off from Chamber's Canyon where that gulch wound through the rocky, pine-studded slopes of a spur that reached down from the Cobble Mountains several miles farther on.

"Git along, horses," Danny said, dragging the back of a sleeve across his face. "You'll get a rest pretty soon and a nice little spring-fed brook to drink from."

He kneed Rattler after the mares, and the old pony strung them out again and got them traveling.

Half an hour later they entered Chambers Canyon.

It was wide, here at its mouth, and dotted with scrub oak whose dusty leaves rattled in the cooler down-draft of air from the mountains. The horses picked up their feet with a reviving interest and two of the mares nickered.

"Like it here, do you?" Danny chuckled. "You'll like it a whole lot better where we're goin'."

They seemed to think so, too, and every little while one or another of the mares would throw up her head and loose a long whinny. This air appeared to refresh them and a springiness came into their stride again. They quit looking around for grass and showed an increasing indifference in the browse they found about them.

"Must have caught a whiff of that water," Danny told himself, noticing the gradual quickening of their pace. He peered ahead uneasily. Be a fine howdy-do if they suddenly up and bolted. Rattler was smart and had a good burst of speed, but with all that cutting he'd done this morning and with the wear and tear of keeping these mares in line, the fine edge of his freshness was probably worn thin. It was not too likely he would be able to head them if they took it in their minds to up and leave for other parts. And if they bolted . . .

63

Danny frowned.

They were two miles into the canyon now. There was no doubt in his mind of the mares' increasing excitement— even Rattler was cocking his ears and every little while he would shake his head, snorting.

At this point the canyon was a quarter of a mile wide, fringed on the sides with sandstone and juniper which in turn gave way to sheer rock walls rising steeply to the rim. Three hundred yards ahead, a side canyon opened off to the right and, even as Danny looked toward it, a horse came trotting out of it and stopped.

Corn yellow, he was, with mane and tail of spun platinum—a magnificent, muscular, fierce-seeming fellow whose lithe, free grace looked to mask enormous power as he stood poised for a moment while the quick, raking roll of indomitable eyes swept over Danny's band and absorbed every detail.

Cold fear gripped Danny as those eyes met his own. He could no longer doubt the evidence before him. The self-same markings. The bald face and white pastern. With a sense of shock he knew that here before him stood Caliban's colt.

But a colt no longer—an untamed stallion in the full, rich flush of his powers!

Dismay rushed over Danny as he recalled, belatedly, that this was the fabled King of the Hills, the devil horse men called *Paleface*; the demolisher of fences and the stealer of mares, on whom an outraged ranchers' association had hung the greatest bounty ever put on a horse.

"Gee-willickers!" Danny cried, shocked out of his

trance as the meaning of the stallion's sudden appearance occurred to him. No wonder his mares had been acting so strangely. They had realized his presence, been excited by it. And now they were ready, like enough, to run off with him!

It was what Caliban's colt intended—no doubt about that.

He suddenly lifted his muzzle high into the wind. He screamed in a clarion call of the wild and the mares, answering, lifted their tails and ran toward him eagerly.

Danny hurled Rattler forward to head them and at once the stallion whirled, rearing and making the canyon walls ring with his challenge. Ears laid back and white teeth bared, he came savagely forward, hoofs spurning the ground.

What a picture of unearthly grace and beauty!

Danny hauled Rattler up with a sobbing groan. It was hard, bitter hard, to let those mares get away—but how could he help it?

That golden devil considered those mares his rightful booty and meant to brook no interference. With head weaving wickedly and white teeth flashing, already he had bunched them, whipped them into a solid unit. Now he was whirling, prancing before them, flinging his screams at Danny and Rattler.

Cold fear and a feeling of terrible loneliness swept over Danny. He knew in his bones that if he pushed Rattler closer, that crazy stallion would fight, would probably tear him from the saddle and kill Rattler out of hand. It was the way of wild stallions.

"Oh—confound him!" Danny growled, and flung himself from the saddle. Dragging the Winchester from its scabbard, he went down on one knee to steady his aim and snuggled the rifle's stock to his shoulder.

The stallion screamed again but Danny did not fire—not even when Paleface drove his mares up the canyon. He just couldn't.

With tear-blurred eyes and a lump in his throat he stood beside Rattler and watched them go.

8

THE BENSON STAGE

DANNY CAMPED that night at Yellow Rock Springs and it was almost twelve before nervous exhaustion overcame the tramp of his disheartening thoughts and he fell into a troubled and harrowing sleep. He dreamed that he was trying to catch Paleface but the yellow devil horse was too smart for him. He saw through Danny's tricks and each time was off with a snort of derision before the young rancher could get his hands on him.

Danny woke with the dawn and found Rattler contentedly cropping the grass at the end of his forty foot stakeline. Downing the last of his cold rations, Danny fetched the horse in and saddled him. He swung off through the sun-rimmed eastern hills in a roundabout way that would fetch him through town, for it was in his mind to seek out Paula's dad, banker J. Cornelius Herald—not that he supposed this would do him much good but because he couldn't think of anything better.

The loss of those mares to Caliban's colt had just about

knocked the props from under Danny. To be sure, he had eighteen broodmares still at the ranch, but if he sold off these, he would be out of the business. And even if he were prepared—or forced—to sell even a part of them, there was no guarantee that he could get them to market—not with that wild devil roving the hills. Of course, he might persuade a buyer to come to the ranch—perhaps this cow buyer Huron had gone to town to meet might be talked into offering him something for them, but Danny didn't think this too likely. What he really hoped to do was to talk Paula's father into making him a loan on them. If he could even get enough to meet the first payment on Crefts' forged note, he would be satisfied, for then he would have a little time to look around.

None of these thoughts, Danny realized, was worth a great deal. His mind wouldn't seem to function right this morning. It was too whipped down from all that thinking last night—thinking which hadn't succeeded in getting him anywhere. No matter how bitterly Danny hated to face it, the plain truth of the matter was that Crefts had him hogtied and there was no circling around it.

Those mares, had he been fortunate enough to have driven them to market, might have stalled Crefts off for another couple of months. But as things stood now, it looked as though he'd reached the end of his string.

Off yonder, to the south and far below him, Danny could see the stage road where it came in from Benson; he could even make out the stage as a minute dot, steadily creeping along before its ribbon of dust.

He smiled meagerly, remembering how, when he had

just turned ten, his greatest ambition had been to be a stage driver. How grand, he had hungrily thought at that time, to be able to sit up there on the box, cracking his whip and, cock of the walk like old Israel Cantos, spinning big windies to spoof the dudes——

Danny pulled Rattler up and sat staring. Why would the stage want to be stopping out there? It *was* stopped, though, and right on that hairpin turn, just this side of that thicket of juniper before the road took the long down grade into Squawberry Flats.

Still watching the motionless speck of the stage, Danny fumbled the brass telescope out of his saddlebags and, hastily adjusting it, put it to his eye. Yep—it was stopped right enough. The spyglass brought the stage up into focus and he could see Old Man Cantos with his red-sleeved arms thrust up over his head—could see him lower one arm and push the shotgun off the seat, could see the bright shine of it falling to the ground.

And then he saw something else.

A slicker-clad man on a big red roan came out from the junipers at the side of the road. With a blue bandanna pulled up over his face, he gestured with his rifle and old Cantos climbed down and went around to the back and heaved a box from the boot.

"Jumpin' frogs!" Danny breathed. "A stick-up!"

He was so excited the spyglass shook like a leaf in the wind. This must be the bandit the whole country was talking about!

"Great guns!" Danny cried, putting away his telescope. "Pop Cantos must be packin' the payroll for the copper smelter!" And he clapped spurs to his horse, lifting Rattler into a headlong gallop.

But not for long. This country was rough, filled with brush and great boulders where spring freshets had torn down the canyon-sides. Despite his furious urge to get over there, Danny knew he wouldn't get far if his horse broke a leg. He reluctantly pulled the bay down to a lope which, while not quite so fast, was less likely to pile them up.

It was like Wishbone often said, this country was changing. It used to be that everyone living here knew everybody else, but now every fifth man you saw was a stranger. The toughs were moving in and a chancy breed was roving the hills, stirring up all manner of devilment. Law and order seemed headed for the discard and if something weren't done pretty darn quick, the honest folks would have to move out to keep living.

When Danny had first laid eyes on the stage it had been pretty nearly two miles away. It didn't look as though he was going to get over there in time to do much toward saving that payroll. Once that robber had the strongbox open, he wasn't going to linger very long in the vicinity. He'd probably dump his loot in a gunnysack and hit for the tules. But Danny reasoned, if he could get there quick enough, he ought to have a good chance at trailing the fellow.

Wishbone had taught him a lot about trailing and he was anxious to put this lore to the test. He urged Rattler along just as fast as he dared and they were making good time, despite the rough going. There was a pretty good chance the man might try to hide his trail, but Danny figured that if he could get there before the winds had a chance to get in their damage, he might at least pick up a clue.

He certainly had one clue, anyhow. He knew the bandit was riding a red roan horse and, while red roans were fairly common, if he could get to see its tracks before the wind flushed them off the beaten surface of the road, it was possible he would know them the next time he came across them. At least he hoped he would.

But it was plain as plowed ground that he'd have to keep his wits about him. This robber would turn ugly at the first sign of pursuit or interference. The smelter's monthly payroll was well in excess of ten thousand dollars—at least, this was the figure claimed to have been lifted when the stage had been stopped last month at Frayne's Crossing. Ten thousand dollars was quite a pile of money and any bandit desperate enough to latch onto it would not be parted from it by anything short of gunfire.

But it wasn't this grim conclusion which so abruptly caused Danny to pull Rattler down to a dogtrot. A power-ful remembrance had just crossed his mind. He was remembering how Starl Crefts had trapped Wishbone.

He rode a couple of hundred yards while the thought juned around inside him. It did not seem at all likely that the influential owner of the Clover Cross Land & Cattle Company would mix himself up in a stage robbery just to pin a charge of theft on the Brockett boy.

Just the same, by golly, if Danny sent Rattler up onto that road and there weren't any other tracks up there, and if some of Crefts' henchmen should happen along, it could look mighty dark for the last of the Brocketts. Mighty dark. And Crefts wouldn't need to be mixed up in it himself—he had plenty of hirelings who could do the job for him.

Not liking the idea, Danny pulled Rattler down to a walk. This was just the kind of a stunt Crefts might try. And the payroll didn't have to be on that stage. If Crefts were behind this, he would know what to do to make it seem the work of Danny. Crefts was slick. If Danny went up there and someone should see him, or if some of the loot were to be found in Danny's possession, he would be a gone goose and no two ways about it.

Then, remembering the color of the bandit's horse, he felt more inclined to play down these notions. Pop Cantos would remember what the robber's horse looked like. No one could mistake a red roan for a bay—no one with any horse savvy, anyhow.

Danny reckoned he was getting kind of soft in the head. Next thing he knew, if he kept on like this, he'd be jumping at his shadow. There were limits to what even Starl Crefts could do, and the Clover Cross boss certainly couldn't have known that Danny would be anywhere near this road today.

Unless, of course, he was having Danny watched.

A most unwelcome thought and about as foolish a one as he had ever had, Danny told himself. He wasn't important enough to put Crefts to such bother. He was just a dumb kid—just the Brockett boy.

But with a man like Crefts a fellow never knew. He had had Wishbone watched or he wouldn't have known where and when to loose Paleface so that Wishbone could be caught apparently trying to make off with him.

Danny began to look around with considerable more care. It was a bright, peaceful morning, already warm with the promise of higher temperature. Mockers sang in the brush and, off yonder, a jackrabbit bounced to his feet and went tearing. Everything looked about the way a man would think it would and if he hadn't seen that darned stopped stage . . .

But not all his wishing could get around that.

A man couldn't witness a robbery and just ride off and forget about it—Danny couldn't anyway. A certain moral responsibility went hand in hand with knowledge and, having seen that stopped stage, he was keenly aware of the obligation it put on him.

He broke open his rifle and slipped in a couple of fresh shells. He examined his six-shooter and peered about uncomfortably.

There was nothing to be scared of, he told himself scornfully. The bandit had doubtless sped away from there long ago and the stage would be rattling hellity-larrup towards town. There probably wasn't another person within five or six miles of him.

He reckoned he must be getting pretty close. He moved his horse forward carefully, rifle held ready across the pommel of his saddle.

The strongbox was probably still up there on the road. It would have been too awkward for the bandit to lug off. He'd probably broken it open already and transferred his loot to a gunnysack. Right now he was probably hunting some place where he could hide it or bury it. He'd want to rid himself of it at the earliest possible moment.

The sound of Rattler's footfalls seemed unconscionably loud. The sudden thrumming of a woodcock from under Rattler's feet almost toppled Danny out of the saddle, and he sat there weak and shaking for several seconds before kneeing the gelding into movement again. A thing like that was enough to unnerve anyone.

If he hadn't been wrestling so hard with his thoughts, Danny knew he wouldn't have been surprised in that manner. He could not afford to be surprised that way if he aimed to go up and look at those hoof tracks. He must keep his wits about him.

He rode carefully now, scanning the terrain about him, probing each thicket and juniper clump with a thoroughness that precluded any further surprises. In another ten minutes he was into the pines and then the road came in sight, less than fifty yards away.

He was a little below where the stage had been stopped, but he could see the place yonder and he approached it carefully. He did not ride onto the road but wound through the brush along its side, working higher. As he had guessed, the road was empty and, looking down into the valley, he could see the stage rolling into Squawberry Flats.

Though he saw no evidence to indicate that the lone-wolf highwayman was still in the vicinity, he worked his way forward with an added care. Thus it was that he came on the scene of the holdup without undue noise and remained lounging in the saddle among the dust covered weeds while he studied the sign left upon the road's surface.

He had no difficulty finding the place. The braked wheels of the coach had left plain sign in the road's dun and gravelly surface, and he could see the unshod tracks of the bandit's horse. He was a little surprised to learn that the man had been riding a barefoot mount. Evidently some horse he'd caught up off the range with this very job in mind. It showed the man was no fool.

Danny studied the tracks, observing where they had emerged from the juniper thicket and how they had gone across to the place where old Cantos had dumped the stage's strongbox. Of the box itself there was now no sign, though several ragged splinters of wood lay about and he did find the pattern of the bandit's gunnysack where the weight of the loot had ground its imprint into the dust.

The box had probably been heaved down into the gulch, Danny thought, but he did not attempt to look for it because he did not want to leave Rattler's tracks on the road. He reckoned it was plain foolishness to suspect Crefts of having had any part in this business, but he didn't aim to take any chances. He didn't want to be caught like old Wishbone.

He looked again at the tracks of the bandit's horse. He guessed he would know them the next time he saw them —unless, of course, in the meantime someone shod the horse. There was a distinctive break in the striking surface of the left front hoof; he thought this would be pretty easy to identify. Also it looked as though the horse was limping slightly. All you had to do was to find a red roan having these characteristics and you would have the very horse the lone bandit had ridden. And, if someone were on him, you might reasonably suspect that such a fellow was the man who had stuck up the stage.

Or so Danny thought as he sat staring at the tracks.

He could see, over there, where the man had remounted. And over here was the place where he'd gone back in the brush. The trail, pretty fresh, appeared to angle northwesterly and, keeping his eyes peeled, Danny decided to follow it a distance. Far enough, anyhow, to make sure the man was really headed that way.

The man was not. Less than six hundred yards from the road, in a dense thicket of thorny brush, the trail dipped southwest and took to a series of ledges where Danny became hard put to follow it. Obviously, without wasting too much time, the man was attempting to hide his trail. Danny found it hard sledding, trying to track this barefoot horse across these rock outcroppings. Unshod hoofs did not easily scratch rock and Danny lost time making certain the man had stayed with the ledges and had not gone hightailing off at a tangent.

But he had stayed with the ledges for as long as they lasted. Then he'd turned south again, slithering down the steep slope, angling back toward the road as though he couldn't make up his mind where he was headed. "Like a dadburned chicken with his head off!" Danny muttered.

It began to look as though the fellow intended to cross the road. And that was just what he did do. Where it went snaking down through dwarf cedars and catclaw the bandit had come up out of the brush and crossed the road, still going south.

It beat Danny, for, despite all this fooling around, the robber still wasn't over a couple hundred yards as the crow flies from the place on the road where he had stuck up Pop Cantos.

It had Danny puzzled. Why waste all this time? Did the fellow think he was followed? But if he thought that, it would be a heap more natural for him to dig for the tules, pull his freight and get out of here. It just didn't make sense, Danny told himself as he followed the roan's plain tracks down the slope.

And then, abruptly, it did.

Not a quarter mile below him, as he came out of the oak brush, Danny's questing gaze picked up the figure of the man. He was on foot!

9

A VERY PECULIAR FELLOW

THE MAN was in a thicket of squatting cedars; and it came over Danny then what he must be up to—he was hunting a good place to hide that gunnysacked loot!

Danny backed Rattler into the protecting shade of the scrub oaks again while he tried to think what he had better do now. Bumping into that fellow at a time like this wouldn't be at all healthy. But it was plain as plowed ground that when the robber came back to his horse again he would not be wearing that slicker and bandanna. He would cache them with his loot and there'd be nothing to connect him with this deal but the horse, which he would probably get rid of at the earliest opportunity.

Another thought struck Danny. What if he'd already abandoned the horse?

Shading his eyes from the glare of the sun, Danny looked around carefully and spotted the red roan again. He was still packing a saddle and had been left on dropped reins. But that didn't necessarily signify anything. If the

78

fellow had grabbed the roan up off the range—but surely the man wouldn't abandon his saddle. A saddle might be traced. And he could just as easily hide it with the loot. But if he had his own horse hidden out around here, he would naturally figure on using that saddle.

Danny suspected the robber hadn't quit the horse yet. He hardly knew what to do. He wanted to get a good look at that fellow if he could—a much closer look than he could get from up here. Yet he realized that to go down there would be taking long chances.

On the other hand, if he didn't find out where that loot was hidden now, he might never be able to locate it. The workers at the smelter would be depending on that payroll. The owners of the smelter might even lay their help off rather than take the risk of losing further money. He was in a position where he might recover this payroll and what kind of citizen would he be if he didn't do his best?

The bandit would be too cunning not to cover up his tracks. But if he'd come down here deliberately to hide his plunder, it looked uncommon odd that he hadn't taken more trouble to hide the tracks already made. Danny guessed he was aiming to take care of that going back.

Danny got down off his horse. Leading Rattler back into the brush a way, he tied him. He pulled his rifle from its sheath. Maybe what he was aiming to do was foolish, but he had to find out where that fellow had gone to, if he meant to get a line on where he'd hidden the payroll.

Careful to keep a good screen of brush between himself and the bandit's horse, Danny cautiously commenced to work his way down the slope. Before he'd moved very far he was wishing he had left his rifle behind. It was no simple thing to worm your way through the brush with a rifle. And there was a greater than even chance that the sun, flashing off its barrel, might give the show away. But he made it to within fifty feet of the roan without any unto-ward incident, without the horse even managing to catch wind of him.

By this time Danny was both hot and worried. The pounding of his heart was like a stamp mill going full blast.

There was no sign whatever of the stage robber.

Crouching in the full glare of the sweltering sun behind the frondlike foliage of a gnarled mesquite, Danny tried to decide what he had ought to do now. His position near this horse was not a thing to take any comfort from; he'd have a lot of explaining to do if he was found here—by the law, that is. If the bandit discovered him, no explanation was likely to do him much good. The man would shoot him out of hand. That would be all there was to it.

Though he was wet with sweat, Danny shivered.

Listen as he would, he couldn't hear anything but the movements of the roan, as it searched out stray wisps of grass among the rocks. Not even a bird call came to relieve the oppressive stillness.

The bandit's choice in horses wasn't anything to brag of. And that saddle wasn't anything a man would set much store by. It was cracked and scuffed and ancient, as though it had been hanging a long while from a peg in some shed.

For a dragging five minutes Danny probed the surround-ing brush without seeing anything of the man he was hunting. Finished with this horse, the bandit probably had abandoned it— Perhaps he had his loot cached and was heating his axles for other parts.

With a soothing word so as not to frighten the horse, Danny rose to his feet and stepped out into the open, eyes scanning the ground to find the outlaw's tracks. He came on them finally and followed them down a dry wash heading east and then up over a bank until, behind a screen of oak brush, they started up the slope.

The guy was crazy as a goon! What had he come down here for in the first place? Just to leave that horse? He could as easily have left it up above on the bench—and he hadn't cached that plunder, not so far anyway. Danny'd been keeping his eyes peeled for that and would have taken his oath there was nothing buried down here. So why had the fellow come down here at all?

He never had heard of such a crazy galoot! Most guys ornery enough to stick up a stage would have cut their string long ago and got to heck out of here. They never would have skylarked around like this fellow.

Danny cuffed back his hat and stood a while scowling. Then he went on again, and the farther he went the more baffled he became. Where was the sense in all this twisting and turning? The man didn't act as though he had all his buttons! Any moment now a posse might come ramming into sight, yet here this fellow was, traipsing round all over the gulchside like he didn't give a whoop if he *never* got away! It didn't make as much sense as a fool pounding sand down a rat hole.

Yet there went his trail, still fiddling around with no more objective than the tracks of a gopher. It would have broken a snake's back had a snake tried to follow it through all this roundabout brush and these boulders. Where Danny stood right now wasn't more than two good stone throws from where the bandit had stuck up Pop Cantos.

Exasperated, Danny took up the trail again, gradually becoming aware of a pattern in the robber's perambulations. Always, it seemed, the bandit kept to the east of rockpiles and brush clumps; this he did with a stubborn persistence there was no getting away from. With a growing unease Danny kept sending glances over the terrain to the west of him, the part of this vicinity the outlaw was avoiding. But he saw nothing over that way that wasn't also over here, and his perplexity grew as he tracked the man's sign across the arduous ground.

Suddenly Danny stopped.

An appalling explanation put cold fingers on his spine as he stared back over the way he had come and saw the outlaw's red roan still searching out grass in the rock-studded pocket nearly a quarter mile below him. His eyes snapped back to the trail, and they grew wide and dark with foreboding as he saw how determinedly the tracks now bore to the west. A dreadful excitement laid hold of him and, throwing caution to the wind, he broke into a run.

String straight the tracks went through the oak brush and juniper, leading Danny directly back to the place from which he'd started. But he knew with a frightened certainty long before he reached it that Rattler wasn't tied in that thicket any longer.

And Rattler wasn't.

10

SNOOPER BORROWS A HORSE

PAULA HERALD as a rule was up and about quite as early as any young sprout in the country, yet here at the impossible hour of 9:30 she was still in her bed and didn't much care whether she got up or not.

When a girl has only just turned sixteen the difference between reality and her most cherished convictions can easily seem catastrophic. She could not understand how a girl's own father could be so utterly heartless, so completely deaf to her voiced desires, so adamant and coldly final.

But there it was. J. Cornelius had said "No!" most definitely and had told her, moreover, to keep away from Wagonwheel. "If you've got to go around making sheep's eyes at boys, at least find a boy who'll amount to something. *That* young fellow will probably wind up in jail!" And he'd stamped off to his bank without further words.

Had the sky suddenly fallen Paula couldn't have felt worse. If it had been young Paul Crefts she had wanted him to help, he would have been all smiles and ready assurance.

Just thinking of the fellow was enough to make her squirm. "Beau Paul"—as Huron called him disparagingly—was a first class drip in the opinion of Paula Herald, who had never forgotten the time she had seen him pull the wings off a butterfly just for the pleasure of watching it wriggle. "Beau Paul" with his rabbity nose and buck teeth, always taking out girls in his yellow-wheeled buggy, buying them pop and then expecting to hug them in return for his investment.

Yet she knew very well her Dad would favor Paul. All the girls' mothers around Squawberry Flats looked on young Crefts as the best catch in town.

Was justice something to be maneuvered around to the particular advantage of a carefully chosen few?

It was a hateful thought. It was especially repugnant to Paula who had always pictured Justice as she appeared in the schoolbooks—a blindfolded woman impartially dispensing merited rewards and deserved punishments to each and every person according to his due. Paula thought if there was one kind of justice for the rich and influential and a separate set of values for the poor, it was a pretty sorry world.

Finally, throwing off the rumpled sheet, Paula swung her long legs over the side of the bed, thrust her feet into slippers and crossed the parquet floor to her washstand where she filled the white bowl with water from the crockery pitcher.

After splashing water on her face she felt a little more

cheerful. She got into clean levis and fresh calico shirt, fixed herself a bite to eat and, afterwards, washed and put away the dishes.

She rather hurried toward the last, remembering belatedly that Huron was coming in to meet an expected cattle buyer. She wanted to see Huron before he got away.

Like a hawk arrested in full flight Danny stood with his eyes sprung wide, the breath trapped in his throat. The thicket was filled with a muted pulsation which resembled the distant banging of a single-jack.

Danny knew, deep inside him, that he'd been right about Rattler, though his mind still refused to believe the evidence of his eyes. Common sense insisted the horse had merely strayed, but horses didn't stray after being securely tied to young oak saplings as big around as a grown man's arm. Of course, Rattler *might* have broken free, but there was no indication that he had done so, no scuffed place on the ground where he had set back and tugged. The only marks on the ground which held a story for Danny were the tracks of high-heeled boots—the very boots he'd been following all over this pocket.

While he stared at those tracks the rhythmic thud he'd been hearing grew louder and louder; abruptly Danny knew it was the hammering of his heart. He knew he'd better face it. The robber had spotted him right from the start, had been laughing up his sleeve while he was laying that trail all over the gulchside, playing with Danny as a cat would with a mouse.

Suddenly Danny found himself panting as though he had run a long way.

It was silly to suspect Starl Crefts of having a hand in this. Danny thrust out his jaw and brushed aside such arrant nonsense. Starl Crefts had better things to do than waste his time to such small purpose. And he—Danny—had better things to do himself than stand here goggling like a fool. The situation was sufficiently unhappy without trying to make it any worse than he found it. What had most likely happened was quite explainable and simple. The bandit had observed him, just as he had observed the bandit. The flash of Danny's spyglass had probably put the robber wise.

A very wideawake fellow, that bandit, and one not easily stampeded. Instead of filling him with panic, he seemed actually to have relished Danny's presence, seeing in it not only the chance of acquiring a fresh mount but a good possibility of saddling his guilt on another. For Danny could not doubt that it could be made to look mighty bad for him, if he were discovered in this vicinity. He might even be taken into custody——

"Great guns!" Danny exclaimed. Supposing the bandit should decide to accost him? And why not? He could take Danny straight in to town with a story of having seen him stick up the stage, of having chased and caught him; and he would have the blue neckerchief and slicker to prove it! He even had the horse—and Pop Cantos would identify it.

Cold sweat came out on Danny's palms. Starl Crefts would be glad to believe such a charge. And so would

Dode Forney, the sheriff. Everybody knew he was just a Clover Cross hireling, led by the nose every time Crefts whistled.

And then another thought came and Danny drew a deep breath. "Whew!" He drew a great breath of relief as he realized that the bandit wasn't fixed to take him in right now. He couldn't take Danny in while riding Danny's own horse.

But he could go fetch his own, Danny suddenly remembered. He could go fetch the horse he'd been riding before he'd roped the red roan off the range. Or somebody else might come along and spot Danny, which would be almost as bad—particularly if that someone happened to be hooked up with Clover Cross.

Danny knew that if he were found in this vicinity, proving his innocence might be more than he could manage. Everything seemed to be conspiring against him. A feeling of helpless anger burned through him and he scowled at the robber's boot tracks again, hoping to find some distinguishing mark. But the only discovery he drew from this study was that the boots which had made them were larger than average. Number elevens, he reckoned.

He looked again at the bandit's abandoned roan, contentedly cropping grass in the rocks down below him. He wanted mightily to take it but good sense prevailed. To be found aboard that horse, or even close to it, would be tantamount to admitting he had robbed the stage. Fiercely as he hated the prospect of walking the hot and dusty miles that lay between himself and town, he realized it was the only safe way he could get there; and he struck out at once.

Paula's resolution to seek out Huron Jones bore little fruit that morning. Fifteen minutes after leaving the house she discovered that Huron had been in town bright and early, had located his buyer and gone riding off with him in the direction of the Turkey Track.

She couldn't decide whether she ought to follow him or not. Tom Lark and his wife, though good Christian people, might think it peculiar that she would want to see Huron badly enough to ride out there. Though they probably wouldn't ask her any questions, in the end they would likely worm it out of Huron and might even forbid him to have any part in it. Starl Crefts was a power in this country and most people roundabout were inclined to shy away from doing anything that might stir up his wrath.

Paula didn't care two figs for his wrath. But there was her father to be considered and Starl Crefts was not only a director in his bank but, in addition, was its largest stockholder.

Since Mrs. Herald's death several years before, J. Cornelius had become much too engrossed with his business affairs to give much attention to his daughter. She had to go to school, of course, and had been enrolled in an exclusive college for girls at some far off town in western Pennsylvania; otherwise he let her do pretty much as she pleased. It was now the middle of May and the local school had closed to enable the boys in the upper grades to help with calf roundup; Paula would not have to leave for the eastern college before the last of September. She didn't have to bother with much housework. A Mexican woman cleaned the place twice a week and Paula cooked the evening meals, the only ones J. Cornelius ate at home. So she had plenty of time on her hands to do what she felt needed doing.

But she knew her father would not like it a bit if he found out what she was up to now. He had very definitely told her to keep away from Wagonwheel.

Paula thought about this for quite a while before making her decision. She was an impulsive girl but did not generally go against her father's wishes. Nevertheless she had a mind of her own and she knew that J. Cornelius was wrong about Danny. He was probably being influenced by something Crefts had said and, anyway, he had not specifically told her to stay away from Danny. Danny might now be Wagonwheel but Wagonwheel wasn't Danny. And, if Danny was determined to hang onto his ranch, he was going to need every bit of help he could get.

Since Duff, her gray gelding, had caught a stone in his frog and lamed himself, Paula borrowed a horse from Ed Stokes at the livery and set off to find Huron Jones.

11

SURPRISE!

WHILE PAULA HERALD, on one of Stokes' livery horses, pushed steadily nearer her determined objective—that needed talk with Huron Jones—Danny trudged the dusty miles that stretched interminably between himself and town. He was always careful to keep off the ridges and utilize whatever cover the range afforded, lest he be seen and suspected of stopping the stage.

A fitful wind rushed across the ranges, sending the dust devils dancing and driving harried white clouds across the blue heavens, but for all of that it was uncomfortably hot and Paula was glad for once that she was not a cowpuncher.

A cowboy's life, pleasantly glimpsed from afar, was believed by dudes to be a thing of romance, but Paula had been brought up in the country and knew its dangers, its cares and monotony. Cowboys worked hard for the wages they drew and lived on beans, sourdough and jerky. They were called from their blankets before dawn broke and seldom crawled into them till long after dark. They had to work in rain or shine, through gales and blizzards, in summer's blazing heat; branding, combing the gulches and chaparral for strays, pulling cow critters from bogholes, doctoring calves infested with screw worms. A cowboy's work never ended and if there was any romance connected with it, someone else could have it, thought Paula.

Yet it had its compensations, she reflected. It was a wild, free life, strongly spiced with initiative and danger. Though it was generally hard and frequently monotonous, it had its occasions of high excitement. Its loneliness and strenuous hours in the saddle were offset by the boisterous celebrations and rough-handed frolics which the cowboys always had when the work was done and the beef was rounded up each fall. She would miss the roundup fun this year, for by that time she would be in the East, drearily wrestling with lessons at the Misses Gilespie's College for Cultured Young Ladies.

She made a face at the thought and wished the Territorial Legislature would get a wiggle on and build that university that was being talked of for Tucson. Perhaps next year she wouldn't have to go so far away. People said the school being planned for Tucson would be the greatest university anywhere in the West and that both boys and girls could enroll. That would be more sport than being cooped up with a bunch of prissy Cultured Young Ladies at some stuffy old place in faraway Pennsylvania!

Paula had never been farther East than El Paso, but she was sure she wouldn't like it. There wouldn't be any coyotes howling at the moon, any rodeos, hoedowns or county fair horse races. Paula thought horse racing was the greatest thrill ever and often wished she were a boy so that she could ride in the races at Squawberry Flats. The Fairgrounds Oval wasn't much of a track but each September, when they held the County Fair, the ranchers came in with their fastest horses and everybody bet their heads off.

Paula sighed nostalgically. Scrinching her eyes against the glare, she looked off across the tawny miles toward the blue of the faraway mountains. Wagonwheel lay over that way and she wondered what Danny was doing now and whether he'd hit on a plan which could hold out the least hope of helping him meet those payments.

Probably not. If there had been any way, Crefts would have blocked it. That was how Crefts operated; it was the way he had made himself a power on this range. Never give a sucker a break—that was Crefts.

Paula's route would not take her very close to Danny's ranch, the trail to Turkey Track swinging directly north just this side of the buffalo flats, which were still several miles ahead of her. She played with the thought of cutting over for a talk with Danny but resolutely put the temptation away. She wished she hadn't mentioned Danny's plight to her father; if she hadn't, he wouldn't have told her to keep away from Wagonwheel. She was sure he didn't have anything against Danny personally. Crefts or Teel must have said something to him to make certain the bank would not loan Danny the wherewithal to get out of the corner they had backed him into.

Common sense told her Danny's fight was hopeless. When Starl Crefts went after anyone that person was as good as whipped right then. Paula had to admit this to herself. But that didn't mean she was abandoning Danny. She intended to do everything she could to help him—and she would do it whether J. Cornelius liked it or not!

Coming up out of a hollow, she saw the Big Rocks before her, the eighty-acre stretch of badlands that divided Crefts' summer range away from his winter range. This was where the Clover Cross boys had framed the fuddled Wishbone and hung a rustler's reputation round his neck.

It was a stark, depressing region of barren desolation, yet it possessed for Paula Herald an insidious fascination, a weird and evil beauty comparable in its fierceness to a crouched and snarling mountain cat. A land of grotesque boulders, some of them towering seventy feet; an irregular sweep of never-used country, crossed and recrossed with tenuous trails that dimmed and faded in the tortuous twists and turnings that led nowhere. Rock piled on rock in a bleak and witless profusion of reds and browns and scabrous yellows, its corridors were littered with the bones of trapped cattle.

The Dragoon Trail wound through this region like an air current through a furnace. In the brassy glare of the noonday sun the sorrel coat of the livery horse turned brown. Dry winds stirred up the stifling dust and drew the moisture from Paula's body. Before she'd gone a quarter mile her burning eyes felt scratched with silt and every breath was a painful effort.

She was halfway through when, crossing a hogback, she

happened to glance west and, through the dust haze traversing a converging corridor, caught a fleeting glimpse of another rider. He was perhaps as much as a half mile away and she at first supposed him to be some ranch hand combing the rocks for strays. He was nearer when she saw him again but still not close enough for recognition. He was traveling a trail that came in from the east and would join with hers before it went much farther. He was on a dun horse and was nearer the intersection than she was, which was probably the reason why he had not yet observed her. A hunch told Paula he hadn't.

The man was garbed in range clothes but he didn't act much like a ranch hand. He wasn't in these rocks to hunt cattle; all his attention was taken up with the trail. And there were other things about him which set him apart from the average cowpoke in this country. He wore a low-crowned hat, for one thing, and he carried a rifle across his pommel, like a man on the watch for big game; only this wasn't a place where big game abounded and the fellow didn't seem to be watching anything but his trail. A burlap sack that looked heavy was lashed behind his saddle where, if he were a working cowboy, he would probably have packed his fish—"fish" being the name usually given to the range rider's yellow oilskin slicker.

There was a lot of wind in this strange fellow's corridor and the dust swirled around him thickly, at times almost obscuring him. Since he was nearer the intersection than Paula was, she had no chance to get a good look at his face but there was something about his shape or posture which began to sink claws into her memory. And then he was hidden by the rocks again and, unaccountably, Paula was shivering.

She could not have told why the sight of him scared her, but suddenly she was panicky. Something warned her this would be a bad place for that man to find her, and she knew by the direction in which he had been traveling that they would be in plain sight of each other pretty soon.

It came to her with a small sense of shock that she hadn't previously known there was a trail over there. She had lived in this Squawberry Flats country all her life and had never even suspected the presence of a trail cutting through these rocks from a southeasterly direction. She would have said that none existed, and the fact that she had inadvertently discovered one did little to restore her confidence.

She and that man were traveling converging lines of a triangle whose apex could not be more than a hundred yards away. A little swift figuring assured her of this. Further figuring made it plainly apparent he would get there first and that, when he did, he would look down this trail at once and discover her. He must be very close to discovering her right now.

Frantic, she looked for some place where she might hide.

There were plenty of rocks tumbled handily about but none of these was big enough to conceal her horse. And up yonder, just ahead, were the last of these boulders where the badlands ended in that windy open which roundabout ranchers called the "buffalo flats." There was not enough cover out there to hide a fly!

Paula pulled up her horse, about to jump from the saddle

and start running. She even had one foot from its stirrup when the folly of such a course occurred to her. If there were anything furtive about that man's presence, the sight of a riderless horse would excite his suspicions in short order. Flight would be a dead giveaway. He would track her down in a matter of moments. Then what could she say as an excuse for having hidden?

And suppose he had a perfect right to be here? There was actually nothing sinister about him except the sight of that ready rifle. A lot of things could account for his carrying it that way. As for the trail he appeared to be using, it might be no different from half a hundred others and may have ended just beyond the point where she'd first seen him.

Common sense told Paula that she was all worked up, that she was creating a mountain out of a two-by-four mole hill. She prayed that she was, but she couldn't believe it. There was something about the sight of that man which raised a cold chill, and it had little to do with reason.

But she was calmer now, even controlled enough to wonder why he hadn't already appeared. One thing was apparent. She'd be wise to put a bold front on the business, to ride straight along as she normally would, as though she imagined herself alone in this rock maze. Since she couldn't hide her horse, he would find her anyway. She would be a lot safer if he didn't think she were frightened. That was sound psychology.

Paula took a deep breath and swallowed. She meant to knee her horse into motion but her legs were as stiff as two petrified logs. She drew another quick breath and shuddered. Then she slapped her horse on the rump and went forward.

She rode fifty yards, seventy-five, the full hundred. There was no one in sight—no trail even. Just a bunch of sprawled rocks like everywhere else. She stopped the gelding and stared, astonished. She sent a glance at the ground. There were no tracks, either.

She looked up and saw the man—watching her!

12

A MAN OF GOOD HEART

IT WAS AFTER dark when Danny, just about done in, reached the outskirts of Squawberry Flats. He'd had time for considerable thinking and had come to the conclusion it would be most unwise of him to rent a horse from the livery. Ed Stokes, the stable boss, might be quite as hard working and friendly as he seemed but, even if he kept his curiosity bridled, he'd be bound to think it queer that anyone from Wagonwheel would need to rent a horse.

Danny could, of course, tell him Rattler'd thrown him and run away. He could say the gelding had been snake-bit or had stepped in a dog hole and had to be destroyed. Such things were not unheard of, and he could explain his lack of gear by saying he'd cached it out there.

But lying, even in the best of causes, went against Danny's grain. Besides, in these present peculiar circumstances, it might well prove a boomerang, a black-powder trail to trouble. Stokes would almost certainly mention Danny's need of a horse to others. If Danny kept his mouth shut and vouchsafed no explanation, speculation would be stirred at every roundup camp and bunkhouse. It would be folly to tell the truth to Stokes, and any substitute he offered would give people something to chew on. Some of those who heard of it might decide to look into it. And Starl Crefts, if he were at all mixed up with that stage robber, would know better and might thus be able to use the tale against him. Danny couldn't forget what had happened to Wishbone. With a fellow like Crefts you had to get up early and stay awake all the time.

So he decided to keep away from the livery. He'd been lucky so far; he hadn't run into anyone and no one—with the sole exception of the robber—had seen him, he thought. On top of the walk he had already had, he knew mighty well he couldn't hoof it clear home. But if he could find Fidelio, he believed the old Mexican would lend him a mount.

Old Fidelio was a saddle maker. He had a shop in the Mexican quarter, in a tumbledown adobe hut that always leaked when it rained. When the water ran into his house the old man always swore he would fix the roof tomorrow, but then when the sun made the tin roof hotter than a seat in a frying pan there didn't seem much use in going to all that bother. Almost everything with Fidelio was *mañana* —tomorrow.

But he was a friendly old codger and one of the best leather craftsmen in the Territory. His hand-tooled saddles were prized above all others; his belts and chaps and quirts and bridles were creations of exquisite artistry. Old Fidelio took pride in his handiwork. "No hurry-up, hurry-up, hurry-up," he would say, and took his own good-natured time to everything. This was probably the reason why he still wore patched clothes and seldom was able to clank two cartwheels (silver dollars) together.

The town of Squawberry Flats was thrown up around a wide central plaza in the old Spanish fashion. A road flanked each side and most of the buildings were of sun dried mud blocks, called "adobes." The more important establishments—bank, assayer's office, the Pinto Bar, an apothecary's shop, Town Hall and Teel's office—were grouped along the southern side of this square. This road, heading east, went past the smelter and on through the greasewood to Sulphur Springs Valley; heading west, it eventually crawled into Tucson.

Otie Clegg's GENERAL MERCHANDISE occupied the southernmost building on the square's west flank. Cattycornered across from this, in the plaza's northwest corner, was the stage station with, beyond it, the corrals, track and horse barns of the Fair Grounds. At the northeastern corner of the plaza, flanking the trail which led to Clover Cross, Wagonwheel and Turkey Track, were the livery stable and corrals run by Ed Stokes.

The Benson road, angling east from this same corner, was built up on both sides with the dilapidated hovels of the Mexican quarter and it was here, among these unplastered and rain-gutted shacks, that old Fidelio had his saddle shop. There were more cur dogs and shrill-voiced, pot-bellied, half-naked brown children to the square inch in this section than in the entire rest of the town. Most of this property was owned by Starl Crefts' Clover Cross Land & Cattle Company. Moses Teel made the rounds on the first of each month and, whenever the rent was not ready and waiting, the family was promptly moved into the street.

Stumbling through the clutter of accumulated junk, tin cans, broken bottles and yapping dogs, Danny thought the most beautiful sight he had ever beheld was the lamp-lighted window of Fidelio's shack. Not until he glimpsed its feeble glow did Danny realize how much he had unconsciously been counting on the old man's aid.

The mongrel pack had left him to go tearing off after a tamale vendor and in the comparative quiet each bumped can or rolling bottle set up a nightmare crash of sound. He thought that never in his life had he felt so done in; he could hardly put one foot before the other.

There was no denying that Fidelio's light heartened him as he limped painfully up to the sagging back door. But with his hand raised to knock he suddenly froze in his tracks. A mumble of voices drifted out of the house.

The old man had company!

Danny almost cried. And who could blame him? To have come so far . . . But feeling sorry for himself would not butter any parsnips. He took a hitch in his belt and squared his drooping shoulders. Backing off a little way, he tried to think what he should do.

Asking Fidelio for the loan of a horse was one thing. To request the favor in the presence of another was quite a different thing, however. It might be fully as risky as approaching Ed Stokes.

He might wait, of course, until the old man's company left; but waiting, too, posed problems. What if one of the neighbors should notice him loitering out here? Or supposing some dog suddenly set up a racket!

He didn't know what to do. He had managed to get here without being detected, but he doubted his ability to slip away as luckily. Though he was much too exhausted for any clear thinking, he understood well enough the dangers of discovery. In this part of town a knife or a bullet was generally used to rout prowlers and, even were he to get off more cheaply, there would still be a multitude of questions. It was to avoid the danger of questions that he had come to Fidelio.

Perhaps if he could get some idea of who was in there . . .

Crouching down, the better to see where he was putting his feet, Danny worked his way around toward the window, praying that his shape would not be seen against it. The window had no shade or curtains and he now observed that it was partially open at the top. The view, from where he finally stopped, showed a section of the old man's workshop, including the front, the back of the saddle maker's tousled head and one arm of the visitor. That arm was not enough to give his identity away, but the sound of his voice started Danny's heart thumping.

There could be no doubt about it. Fidelio's visitor was young Paul Crefts and, judging by his tone, he was in a sod-pawing mood.

"I don't care!" he was saying arrogantly. "I gave you

the order for that saddle last week—you lazy pelados are all alike! A dirty, thieving, shiftless lot whose word——"

"But, *Señor* . . . I 'ave tol' you to make the good saddle take time. I 'ave tol' you other mans also want saddle——"

"They can wait. Confound you, I told you this was special and must be ready for me today! You know who I am! If you want to stay in business, you'd better hump yourself. I'll send Coffin Creek Charlie after that saddle the day after tomorrow and you'd better have it ready!"

The arm disappeared and then Danny saw young Crefts move across the room, plainly aiming to depart. But at the front door he paused to regard Fidelio with a scowl. "Now don't forget! It must be made of yellow leather. I want it hand tooled in that twined roses pattern. I want silver conchos every place you put a string. And remember—day after tomorrow! If you figure to stay in business here, you'd better have it right!"

He went out, slamming the door behind him.

Danny could hear old Fidelio muttering. He heard the creak of springs as "Beau Paul" got into his yellow-wheeled buggy, and the larruping thunder of flying hoofs as the disagreeable youth gave his horse a taste of the whip.

The smell of lifted dust drifted back but Danny waited a moment before getting to his feet. The way young Crefts had acted almost made him ashamed he belonged to the same race.

He wondered what Beau Paul's rush was, why he should be wanting a new saddle in such a hurry. But it wasn't until he reached the door that the significance of

103

the matter finally came to him. The day after tomorrow would be Snooper Herald's birthday!

"Golly Moses!" Danny exclaimed in dismay. He had completely forgotten all about it. He'd been intending to get her something himself. It was too late now to send away for anything. But, now that he knew about that mortgage, he couldn't afford to anyway. He might get her some candy. . . .

Clamping shut his lips, Danny knocked on the back door of the saddle shop.

"*Amigo!*" Fidelio cried with delight when he saw who it was. "My house is your house." He brushed a pile of tools and scraps from a chair and conscientiously puffed upon it, afterwards wiping it off with his elbow. "Sit down, *amigo,* an' tell me how you are."

Danny flopped into the chair with a sigh.

"You are tire'," Fidelio said and considered him with deep concern. "You no come by *caballo?* You *peon*—alla time walk, walk, walk?" He laughed at his joke, then put a finger to his lips. "Come here, *amigo,*" he said, beckoning. "You look."

Moving over to a rack by the wall, he snatched a dark cloth away and Danny's eyes went round in amazed excitement. "*Mira,*" Fidelio said—"Ees no *bueno?*"

"You bet!"

The subject of the old man's dramatic unveiling was a brand new yellow saddle, lacking little to be ready for delivery. It was easily one of the finest ever seen in that part of the country, Danny thought. Every stroke of the

104

twined roses pattern stood out bold and free, a piece of hand tooling that was almost perfect. The oxbow stirrups were encased in the sort of tapaderos seen only on the saddle of a *rico*. Here was the work of a master craftsman and Danny asked with a twinge of envy, "Is that the one you're making for Paul?"

"For Paul!" Fidelio stared. "*Chihuahua*—that noisy worm! Would I make such a niceness for such a one?" Then he smoothed his scowl away with a shrug. "Pretty soon complete—maybe *mañana*. I don't know. You like?"

Dry of throat, Danny nodded. "It's beautiful," he said at last. "Someone's goin' to be mighty proud——"

"Someone!" Fidelio laughed. "Ees for you, *amigo*."

"For me! Oh, no—" Danny sighed. "I couldn't possibly afford it."

"Afford? What ees this?"

"Too mucho *dinero*," Danny said. "I have no money—broke!" he explained, pulling out his pockets to show there was nothing in them.

The old man smiled, patting him on the shoulder. "*No le hace.* No matter. Between friends what ees money? You no pay—me give."

Danny's eyes filled up. He couldn't trust his voice for a bit. At last, he managed to say, "I—I couldn't let you do that. Too *grande*, Tio Fidelio. Too *mucho trobajo*—too much time, too much work——"

"Ah—*trobajo*. Say no more. It ees yours."

But Danny shook his head. "You're forgettin' Paul Crefts. You can't make a saddle between now and the

105

mornin' of the day after tomorrow—not the kind of saddle he's ordered. No, Fidelio; put on the silver conchos and sell him this one. He's aimin' to give it to the Señorita Paula. Since it is for her, I would like for you to do this."

Forestalling further argument, Danny told the old man how Beau Paul's father had produced a mortgage on Wagonwheel, and of his own determination to pay this off if he could. Then he told him about the stage robbery, and what happened afterwards, concluding: "So if you can loan me a horse to get home on, I will sure consider it a favor."

"*Chihuahua!*" Fidelio exclaimed. "This ees bad, this thing—no *bueno*. You must watch the step. Thees man, she's no stop for no thing. Pretty soon take ranch—*no bueno por nada!*"

"They may take it," Danny scowled, "but not if I can help it."

"Ah, *pobrecito*. But what can one man do? Already they 'ave put big reward for catch thees *coyote bandido*— five hondred pesos. Maybe put you in jail, take ranch!"

Danny shook his head. "I've got to be gettin' home, Fidelio——"

"I get *caballo*. You wait."

In a few moments he was back with the horse. Danny climbed aboard, shook the Mexican's hand. "Now remember, Fidelio, you sell the saddle to 'Beau Paul'—if for no other reason, do it to please me. Don't tell him a thing, just give him the saddle and be sure he has the money to pay for it."

"Ees no *bueno*, *amigo*. Use the head, not the elbow. If he give saddle to *señorita*, what you give?" He pulled a long face. "Pretty soon *señorita* say you no like. Ah, Danny!" He grinned, digging a thumb in his young friend's ribs. "Pretty soon *señorita* maybe marry coyote!"

FOR A MOMENT Paula couldn't say anything.

The man was sitting his horse twenty feet away. No telling how long he had watched her. He had one knee crooked about the horn of his saddle and his shoved-back hat showed a sweat-beaded forehead that was a whole lot whiter than the rest of him. There was an amused kind of grin on his face, half compounded of malice, and his eyes were scrinched from the smoke of his cigarette.

It was Forney, the sheriff.

Amazement and relief struggled for mastery of Paula. She stared at the lawman in complete bewilderment and could not have been any more surprised had he been some queer monster from another planet. Dode Forney, of all people!

She managed a shaky laugh and Forney said: "Reckon seein' me give you kind of a turn. Guess you thought, like enough, you had this trail to yerself." He looked at her a moment before he asked, "Yer pappy know you're out here?— Humph! Never mind. I kin see he don't."

He sat a while then, rubbing the brass horn of his saddle and smiling. "You ever hear tell of a girl called Red Ridin' Hood?"

"I don't believe," Paula said stiffly, "that I quite catch the illusion. What has Red Riding Hood to do with my father?"

"Well, that's a question," Forney admitted. "Mebbe we'd better go ask him. Turn that crowbait around an' I'll ride back with you——"

"I'm not ready to go back."

"Just feature that!" The sheriff chuckled; then he looked at her obliquely. "If you're just out ridin'; you kin ride just as well in the other direction. I'd be failin' in my duty if I was to go off an' leave you out here. Badlands ain't no place for a young lady. Lot of rough characters driftin' through these hills. If you'll turn your horse around now——"

"Leave my horse alone!" Paula flared. "I'll ride where I feel like——"

"Hoity toity!" Forney mocked. "You'll ride where I tell you, an' it won't be to Wagonwheel."

Paula gaped at him, astounded. "Have you taken leave of your senses?"

Forney grinned. "I expect you catch my meanin'. You've got past the eighth grade."

Paula didn't care for the look in the sheriff's eyes. She didn't care to be kept here talking, either. She had another ten miles still to go and time was passing. She took hold of her reins to ride past him and he put his horse squarely across the trail, blocking it.

"Get out of my way!" Paula cried.

But the sheriff held his horse right where it was, grinning like a cat. "I don't think yer pappy'd want you messin' around that outfit."

"But I'm not going to Wagonwheel——"

"You kin say that again. Turn your horse around now an' I'll ride back with you."

Paula bit her lip. She had an angry impulse to use her quirt on him, but something about the way he was eyeing her told her she had better not try it. Inwardly furious, she managed to sit tight until she was able to say with some semblance of control, "Has my father asked you to look out for me? Because if he hasn't, you're not my guardian. And if you're not my guardian, where I ride is no business of yours."

The sheriff nodded. "I expect most times you'd be right about that. But this ain't most times. An' you ain't most people. Any time I see a banker's daughter throwin' up dust in this kinda country I'm bound to make it my business."

He smiled at her sourly. "Lucky for you I come along when I did. If I hadn't been out to see Tom Lark . . . well, no matter. Point is, you're old enough to know what could happen if one of these tough mugs driftin' through the hills come onto you like I done. He'd have you trussed up in a cave some place before you could say abracadabra."

Paula said, "That's ridiculous!"

"I'm glad if you kin see any humor in it. Yer pappy wouldn't be doin' much laffin' about the time he unfolded a demand for ransom. It's time you growed up an' quit tomboyin' round. Come on, let's git started. A man in my job has enough on his hands without playin' nursemaid to a dang spoiled kid."

Paula felt more riled than ever. Her brain seethed with her effort to think up some suitable comeback, but she knew the futility of further argument. Chagrined, resentful and angry as she was, she realized that physically she was no match for the sheriff. If he was really determined to take her back to town, she was going to have to go back whether she wanted to or not. And there was still another factor adding weight to her surrender. Forney had implied that he'd been out to see Tom Lark but he certainly hadn't been coming from that direction. And when she'd first sighted him he'd had a burlap sack lashed behind his cantle, but there wasn't any sack behind his saddle now.

She really had wanted to talk with Huron. But, because she had no choice in the matter and because she felt the need of thinking this thing over while she had all the details fresh in her mind, she turned her horse around and let the sheriff have his way.

When Danny, mounted on Fidelio's pinto mare Querida, left the old saddle maker's yard, he hardly knew what to do, or even where to go. He supposed he ought to go home, and he'd been aiming to, but Fidelio's remarks concerning the stage robber had channeled his thinking along a different track. Fidelio had said there was a five-hundred-dollar reward on that fellow. Five hundred dollars would take care of the first payment on that mortgage —if he could get it. And after the way that fellow had tricked him, Danny was certainly feeling in a good mood to try. Besides, hadn't the Mexican said very plainly a thought which had been hounding him all afternoon?

They might put him in jail for that business. They might, indeed, if that grasping Starl Crefts had anything to do with it—or could figure how to work it. There was a better than even chance they might manage it. Just let Starl Crefts discover that he'd been out there and he would find some way of pinning it on him, never fear.

Unless, of course, in the meantime, someone managed to catch the real culprit.

This was not likely, for what did they have to go on? For the matter of that, what had Danny? He would not be found with that red roan horse and the roan, by itself, proved nothing. Which reminded Danny that by last accounts that dadburned robber had Rattler. Good old dependable Rattler, with the Wagonwheel brand plainly stamped on his hip.

Danny began to think that maybe he should have put in more time trying to find old Rattler. As soon as that fellow had come to where he'd cached his own horse he would have turned Rattler loose.

Against the obvious wisdom of this, however, was the thought that if Crefts should be mixed up in the robbery, Rattler would probably be shortly in evidence—would probably turn up along with the robber's hat, neckerchief and slicker. Which would really be something!

Danny, sitting his borrowed horse in the darkness, reckoned he was in a mighty bad spot. Danged if he did and plainly danged if he didn't. He could sure use the five-hundred-dollars reward money, but going after the robber would be no Easter egg hunt. That scalawag would know him—would know anyway, after getting hold of Rattler, that it was someone from Wagonwheel. It might enter his head to shut both of their mouths!

Golly! That thought straightened Danny right up in his saddle.

He would have to warn Wishbone to keep his eyes peeled. The more Danny thought about it, the more convinced he became that both he and Wishbone were in danger from that fellow. He wouldn't know how much Danny had observed and, just to play safe, it was entirely in the cards that he might lay for them some place with a loaded rifle.

It was not the kind of thought that made a fellow feel exactly comfortable.

Danny looked about him nervously and wished rather wildly that he was safe home in bed. The night seemed a lot colder than it had been and his throat felt drier than a dusty boot.

Why, that fellow could be almost any place! How was Danny to know him before it was too late to do him any good? How did you go about guarding against an enemy you didn't even know?

And supposing it were someone he *did* know!

"Thunder!" Danny exclaimed, and kicked the mare into motion, pointing her head toward Wagonwheel. He held her down to a walk until he got well clear of town, and then he hit her a lick with his quirt and prayed she wouldn't stumble or throw him.

But after ten minutes of that headlong travel some vestige of reason reasserted itself and he pulled her down to an easy lope. A little more thinking and he pulled her down to a walk.

If he was going to be shot at, he was going to, that was all. He couldn't rush through life at a headlong gallop, just because someone aimed to take a shot at him. There was no use getting in an uproar about this. Sure that robber would be after him. If he had the least suspicion Danny might be able to identify him, you could bet your last nickel he would do his best to put Danny where the law couldn't reach him.

But other men had been in that same boat and survived.

When he'd grown more used to the notion, it occurred to Danny that it might not be such a bad idea to have that fellow come after him. If Danny stayed close to home, the man would have to come there. If any stranger showed up, you could feel pretty sure that—but supposing the robber wasn't a stranger?

That would make it kind of tough, and no mistake. Still, if Danny and Wishbone were to put their heads together, maybe they could hatch up a plan that would trap the bandit. It was worth thinking about. When it meant staying alive a man could do a lot of things.

It was after eleven o'clock when Danny reached Wagonwheel. No lights showed, nor had he expected any. Wishbone was in the habit of retiring fairly early and had probably gone to bed a long while ago. Danny didn't approach the house right away though. Tired as he was, he was much too excited and worried to get careless.

114

He studied the buildings from a distance for a considerable while before working in closer, and even then he kept his eyes skinned, probing the shadows for any sign of movement. Everything looked about the same as when he had left it, but he was taking no chances. Keeping to the deepest shadows, he wormed his way into a thicket of mesquite and tied the borrowed mare. Then, afoot, he moved in slowly.

But there was nobody around, no one but old Wishbone stertorously "sawing wood" in the bunkhouse. Danny went and got the mare, rubbed her down and stabled her, leaving her with an armful of hay. Then he went in the house and climbed into bed.

He was late getting up the next morning. He felt as though he'd been dragged feet first through a knothole. Every muscle ached like blazes, but he felt a little better after eating the hearty breakfast Wishbone threw together. Then he shoved back his chair, watching the old man pack his pipe.

Wishbone wanted to know what he had got for the mares. The old foreman had guessed the reason for Danny's trip away.

"Nothing," Danny answered, and told him how the wild stallion, Paleface—that had been Caliban's colt—had lured the mares away.

The old man shook his head. "He's a devil, that one. I dunno what folks is goin' t' do around here if that dang hoss ain't took care of. Most hands figured, when the Stockmen's Association put that whoppin' big bounty on him, somebody'd git his scalp inside of a fortnight. But that rascal ain't like no ordinary hoss. He's got a head on his shoulders an' he sure knows how t' use it."

Momentarily distracted from his own gloomy thoughts, Danny showed a stirring of interest. "You mean people have tried to catch him?"

"Tried! Aye, they've tried, all right. Half the ranchers in this Territory have worked a spell at it, one time or another. But that hoss is smart. He ain't goin' t' be caught by no home-growed methods——"

"How much bounty have the stockmen put on him?"

"Biggest bounty ever put on a hoss—one thousan' dollars in good, hard cash."

Danny's eyes got big. "One thousand dollars!" he exclaimed as though he couldn't believe it. "Golly, that's a lot of money, Wishbone."

"Anybody catches that hoss'll *earn* it," the Wagonwheel foreman declared. He considered Danny with a curious expression. Then he scratched a match on the heel of his boot, cupped the flame to his pipe, broke the match and dropped it. "I kin see what you're thinkin'. You might as well fergit it. We could sure use the money but the rope ain't been twisted what'll ketch that hoss. Ol' Jack Stebbins spent a whole dang winter tryin' t' drop a loop on him an' never got nearer'n a long rifle shot. It jest can't be did, an' that's all there is to it."

"He could be walked down, couldn't he?"

Wishbone answered that question with a snort. The look he gave Danny was one of mixed contempt and pity.

"Boy," he said, "that bounty was put on Paleface better'n six year ago. Every busted-down tramp in this country has been after it an' that dang yaller devil is still runnin' loose. Still stealin' mares an' tearin' down fences."

He puffed on his pipe and watched Poncho, the shepherd dog, chasing a lizard. "Algie Perkins got a rope on him onct—thought he had 'im fer sure. Got 'im snubbed ag'in' the bole of a sixty-foot cottonwood. Had him dang nigh choked down—an' what happened? Algie's rope popped like it was made outa paper an' that hoss took off like a bat outa Carlsbad. No one ever come nearer t' gittin' their hands on that money an', if you want my opinion, no one's gonna."

Poncho came trotting up and licked Danny's hand. He was a good-looking dog, with his shaggy black coat and brown, soulful eyes that were always so quick to see what was needed. Danny'd raised him from a pup and he thought the world of Danny.

Danny sighed and let Paleface slip out of his mind. He had more urgent things to think about now. He said, "The Benson stage was held up again yesterday," and told Wishbone how he had seen it from afar, and how he had gone up there and how the robber had craftily stolen his horse.

Wishbone's eyes goggled. "Jumpin' jackrabbits!" he exclaimed excitedly. "I hope you didn't ride in on that roan!"

Danny smiled wanly. "I wasn't quite that foolish." He explained how he had feared the whole deal might have been some elaborate trap Crefts had set to put the onus of banditry upon him. "I don't suppose there is anything in it," he added, "but I wasn't aiming to get caught the way you were. I walked back to town and I was almighty careful to make sure no one saw me. I got in after dark and borrowed Fidelio's paint mare."

Wishbone sighed lugubriously. "Now it's startin'," he growled darkly. "You never should of sassed that dadburned lawyer. Talkin' t' him the way you done was jest like signin' your way into the poorhouse—or worst. You shoulda sold out t' Crefts like I told you. Nothin' good'll come of this. You mark my words! Crefts'll git this place one way or another an' you'll be powerful lucky if you don't wind up in jail."

"Then you think Crefts is back of that stick-up?"

"I dunno what t' think. But it's plain as the nose on your face he's mixed up in it. Who knows where we'll find ol' Rattler? They're apt t' ride him right over the trail this robber took gittin' away from where he stopped that stage. Then our goose'll be cooked fer sure."

Danny looked puzzled.

"Cripes!" Wishbone scowled. "Can't you savvy plain English? What way could they hit on of smashin' Wagonwheel quicker? You didn't fall fer their stunt of leavin' you afoot with that roan. They prob'ly counted on you ridin' away on that critter. When you dodged that trap, they had to figger out another. All they had t' do was t' rub out any tracks on the road an' put another double set there—the roan's on the road an' Rattler's in the brush. Then they show both sets travelin' into the hills up north of the stage road. Then they lame up ol' Rattler an' turn him loose or shoot him, the roan goin' on an' cartin' off a double burden. Where does that leave you an' me when the sheriff reaches Rattler?"

"You mean—" Danny moistened his lips. "You mean," he said, abandoning school talk and falling into ranch vernacular, "the sheriff will figure it was me an' you that done it?"

"What else'll he figger?"

After a moment Danny said, "But we don't know that they've done that. We don't know that those tracks have been tampered with."

"We don't *know* tomorrow'll be sunny," Wishbone grumbled, "but it's a pretty safe bet."

"But you're figuring, as I did, that this whole peculiar business is some kind of trap Crefts has set. Supposing it isn't? Supposing Crefts had no part in it—what then?" Danny asked.

Wishbone looked at him pityingly.

Danny, flushing uncomfortably, doggedly stuck to his point. "I know it's hard to think this isn't some kind of plot, but it doesn't have to be. That robber could be the very same fellow that held up the stage last month; maybe he doesn't know Crefts from Adam. He might be just some saddle bum or grubline rider holing up in the hills, figurin' to get himself a stake by holding up the stage——"

"He might be a alligator too, but he ain't."

"Let me finish," Danny said. "Whatever he is, let's suppose for the moment he has no connection with Clover Cross or Crefts. Now then, he sticks up that stage. He discovers me makin' towards him. He sees a good way to

119

get rid of that horse and maybe saddle me with the blame for that robbery. I do just what he thinks I'll do. He grabs my horse and rides off.

"Now, supposing," Danny argued, "that after he gets away from there—to wherever he has his own horse hidden —it suddenly comes over him to wonder how much I saw. Supposing he gets worried. Supposing he decides I may know a lot more than would be good for him. What would *you* do if you were the robber and figured things out that way?"

Wishbone stared a moment, turning it carefully over in his mind. "I don't see that this notion leaves you any better off——"

"Never mind that. What would you do?" demanded Danny.

"I reckon I'd shut your mouth."

"Exactly! All right," Danny said, "he would know from Rattler's brand where to look for me, wouldn't he?"

"If he was a stranger, he wouldn't. But I guess he could find out." Wishbone said, abruptly anxious, "Mebbe you better stick close around here for a while——"

"That wouldn't stop him from holin' up in the brush and waitin' his chance to cut me down with a rifle."

"Great Jehosophat, boy! Don't talk like that—it gives me goose pimples. Mebbe you better git clear outen the country."

Danny shook his head. "What I'm getting at is—if this notion is the right one—don't you reckon he's bound to come here? But supposing he didn't get too good a look at me? What if all he knows is that I'm someone from this

120

outfit? Then first of all he'll scout around, wantin' to look this outfit over——"

"Golly!" Wishbone whispered. "There was a strange galoot here yesterday—yesterday evenin' it was, jest after I'd et my supper . . ."

14

THE IRON FIST

PAULA WAS JUMPY as a cat with wet feet. She scarcely knew what to do. She was caught hard and fast on the horns of a dilemma. Right was right, no getting around that; but there was such a thing as justice—at least she hoped there was—and where could there be any justice if she ignored her promise and let the forces of greed and evil take Danny's ranch away from him without ever lifting her hand? For that was what it amounted to, and it could easily turn out to be a great deal worse.

Her father had told her to stay away from Wagonwheel. But she could not keep her thoughts away and these, ever and always with mounting insistence, kept bidding her go there before it became too late.

True, Danny might scoff at her story, might shrug it away with a contemptuous sniff or ignore it entirely. And that rattle-brained Wishbone was submerged in the past with the ghost of a horse and Starl Crefts' fury that could set him to quaking if you so much as said "Boo!" Yet it was Danny's right to know what was on her mind, for she had promised to help him all she could.

That she might get Huron Jones to carry her story to Danny had, of course, already occurred to her. It was the obvious answer to her inability to reconcile right with justice. But there were complications which made her hesitate to put her ideas in writing. Besides, her strange assortment of news was much too urgent to be put in a letter which might lie for days in the Squawberry Flats post office before anyone from Turkey Track came in for the mail. Yet she dared not trust this verbally to a messenger.

Her original need to see Huron had, after her forced return to town with Dode Forney, been swallowed up and forgotten in this need to get her thoughts before Danny. And how ridiculous it would be for her to ride clear out to Lark's ranch after Huron when, to reach Turkey Track, in the first place, she would have to pass Wagonwheel.

Paula spent two miserable days frittering round the house after returning from that first blocked attempt to see Huron. She could not get away from her thoughts or from the conviction that Danny should be made aware of them. Not even her birthday could change that.

After all, her father had not known what the score was when he had handed down the law about Wagonwheel. She was sure that, if he knew all the facts, he would offer no objections—and yet, she wasn't as sure as she would like to be. And she hadn't been able to bring herself to tell him. That worried her, too. There was no denying that, over the past three weeks, her father had grown more distant than ever. Not a demonstrative man, J. Cornelius

Herald was always wrapped up in deals—*big business* was the way the townfolks put it. But of late, it had seemed to Paula, he'd become more remote than ever. One might almost suspect the bank wasn't prospering, if an opinion were to be based on the way he was acting. He seemed hardly to notice that Paula was around and, at dinner, he would frequently sit staring off into space while his food got so cold it was a crime to eat it. Other times, he would sit glowering at his plate as though the good, tasty meal she had prepared offended him. And it was useless to try to talk with him. Half the time her remarks passed right over his head. When he did condescend to notice them, he seldom bothered to do more than irritably grunt a reply, which, more often than not, had no bearing on the subject.

And so a second day passed, a second night of restless tossing.

The next morning, bright and early, Paula headed out of town, in the direction of Lark's ranch. She had finally decided that she would make up her mind on the way as to just what she had better do.

When she'd planned to visit Huron, the time the sheriff had turned her back, she had been obliged to rent a horse at Stokes' livery because of Plumb Duff's lameness. He still wasn't feeling up to his normal pranks, but something warned Paula not to go to the livery. If it was Dode Forney's intention to keep her immobilized in town, she would not put it past him to have told Ed Stokes her father didn't want her riding out on the range. Or, again, Forney might have somebody watching the livery, in which case, if she left from there, Forney would follow her. So Paula started off on Plumb Duff.

It was around ten o'clock when she caught her first glimpse of Wagonwheel. It looked as calm and peaceful as though it had nothing to worry about, and this appearance of serenity halfway spurred Paula to resentment. It would not be looking so smug if it knew what she knew!

But as she drew nearer a vague unease began to lay hold of her. The place looked entirely too calm, she thought. There was an air almost of desertion about it.

Premonition put its chilly breath about Paula. What if Dode Forney had been here already and dragged Danny off to the Squawberry Flats jail? But could a sheriff do that without a definite charge? And what charge could anyone bring that would ever hold water?

Of course, there was that stage robbery. The whole town had been agog with it the evening the sheriff had fetched her back from the badlands. Suppose they'd found something to connect Danny with that! It was said that Dode Forney was still combing the country and almost any excuse would look good enough to Crefts, if it served to put Danny back of bars for a while. He would not care two figs whether Danny were really mixed up in it, for he would know very well that Danny, in jail, could not possibly hope to pay off that mortgage.

Forgetting her father's orders and her own arguments with herself in her anxiety about Danny, Paula turned Plumb Duff, and urged him toward Wagonwheel. Her cheeks were pale as she pulled up and looked about the yard. She could not see any horses in the old pole corrals.

125

She did not hear any sounds—not even a bird call. There was no sign of any movement. Wagonwheel had every appearance of an abandoned ranch.

She rode ahead slowly, worried eyes nervously flicking about the empty yard, her apprehensions mounting. She was further disquieted when she saw how the battered screen door on the sagging front porch stood open, creakily swaying to each vagrant breath of the capricious breeze.

It made her throat squeeze shut just to look at it.

She was heading her horse toward the porch when a voice, coming out of that dim front room, said: "Get your horse in the barn and slip in the back way."

Paula almost fell out of the saddle.

"Oh, Danny!" she cried, when she could get her tongue working. The sudden relief of discovering him safe had left her feeling limp as a dishrag. "Oh, Danny, I——"

But Danny's voice cut her off. "Put your bronc in the barn and get out of that yard!"

Taken aback, Paula looked toward the porch with her mouth open. Then resentment chased the surprise from her face. To be talked to like that, after all she'd been through, was enough to make anyone furious.

With blue eyes snapping, she spun Plumb Duff around like a twister.

Danny Brockett was due for a rude awakening if he thought he could order her around like that! He could take his rundown ranch and go jump in the lake!

With her back ramrod straight, she was almost to the gate when, through a shimmer of tears, she beheld a great dust boiling up just beyond it. *There must be somebody coming*, she thought, and swiped the back of a hand across her wet lashes.

She saw a spring wagon then, behind a team of bright bays. These went clattering past at a headlong gallop and, if Plumb Duff hadn't jumped back out of the way, they would have run her down just as sure as squeezed apples make cider.

Blowing dust off her face, Paula called indignantly after them, "Why don't you watch where you're going!" And then her eyes went round and big with interest. She had recognized the driver as Moses Teel, the Clover Cross attorney, and the man taking up what was left of the seat was the Starl Crefts hardcase, Coffin Creek Charlie!

"Save the women and children first," Paula mumbled, and stood up in her stirrups so as not to miss anything.

She saw a black, bounding shape come off the porch and make for the team with its teeth bared, growling.

"Poncho!" Danny shouted, coming out of the house; and the dog reluctantly stopped, still bristling, as the team drew up before the porch with a flourish.

Moses Teel eyed the dog vindictively through his cheaters and the look he gave Danny would have split an oak rail.

"I told you to keep that dog tied up," he said as though he were having a little trouble with his breathing. He reached underneath the seat for his umbrella. "Now I'm telling you to get rid of him—I don't want no nasty mongrel around here!"

Paula saw Danny ram his fists in his pockets. She could

see he was seething but he kept hold of himself. His chin made a stubborn line. His eyes were level.

"When you own this place, you can start giving orders——"

The man beside Teel slapped his thigh with a guffaw. Teel's face turned red and then went white with anger. But he didn't explode as Paula expected him to do. He just sat there a moment, glowering down at Danny, and then he said with a grunt, "Where's that no-account Reilly?" And when Danny didn't answer, "Well, no matter," he continued crisply, "I can just as well tell you. We'll want a count of your stuff—an itemized account of every animal wearing the Wagonwheel brand. The first payment on your note comes due on the first—that's two weeks from tomorrow. When you come in, bring that list along with you."

He waited a few moments and then he asked, impatiently, "Cat got your tongue?"

"Mister Teel," Danny said, "what you ask is impossible."

"You mean you can't meet that note?"

"I can't give you that list. All our help has gone off——"

"Gone off where?"

Danny shrugged. "I don't know. They've quit. It would take Wishbone and me a good month to comb this range——"

"Duke Brockett kept books, didn't he?"

"Yes, but——"

"Fetch them out here then. I'll take a look at them."

Danny hesitated. "I'm not sure you've got the right——"

"Never mind the right, sonny. It's the *left* you wanta watch." Teel's companion grinned, slapping his gun butt.

Danny swallowed a couple of times, closed his mouth and tramped into the house. Paula saw the pair in the wagon put their heads together, whispering; then the Clover Cross gun fighter twisted around in his seat, swept his eyes up and down and gave her a leer. "Hello there, sweetheart. Was you waitin' fer me?"

Paula fetched up her chin and pretended to ignore him.

Coffin Creek Charlie chuckled. "I bet you get a real hidin' when Teel tells yer ol' man he saw you out here."

Before she could think up a fitting reply, Danny came from the house with the old, faded ledger his dad had kept the accounts in.

Teel got ponderously down from the wagon under the watchful eye of black Poncho, took the book and went over the figures. Paula wondered if Danny was here by himself and, if he wasn't, why Wishbone had not made an appearance. Then the lawyer put the book down and took off his spectacles.

"According to these figures," he told Danny, "you've got one stallion; thirty-eight mares, of which seventeen are still in their prime; three horse colts; four geldings; fourteen fillies; twelve mixed yearlings and nine sucklings. Is that correct?"

"Well, I don't know," Danny answered. "That's what we *should* have, but wolves and weather are bound to have cut that down some. And then, of course——"

"I understand all that," Teel said testily. "Naturally

129

you've lost a few here and there. But these numbers are substantially correct, are they not?"

Danny licked his lips. "Well, no," he said finally, and took a quick glance at the lawyer's companion. "We've had a little trouble with that wild horse——"

"Paleface?" Teel took off his glasses and tapped his teeth with them. He peered at Danny irritably. "You mean that confounded stallion your father sold Mr. Crefts?"

Crefts' gun fighter shifted his seat on the wagon. He spat out his match stick and leaned balefully forward. "You talkin' about the stud that guy Reilly run off with?—that the one? The horse you cheap crooks drove off into the mountains?"

Danny appeared minded to exchange words on that subject and Paula held her breath apprehensively. But in the end Danny nodded without opening his mouth.

"You mean to tell me," Teel scowled, "that horse came through your fences and made away with a bunch of this Wagonwheel she-stuff?"

Danny looked uncomfortable. "Well . . . not exactly. I was fixin' to take a few head to market——"

Moses Teel's brows shot upward. He puffed up his chest like a prodded toad. "You *what?*"

"I was trying to get some cash to make a payment on that note. Only way I could figure to do it was to sell off a few of my horses——"

"*Your* horses! You don't own any horses," Teel snapped indignantly.

"I own the Wagonwheel horses——"

"You don't own a durn thing!" Teel shouted; and Poncho, the black shepherd, lifted his hackles. In his perturbation the lawyer never noticed the dog. "Everything on this place is tied up with that mortgage—*everything*, do you hear? Every last stick of furniture! Every horse! Every fencepost!"

He slammed a fist in his palm and looked mad enough to bend bar iron with his fingers. His wattles turned red and he grabbed up his umbrella from where he'd stuck it in the ground while going over the accounts.

To Poncho that reefed stick must have looked like a weapon. He came up off his haunches with a furious growl. Danny collared him in mid-spring, but the lawyer hadn't waited. He went scampering for the wagon as fast as he could hike it. Poncho loosed a fierce bark and Teel went up over the wheel without touching it. He just rose right up off the ground like a jackrabbit and stood there puffing with his feet in the wagon bed, his hat nearly off, his steel-rimmed spectacles dangling from their ribbon like a hanged rustler twisting at the end of a rope.

It was terribly funny, but Paula had never felt any less like laughing. Teel would never forget this as long as he lived. His hands shook, his cheeks shook—even his voice had a shake in it. But he hadn't been sidetracked. "H-how many head did you lose?" he quavered.

Danny frowned at the dog and let go of his collar. "Five fillies, seven young mares and eight aged ones."

"Twenty head!"

The lawyer's voice was a cry of anguish. Paula thought he was going to have a fit for sure. He flopped down on the seat and then jumped up again as though a centipede had crawled up his pantsleg.

"I ought to have you arrested!" he cried hoarsely. His mouth opened and shut several times before further words found traction. He glared and glowered and waved his hands. "You had no right whatever to move those horses off this ranch. I don't know what Mr. Crefts will want to do about this, but I'd be serving his interests in a mighty poor way if I didn't take steps to protect his property."

He scowled at Danny grimly. He spoke briefly under his breath to the heavy-set man beside him and the Clover Cross gun fighter got out of the wagon.

Swinging back to Danny, Teel said, "Mr. Prebble's going to remain here until I find out what Mr. Crefts wants to do. I would strongly advise you not to attempt to dispose of anything further unless you care to find yourself in very grave trouble."

He sat down gingerly and tucked his umbrella underneath the seat. Then he picked up the reins, gave a cluck to the horses and sent them on across the yard in a clattering circle. He had them almost straightened in a run for the gate when Poncho left the porch in a flying leap.

A grin twisted Coffin Creek Charlie's tough face. His left hand dipped and came up spouting flame. There was a loud report and Poncho—almost onto Teel's horses—went head over heels in a trail of lifting dust. He staggered up on three legs with the other paw dangling and

Teel swung his team before the dog could catch his balance.

Paula shut her eyes quickly, but she heard bones snap as the wheels went over him. One thin, frightened wail fled upward through the sunlight and then no further sound disturbed the noise of Teel's departure.

15

SOMETHING TO THINK ABOUT

COFFIN CREEK CHARLIE slipped his gun back in leather. He took one look at Danny's face and loosed a hearty guffaw. "What's the matter, sweetheart? You look gant as a gutted snowbird," he sneered, and threw back his head and laughed again; after which he went off toward the bunkhouse.

Wishbone's voice, sunk lower than the cream in a tom-cat's saucer, crept through the screen of the open porch door. "Is it safe fer me t' git up off the floor yet?" And the parrot he'd fetched back from the war in the islands let out a raucous squawk and cried, "Batten down the hatches!" and hid his bald head underneath the porch step.

But Danny was too sick to say anything. His dad had bought Poncho for him on his tenth birthday, a rollicking, frolicsome, little black pup whose tail, when he wagged it, used to shake his whole body. Danny had practically grown up with that dog and the sight of him now, stretched so still and unmoving in the wheel-tracked dust

134

of the empty yard, was like a knife twisting in him. Never again would this place be the same. Never again would Poncho chase lizards, help out with the horses or come like a twister at the cook's call to grub. Never again would he lift his paw to shake hands or hear Danny's loved voice singing his praises.

Danny's mouth twisted, trembling, as he fought his silent battle. What kind of guy was he to be standing here like this?

He dreaded to go out there, to have to look at Poncho closer, yet he knew that he must do it. No man would leave a partner lying out there in the dirt.

He drew a shuddery breath. But there was no good delaying this. "Get a sack," he called to Wishbone. "Fetch a good one without holes in it."

He had to exert all his willpower to force his dragging feet across that sunlit yard. He reckoned dust must have got in his eyes because all he could see was a kind of bright glimmer, and his lids felt hot and scratchy.

But he finally made it, and back again, with the limp form cradled in his aching arms. He crossed the warped porch, stumbled past the sagging door that still stood drunkenly open; and it wasn't until much later that he realized Snooper was with him. By that time he and Wishbone, between them, had got Poncho ready.

"And now what will you do?" Paula asked. "You're not going to have any picnic with that Charlie bedded down in your bunkhouse."

Wishbone let go of the sack and stood up. "You mean he's fixin' t' hole up here?"

"You heard what Teel told him," Paula answered. "He's to camp right here and keep an eye on you till Teel learns from Crefts what he wants done about those mares—about their loss, I mean."

"Yeah," Wishbone said, with his mind plainly wandering. For the fifth time in the space of five minutes he sent an edgy look across the yonder outside silence. When he looked again the parrot, who had been watching him, nervously flapped his wings and squawked, "This ain't no place fer a weak heart, matey."

The old man gave him a nasty glance and Paula said to Danny, "I've come onto something you may want to look into. You know where the— Well, after all, Danny, the least you can do is *listen!*"

Danny's eyes came around like the eyes of a sleepwalker. "Sorry, Snooper. You were saying?"

Paula shook her head at him. "You know where the trail to Squawberry Flats goes through that mess of scattered rock that locks away Crefts' winter range from his summer? Well, the other day, when I was on my way to the Turkey Track, I had almost come out of them when I happened to notice another rider off west of me——"

"Off west!" cried Wishbone. "You must be mixed up. There ain't no trail——"

"Let me finish," Paula said. "I didn't think there was either, but this fellow was certainly riding in a way that suggested he had come from somewhere southeast of there. And he seemed to be following some kind of a trail. He was a little bit ahead of me and the dust was blowing pretty badly. I couldn't see his face but there was a burlap sack lashed behind his saddle."

She looked at Danny appealingly. "I don't know why the sight of him scared me, but it did. I got panicky. I had almost reached the buffalo flats. I couldn't see any place at all where I could hide; and by this time it had become pretty certain that his trail was going to run into mine—or come out so darn near it he'd be sure to see me."

"Gosh!" Wishbone exclaimed. "I'll bet you was fit to be tied."

"I was. And I was sure by then that there was no way to avoid him. I didn't dare let him know that I was frightened, though. If he'd been up to anything he didn't want discovered——"

"All right," Danny cut in. "What happened?"

"I came out on the flats and didn't see a soul."

Wishbone's jaw dropped. "You didn't see *no*body?"

"Not at first," Paula answered. "I couldn't understand it. I looked for tracks and didn't see a sign. The only trail I could see coming out of those rocks was the one I was on, and it was plumb empty. Then I saw him. He was sitting his horse in a clump of mesquite, watching me."

"Gee willickers!" Danny cried. "Who was it—did you know him?"

"It was Sheriff Dode Forney."

"Forney!"

"Aw—heck!" Wishbone straightened up disgustedly. "All that lather an' nothin' but Dode Forney."

Paula looked at him resentfully. "You can scoff if you

137

want to. I was pretty relieved myself. But what was he doing there? Where had he come from?"

Wishbone brushed that aside. "Prob'ly chasin' some cows——"

"Whose cows? And why? And where had they gone to? *I* didn't see any cattle. Or any tracks of cattle. Or of anything else."

"What did he say?" Danny asked after a moment.

"He wanted to know if my father knew where I was. He asked the queerest thing then. He wanted to know if I'd heard of a girl called Red Riding Hood; then he told me to turn my horse around. He seemed to think I was headed for Wagonwheel. He made me ride back to town with him——"

"*Made* you?"

"Well," Paula said defensively, "he wouldn't let me by. He put his horse across the trail and sat there giving me the strangest look till I'd turned mine around."

"What d'you s'pose ailed him?" Wishbone wondered.

Paula shrugged. "He seemed to have it in his head that I was on my way to Wagonwheel. He was very determined that I should go back to town. He pretended to be worried for fear I might be carried away by outlaws or something, but you know that's preposterous. Why would anybody want to run off with *me!* There was a lot more to it than that—I *know* there was."

They all stood around without talking for a moment, Danny and Wishbone thinking over what she'd said. "I expect it will sound outrageously dramatic," Paula explained a little sheepishly, "but I had the idea he didn't want me to see his tracks."

Wishbone blinked. He looked at her carefully. "You ain't sick or nothin', are you? You ain't been touched by the sun?"

Paula tossed her head. "You see," she said to Danny, "he had told me he'd been out to Tom Lark's. You know well as I do how the Turkey Track lays—it's northeast of there. Yet the first time I saw him he wasn't coming from that direction; he looked to have been coming from out of the *south*east, and he was heading north*west*. And I guess I forgot to tell you, but he was carrying a rifle."

"You mean carryin' it in his hand?"

"He hasn't got to using his feet that I could notice."

Wishbone grunted. Danny looked thoughtful. "What's to prove he wasn't huntin'?" Wishbone asked her.

"In that pile of rocks?"

"There's prob'ly jackrabbits in there——"

"Jackrabbits!" Paula exclaimed scornfully. "Would you go hunting jackrabbits with a .45-90? And here's another thing. When I first saw Dode Forney—when he was cutting through those rocks—he had a heavy-looking burlap sack behind his saddle, but when I met him on the trail, he didn't have it any more."

An odd look of intentness had come into Danny's eyes. He went over to the door and scanned the yard for several moments. Then he said to Wishbone, "That give you any notions?"

"I think," declared the old man carefully, "we better sell this place an' git outa here."

And Corpus Christi, the parrot, wagged his bald head emphatically. "I'll call that bet an' raise you five."

"Snooper," Danny said, "when you came by that place today, did you look around for tracks?"

Paula shook her head. "I didn't dare," she answered frankly. "Do you think there could really be a trail in there? I mean a secret trail that no one ever heard about?"

Danny said grimly, "I aim to find out. If there is, and the sheriff's been usin' it . . ." He let the rest go, frowning thoughtfully.

Wishbone said, "I wouldn't trust that feller no farther'n I could throw him. An' I'd keep plumb away from them rocks if I was you."

"You say he seemed to be coming from the southeast, Snooper?"

"Well, I couldn't be sure, of course, but that's what it looked like. There was a lot of dust blowing over there where he was riding. I judged he was half a mile away when I first saw him—pretty near due west of where I was. If he wasn't on a trail, he was certainly traveling like it."

"First chance I get, I'm goin' over there," Danny said. "If there *is* a trail——"

"But what do you suppose happened to that burlap sack?" asked Paula. "And what do you suppose was in it?"

"That's one of the things I aim to find out. I guess you know the stage was robbed last week? Well, I happened to be ridin' around in that neighborhood and I saw the actual holdup."

"You did!"

Danny nodded. "I don't want you to mention this,

Snooper, because the facts of the matter is I'm scared half to death. But I saw the whole thing through my spyglass."

He told her all about it. About how he had gone over there, and about following the tracks and about how the holdup man had tricked him and ridden off on Rattler. He told her of his suspicions, too, and of how he'd finally decided the stickup man was a stranger; and about the stranger who had come to the ranch, pretending an interest in buying horses.

"Now," he said, "I'm not so sure about that guy. Maybe he did want to buy horses. Maybe he didn't have anything to do with that holdup. You see, after Pop Cantos had gone off with the stage, the robber broke open the strong-box—which would have been too awkward to carry off on a horse—and put whatever was in it into a burlap sack. I could see the print of the sacking in the dust of the road up there."

"Gosh!" Paula said, and then she said it again. Excitement put a thin tremble in her voice. "And you think maybe the sheriff——"

"I don't know." Danny frowned. "It hardly seems like Dode Forney would be fool enough to stick up that stage——"

"He'd be ornery enough——"

"But where's the percentage? Starl Crefts owns a big chunk of smelter stock. If he ever suspicioned Forney'd pulled those holdups——"

"I doubt if Forney'd have the nerve to do it on his own," Paula declared. "But it would be just like Crefts to rob his own company— Don't look at me so foolishly! Why wouldn't it? Anything he took in that way he could put right in his pocket and who would be the wiser? That would be clear profit; he wouldn't have to share it with the rest of the stockholders."

"He'd have to split it," Danny said, "with whoever was pulling the holdups."

"Maybe he wants to close the smelter down. He might figure that would force the other fellows to sell out. I wouldn't put *anything* past Starl Crefts—besides, as you've already said yourself, the whole deal might be a stunt to get you put in jail."

"But they couldn't have known I'd be out there," Danny protested. "They didn't know I was planning to sell those mares. They sure as heck didn't know Caliban's colt would run off with them. That's for certain! And if I hadn't finally decided to go along to town, I wouldn't ever have seen that stickup."

"Well, the facts are plain enough," Paula said. "Whether they knew you'd be around or not, the stage was robbed. You saw the robbery and the robber saw you. Whether he recognized you or not, he would have known the minute he got your horse that you were someone from Wagonwheel. We'll say, just for argument, that Crefts had nothing to do with this business. But you say the robber put his loot in a burlap sack and we know for sure that Dode Forney was in the badlands that day with a burlap sack tied back of his saddle. We know that he was carrying a rifle. And that when I found him watching me, he didn't have the sack. Whether Forney robbed the stage or not, he *did* leave a burlap sack in those rocks."

Wishbone looked as though he were about to come down with another fit of the shakes.

"It's just like handwriting on the wall," Paula said. "It's just like an arrow pointing right straight at Wagonwheel. And they've still got your horse. You'd better think about that. If I were you, I'd get right out there and try to find that sack before it winds up in your ranch house and puts you behind the bars."

16

"WELL, WELL, WELL!"

THERE WAS NO doubt but what Snooper had something there. Much the same notion had been juning around in Danny's own head. If Starl Crefts had any part in this business, he would turn every wheel that would offer any chance of putting Danny in jail. And the Clover Cross boss didn't have to be mixed in it; the stage robber himself would be glad to see Danny given the blame for his actions. And if that robber were Dode Forney, he might be laying the groundwork for Danny's arrest right now.

Swift action was plainly indicated.

Danny reached for his hat and Wishbone said, "You ain't takin' such foolishness serious, are you?"

"What's foolish about it?" Danny wanted to know. "I'd have a fat chance of savin' this outfit in jail."

"Jail!" Wishbone scoffed. "That's a girl's gab, boy—an', even if she's right, what's t' prove goin' out there ain't the very thing they're hopin' you'll do? Gosh, boy—use yer head! That sack's the last thing you wanta git close to."

"What's your idea, then?"

"Let 'em hev the durn place! You can't beat 'em any-how—they're bound t' git it one way or another. Sell out t' Crefts. Take what you kin git an'——"

"Nope," Danny said, "I ain't the sellin' out kind. I'd as soon be dead, as knuckle under to that polecat."

Wishbone said darkly, "You may *be* dead before you git done with this. Tougher guys than you hev tried t' buck Starl Crefts—an' where are they now?"

But Danny's jaw was set stubbornly. He said, "Think back a bit, Snooper. When you were on your way out here, are you sure you didn't poke around a little, tryin' to find that trail?"

"I was too scared to do much looking. I was afraid maybe Forney would be around there some place. I just went over by that mesquite thicket where he'd been watching me. Between the wind and the dust, there wasn't much left of his tracks—not enough, anyway, to trail him."

Her cheeks flushed a little when Danny kept watching her. "Well," she said defiantly, "I *did* look a little. Thinking of his general direction—the way he was headed when I first caught sight of him, and using the mesquites as a starting point—I went into the rocks about a hundred yards. But I didn't find anything. Except around those trees, I didn't see any tracks at all."

Danny put on his hat.

Wishbone didn't say a thing until he'd reached the door with Paula close behind him. Then the old man got up and said, "How far d'you think you'll git from this place with that two-legged centipede curled up on the doorstep?"

"Coffin Creek? He won't care where I go. All he's hangin' round for is to make sure I don't try to move any more horses."

"I wish't I could believe that."

"He'll just figure I'm fixin' to ride a ways with——"

"An' what about that stranger we been watchin' fer—that hoss-buyin' jasper? If he's the one that stuck up the stage, he may be camped out there in the brush with a rifle."

"I can't help it." Danny sighed. "I've got to locate that sack."

Paula, meanwhile, had been looking oddly thoughtful. Now she said, "Perhaps we'd better kick this round a little more. Wishbone could be right about one thing. Maybe they *are* kind of hoping you'll go out there. If the sheriff were to catch you with that sack in your hand——"

"I'd be just as bad off if they found it on this ranch," Danny said. "Or if old Rattler turned up with the bandit's mask and slicker. I can't spend all my life sitting round this place waiting. That's why Crefts always wins—the fellows he goes after never dare to lift a finger lest they bring him down on them harder than ever. By the time they see they've got to fight, the fight's over."

"But if you're caught with that sack, you'll be a cooked goose, Danny. No jury would ever believe in this world——"

"Then we'll *all* go out," Danny declared. "We'll all go out there together."

"Lovely," Wishbone muttered.

"Well, at least," Danny growled, "you two could testify you saw me find the durn thing."

"An' we'd all wind up scratchin' fleas in Yuma."

"You're forgetting who Snooper is," Danny countered. "They wouldn't dare accuse the daughter of J. Cornelius Herald——"

"No?" Wishbone eyed him with a pitying contempt. "It's plain you don't know much about sidewinders. That bunch would dare *anythin'*! As fer that precious banker, he's up to his neck—" He came to a full stop, peering at Paula. "He's got all he kin do t' look out fer himself."

"No jury in this country would ever send a girl to jail——"

"But I ain't no girl," Wishbone said. "An' you ain't, neither."

Paula took a long breath. "We've been overlooking something. Danny needs money; he needs a lot of money quickly. I guess you probably know the smelter has offered five hundred dollars for the arrest and conviction of the man who stopped the stage. But it's the express company who's responsible for the loss of that money. They've come into it now with an outright offer of five hundred more for the return of that payroll."

"Gosh!" Danny exclaimed.

Paula said, "There'd be a lot of risk to it, but if you could earn that money, it would sure help you out. For the moment, anyway."

"It sure would." Danny nodded. "Far as the risk's concerned, I'm up to my neck in risk right now——"

"I can't see what good them rewards'll ever do him."

147

Wishbone scowled. "T' collect either one, he's got t' first git his hands on the evidence. Soon's he latches onto that, he's played right into their clutches. That's what they're wantin'—t' git him caught with the evidence. Soon's he gits it, they grab him, an' that's all they need t' send him up fer . . ." He let the rest trail off, standing stiffly as though listening.

"Thought I heard a hoss," he muttered after a moment, and moved over to the door. Danny looked out, too, but didn't see anything suspicious. "Probably Coffin Creek——"

"He ain't got no hoss, unless he's lifted one of our'n. You hear anythin'?"

Danny shook his head.

Wishbone scowled uneasily. Then he tiptoed out on the porch and stood a moment. "I'd of swore I heard hoof-beats," he grumbled, coming back.

"Well, if Coffin Creek's gone, I won't do any bawlin'," Danny promised. "As for Forney catchin' me with the goods——"

"We can get around that, I think," Paula told them. "Danny can go into town and have the express company get him appointed as a special officer to look into this business."

"By golly!" Danny cried, brightening visibly. "That's the very idea. I'll ride in with you, Snooper, and see them right away."

"They won't appoint you," Wishbone growled, "because they'll claim yer too young."

"I think they will," Paula countered. "They're desperate to get that money back. They may not think

Danny'll have much of a chance to succeed, but they'll appoint him. You wait and see. They can't afford to lose all that money and, besides, their reputation's at stake."

"Well, then, mebbe they will appoint him," Wishbone said, "but if he latches onto any evidence, Forney's goin' to jump him sure as cows hev calves. Time him an' Crefts gits done twistin' things around, he won't know up from down—nor anybody else."

"At least he'll have the express company's backing, and that's better than nothing," Paula said. "I don't be-lieve——"

"*Shh!*" Wishbone hissed; and they all heard it then, the clipetty clop-clop of approaching horsemen.

Paula looked askance at Danny, over by the door. He was staring round-eyed into the yard. Wishbone, coming out of his trance, moved across for a glance over Danny's shoulder.

His jaw flopped down to where it would almost do for an apron and his hands began shaking so that he couldn't have poured a cup of water into a cattle-trough without spilling some.

Paula looked for herself and found the yard filled with riders.

"Whatever in the world—" she began and then stopped, suddenly knowing, as her alarmed eyes recognized the face of Sheriff Forney.

He stopped his horse before the porch, touching his hat when he saw her, and a grin licked across his teeth like a cat's. "Well, well, well," he boomed. "Jest imagine seein' you away out here, little lady!"

149

Then his grin dropped away and he fixed his stare on Danny's face with a cold and wolflike glitter.

"I got information you're harborin' a criminal. We're goin' to hev to search this place—any objections?"

Danny swallowed a couple of times and then said, "No," too loudly.

"All right, boys," Forney said to his posse. "Spread out an' look around."

17

NO ROOM FOR LOAFERS

AS THE MEN piled out of their saddles and scattered, a dark suspicion crossed Danny's thoughts. He'd supposed, when Teel had quartered Coffin Creek on them, that the man had been left for his nuisance value as much as for anything else. Yet this visit from Forney so soon after Crefts' man had taken up residence seemed a deal too pat for just plain coincidence. The sheriff had announced that he was scouting for a criminal, but it appeared considerably more probable to Danny that what he was actually after was evidence—and Coffin Creek had been here plenty long enough to plant it.

Danny shifted his weight uneasily, glancing from the sheriff to Wishbone and back again.

Forney wasn't doing any hunting himself. He sat his blue roan horse in indolent ease, with a knee crooked around the horn of his saddle, a brown-paper cigarette stuck on his lip and his droopy-lidded eyes filled with smug malice.

Danny squared his shoulders. "I don't expect you're talkin' about Coffin Creek Charlie, are you?"

"Charlie? Nope," Forney said. "I don't hardly think so. I didn't know Coffin Creek was here, far as that goes. I'm campin' on the trail of that galoot that got off with the smelter payroll."

He paused a moment, running his eyes over Danny. "I can't think what Charlie would have to do with him. I don't suppose he happened to fetch a sack out with him, did he?"

"A—a sack?" Danny echoed, and his voice jumped in spite of him.

"Sure. You know—a tow sack. One of them burlap affairs. This stage-stopper couldn't git away with the strongbox, so he busted it open an' dumped his loot in a gunnysack."

Danny's thoughts leaped halfway to Benson but he didn't say a word until he had them corralled. "Charlie didn't have any gunnysack with him. He came out here with Teel in a wagon. Teel left him here, he said, to keep an eye on the place."

"Good idear," Forney nodded. "That Teel's a smart jasper. Understand you had a few words with him last week."

But Danny wasn't thinking of Teel just then. He was remembering the actions of the Clover Cross hardcase. After demonstrating his proficiency with that long-barreled pistol, he'd gone straight to the bunkhouse. But this did not prove he hadn't come out since, any more than his not having a sack proved he'd come here empty-

152

handed. He could easily have concealed a blue bandanna on his person or a big wad of bills from the smelter payroll——

Forney demanded impatiently, "Did you or didn't you?"

"Uh—what was that? Afraid I didn't catch your——"

"You better dig your ears out! What, I asked, was your idear in movin' twenty mares off this place?"

"I didn't know I wasn't supposed to. I naturally figured it was mine——"

"That ain't what I asked you."

"I know. I'm tryin' to explain," Danny answered, doing all he could to keep his voice level. "I've been told my father aimed to put this place in shape; that Mr. Crefts advanced him money on a note secured by a mortgage. Mr. Crefts' lawyer said if I wanted to keep this ranch, I would have to lift that mortgage. I told him I figured to keep it. So, on the first of the month, there's a payment coming due on that note—four hundred dollars."

Danny stopped a moment to swallow. "That's a lot of money, Sheriff. There's not many ways I could get it. I figured the best thing to do was try and sell some horses."

Forney nodded. Then his lips squeezed together. "I see," he said in a voice dry as dust. "You mean to keep this ranch an' the first of the month is less than three days away. Yep," he said, "I see a lot of things now."

Danny didn't like the way he said that. Paula didn't, either.

"Well, I guess I'll be weaving along," Paula said. "It's about time I was putting the potatoes on to boil. Take care

153

of yourself, Danny, and don't forget you've got a date to eat at our house tonight."

Danny hardly heard her. He understood she was trying to remind him to ride in and talk with the express company, but he was too worried and engrossed at the moment with the bland and yet inexplicably ominous manner in which Sheriff Forney was eyeing him—with the sense of alarm which the sheriff's queer tone had aroused in him—to answer her.

He finally turned to look at Paula but he didn't really see her. He waved a hand as she rode off but it was hardly more than a conventional gesture. All the time he was wondering, with a sense of impending calamity, about what had put that calculating look in Forney's eyes.

The sheriff didn't leave him long in doubt about the matter. A couple of his men came out of the harness shed and, when they shook their heads, he turned back to Danny.

"So," he said, "you're needin' money. You're needin' a lot of money—quick. You're feelin' desperate. I wonder if you'd be desperate enough to stop the Benson stage?"

Wishbone said, with his gray cheeks shaking. "That's a awful thing t' say to a boy——"

The sheriff skewered him with a look of contempt. "When I want your gab, I'll ask fer it." He brought his stare back to Danny. "I don't suppose you're prepared to admit it?"

Danny's voice, when he spoke, seemed to come from miles away. It seemed strange even in his own ears, yet the strangest thing about it was the remarkable fact that it

154

was steady. "No," it said, "I don't imagine I would ever be that desperate, Sheriff. It never entered my mind to rob the Benson stage or do anything else to get money that wasn't honest and aboveboard."

"You call it honest to sell horses that don't belong to you?"

"I didn't sell any horses."

"But you intended to."

"Yes, but I told you about that. I didn't know the mortgage tied everything up."

"Ignorance is no excuse," Forney said, "and I don't know that I can take your word for not knowin'. Mind you, I ain't sayin' I *can't* take it, but people's had trouble with this outfit before."

The look he sent Wishbone needed no interpreter.

"You can see how this thing stacks up to the law. Here's you needin' money so bad you can taste it. There's a stage comin' through with the smelter payroll. The stage gits stopped an' the payroll took off. You claim you didn't hev nothin' to do with it, but the facts of the matter is you're desperate. You don't wanta lose this ranch. You got to git your hands on some money quick. An' you got the nerve to do it. No Sunday school kid's goin' to tell Moses Teel if he comes back with the sheriff he had better come armed."

He threw his smoke away and looked at Danny narrowly. "What day was it you moved them horses?"

Danny thought back and told him.

Forney pursed his lips. "I been told that yeller stud run away with them. When was that, an' where?"

"The same afternoon. Up in Chamber's Canyon."

"What'd you do then?"

"It was gettin' on towards dark," Danny said, all too well aware of where this talk was heading. "I camped out."

"In Chamber's Canyon?"

"Yes, sir."

"What'd you do the next mornin'?"

Danny had one moment of extreme regret for the strictness of his dad's precepts. Always tell the truth, Dad had said; and he guessed he would have to do it. Or as much of it, anyway, as Forney's questions called for, and he reckoned that would be about all of it. It was plain as plain could be that he wasn't going to be believed, but there wasn't anything he could do about that, either.

He took a deep breath and said, "I started for home."

"Didn't spend no time lookin' round for your mares?"

"No, sir."

Something tugged at the corners of Forney's mouth. "What time would you say you got started?"

"Don't you answer that question!" Wishbone cried. "Don't you tell him!"

Forney lifted the anchoring leg from his saddle and dropped to the ground, light and quick as a cat. He caught the old man by the shirtfront. "You asked for this," he breathed wickedly, and slammed his fist into Wishbone's face.

The old man spun half around, eyes rolling. He got hung up in his spurs and went down. The sheriff's wild look beat at Danny's blanched features. "I asked you what time you got started."

Danny's knees knocked together like the thumps of a rabbit. He had to try three times before his voice would make sound and then all he managed to squeeze out was "Daybreak."

Some of the posse drifted up and stood around, watching Wishbone trying to get himself up off the ground.

"Daybreak, eh?" Forney pushed it around. "What time did you git home?"

"I expect it was pretty late."

"How late?"

"I didn't look," Danny answered.

"You can make a guess, can't you? That's the day the stage was stopped, the day that bandit grabbed the payroll. You prob'ly wasn't anywheres near there but, considerin' how bad you need money, it's my plain an' bounden' duty to find out how you spent your time. I reckon you could make it home from there in about six hours."

Danny licked his lips. "I—I didn't go straight home. I was closer to town than I was to the ranch. I wanted to talk with Mr. Herald——"

"I can understand that, needin' money the way you do. Herald can tell me what time you got there. How long did you talk with him?"

"I didn't see him."

"Oh. You didn't see him, eh? Why not?"

Despair's cold fingers suddenly closed around Danny's throat. It was hard to tell the truth with the grim result so clear before you. The simple facts were a plain trail of evidence that would take him straight to the jailhouse. Who would believe his dark suspicions and guesses? Not Dode Forney who'd been out in the badlands, hiding a sack.

Beckoning two of his men, Forney sent them in to take a look through the house. Then he repeated his question. "Why didn't you see him?"

"Something happened to my horse. I had to walk in to town. The bank was closed——"

"Herald's bank don't close till four o'clock!"

"I had to walk ten miles."

"What happened to your horse?"

"Someone stole it."

The sheriff's hard eyes went over him coldly. "Must've been a better nag than any *I*'ve seen round here. What'd he do—knock you off it? Stick a gun in your face?"

"No. I wanted to see about something. I left him tied to a——"

"Just a minute," the sheriff said. And then, to someone back of Danny, "What've you got there?"

Danny twisted his head and saw one of the possemen coming from the barn with Fidelio's mare. Before the man could answer, there came a shout from the house. A man stuck his excited face out the door. "We've got it! We've found the loot!"

The sheriff's jaw kind of sagged and then he said, brightening up, "So I was right! Where'd you find it?"

"Right behind the kitchen door—still in the sack."

"Good. Fetch it out here an' let's git goin'." The sheriff

gave Danny a stern and ominous look. "You can see for yourself how far a man gits when he tries to buck the law," he said sententiously. He snapped his handcuffs on Danny. "Can't afford to be takin' no chances with any customer desperate as you are."

Danny was too overwhelmed to protest. Old Wishbone had been right. He should have sold this place and cleared out of here. Now he'd go to jail and they would get the ranch anyway.

"Where'd you git this paint?" Forney asked, looking at the mare the man had led from the barn. "Humph—one of them fluidy mustard brands! Didn't even git time to run your iron over it, did you?"

"That mare's not stolen. I borrowed——"

"Sure. That's what they all say. Reckon that's why you had her hid in the barn! Pretty much of a all-around scamp, ain't you, Brockett? Put a saddle on that critter, Haines; we're takin' this rough actor in with us."

A short, bowlegged man came up, dragging a sack. "You want I should open this up?" he asked Forney.

"You keep your paws out of it," the sheriff said gruffly. "It goes straight to the express company. I want you boys to witness it ain't been tampered with."

Wishbone looked as though the end of the world had come. As they were hoisting Danny into the saddle, the Clover Cross hardcase strolled up from the bunkhouse and told the old man crustily, "Stir your stumps an' go rustle up some grub fer my supper! This outfit's under new management now an' there won't be no room here fer loafers!"

18

THE BEST LAID PLANS—

IT WAS GETTING along toward the shank of the evening when the dust-covered posse finally rode into town. A scattering of lights shone from the more pretentious dwellings and the smell of cooking suppers tantalized the tired men's nostrils. They'd been combing the hills for the past three days, living on jerky and warmed-over beans, and would be glad to slide their feet beneath their own well-laden tables. It wasn't every man who had enough civic pride to drop his own work and go tearing through the brush on a chase after fellows who might shoot if they were cornered. They were glad to get back and be done with it.

All this Danny realized with that part of his mind which wasn't pawing over his own problems. Of course he very well knew his direst problem right now was tied up with this arrest and what might come of it. There didn't seem to be much doubt about the outcome; he would be tried and convicted and probably sent to Yuma. And Starl

Crefts would get Wagonwheel and all that was left of Duke Brockett's horses.

He could see that much without any trouble. What he couldn't understand was how the stolen payroll had been planted in his house.

As the posse turned into the plaza, he saw the sheriff scowl when he beheld the growing crowd rapidly collecting in front of his office. Swearing under his breath, Forney fingered his gun butt nervously, as though he more than half suspected they might attempt to take Danny away from him.

Danny shivered a little himself, for he had heard wild tales of the things mobs sometimes did to prisoners; and he scanned the faces apprehensively, trying to determine the pitch of their tempers.

The sheriff's mouth settled into a hard, tight line, and he rode straight into the crowd after the manner of a cowman going through a flock of sheep, the posse trailing after him.

But nothing happened. The sheriff's manner took on more confidence and, though his surly eyes remained alert for trouble, his cold-jawed mouth became arrogant and scornful. He brushed all questions aside and got down from his saddle, flipping his reins across the tie rail.

"Haines, you take this young ruffian inside," he said, and gave the assemblage a grudging grin. "Yep," he nodded, "Brockett done it all right. We found the loot in his kitchen. Nope, he didn't put up no resistance; when we found the payroll, he come along meek as Moses. I reckon he's realized crime don't pay—not in *this* county, anyhow. When I go after a man, I git him."

Danny could tell by their faces the sheriff had assumed a new importance in the community. And then Haines was lifting him out of the saddle and hurrying him up the steps and into Forney's office.

The dark room seemed filled with people. Then somebody snapped a match to flame and the lamp's yellow light drove back the shadows and disclosed the solemn countenances of Huron Jones, Lawyer Clancy O'Toole and a tall, rawboned fellow Danny'd never seen before.

The sheriff's deputy stopped just inside the door, surprise stiffening him up and putting a frown across his features.

"Come right along in," O'Toole said pleasantly. "We've been waiting for you." Then he sent a smile at Danny. "Keep your chin up, young fellow. You're going to have a chance to tell your side of this story."

Danny felt grateful toward Huron for having fetched the lawyer here, though he couldn't think how his friend had caught wind of what was happening or how the telling of his story was likely to do him much good. Just the same, it was encouraging to know that someone was standing back of him.

Haines edged Danny toward a chair and went to lean against the wall, not looking very pleased at finding O'Toole on the premises. The Irish lawyer was an outsider who'd come to Squawberry Flats a few months ago from someplace in Illinois. He was just a bag of skin and bones, no taller even than Danny and just about twice as thin. He'd come here for his health, he'd said; and none who were friendly to Clover Cross had so much as an ounce of use for him. These called him a "conniving shyster" and he certainly had a knack for getting into Starl Crefts' hair, representing with considerable gusto every drifter, squatter and small-spread rancher that Clover Cross had any trouble with. He seldom succeeded in solving their problems but he did put Crefts to a great deal of inconvenience; and Moses Teel got red in the face every time his name was mentioned.

The old-timers around here liked O'Toole but frequently shook their heads, predicting a swift and uncomfortable end for him if he didn't wake up and pull in his horns.

Forney's spurred boots clattered up the steps and then he was standing framed in the door with his windburned cheeks creased in lines of surprise. He pulled up his dropped jaw with a sharp clack of teeth as his ugly little eyes fixed themselves on the lawyer.

"What're *you* waitin' fer?"

"I've been waiting to see you——"

"All right, you've seen me. Now git, an' take your friends along with you!"

"I intend to, when I leave," O'Toole smiled. "This is a bad business, Sheriff. What's the charge against this boy?"

"None of your blankety-blank business! Git out!" Forney yelled. "Git outa here while you're able or I won't be responsible!"

Danny held his breath as Forney clenched his big fists

and came belligerently forward, but the little Irishman stood his ground.

"Take it easy, Forney, or you may dig your own grave. This is a public office and you're just a paid public employee. Suppose you cool off now and answer my question."

Forney stood glowering as though he intended to hit him but the lawyer's blue eyes never wavered and, finally, Forney sat down. "I ain't made no charge yet," he said sullenly.

"You had better be thinking one up then. I've sent for Judge Botts and if that's the payroll you've got in that sack by the door, you had better get word to the express company's agent."

"They can hev it when I git done with it," Forney growled, but he sent Haines off with a message.

Judge Botts came in then, a wrinkled old man in an alpaca coat with a huge "walrus" mustache and tobacco-stained teeth. He looked at Danny with surprise and then said to the sheriff, "What in tarnation's goin' on around here?"

"I've caught the smart monkey that lifted that payroll off the Benson stage."

The judge's brows shot up. "You mean," he said, forgetting his grammar, "the Brockett boy done it?"

"I ain't makin' no accusations. I'm just tellin' you we found the loot from the stage back of a door in his kitchen. That's good enough fer me."

The judge considered the implications a moment, with his shrewd eyes keeping his thoughts to himself. "I ex-

164

pect," he said dryly, "you can safely remove those shackles now. Did he put up much of a fuss?"

"He didn't give me no trouble," Forney answered grudgingly. Pawing through a bunch of keys, he finally found the right one and took Danny's cuffs off, dropping them clanking into one of his hip pockets.

"Well, what's his story?" the judge asked impatiently.

Before the sheriff could answer, O'Toole cut in smoothly, "If Your Honor will permit it, I think perhaps his lawyer should hear it first."

"You his mouthpiece?" Forney sneered.

"I have that privilege."

"Very well," Judge Botts decided. "I can give you ten minutes. Take him out in the hall."

"If he gits away," Forney glowered, "just remember it was *you* that let him go out there!"

Nobody paid any attention to that. Danny followed O'Toole out into the corridor. Despite the encouraging trend the affair appeared to be taking, Danny wouldn't let himself put much hope in his prospects. O'Toole, it was generally conceded, was a pretty sharp lawyer; but Starl Crefts was a hard man to stop and Crefts, Danny knew, was determined to have Wagonwheel.

The lawyer's crisp voice pulled him out of his thinking. "Just hit the high spots and let's have it quick."

"I'll do the best I can," Danny answered, and told him first of all about the unexpected mortgage and the loan money Teel claimed to have turned over to Wishbone. Then he recounted how the Clover Cross had framed old Wishbone with the theft of Caliban's colt.

O'Toole nodded. "I can see we're up against some pretty unscrupulous people."

Danny told him then about the mares he'd attempted to market in the hope of raising money to meet the first two payments, and of how the wild stallion had disrupted his plans. "I camped out that night at the springs in Chamber's Canyon. I got up at daybreak, ate the last of my rations and decided to go to town and have a talk with Mr. Herald—Paula's father—about a loan."

He told of witnessing the robbery of the stage and of afterwards going over there and seeing the marks left in the dust by the sack into which the robber had dumped the loot from the strongbox. He told of tracking the robber and of losing his horse, and of the suspicions which had prompted him to walk the ten miles to town.

"Did you tell Mr. Herald of these things when you talked with him?"

"I didn't get to see him. That was a mighty long walk, Mr. O'Toole, and I took more time than I should have, I guess, making sure I wasn't seen. It was dark when I reached town. I borrowed a mare—it's outside now—from old Fidelio, the saddle-maker, and hit straight for home."

"So that, actually, you have no alibi for what you did with your time that day. I mean, no one saw you until you went to Fidelio's to borrow the mare?"

"Well—no one but the robber. I expect he must have seen me or he wouldn't have known where to find my horse."

O'Toole nodded. "I'm afraid he's not going to be of much help. What I'd really like to have is some disinterested witness who could prove the truth of your story. If you tell the judge what you've just told me, he will probably remand you to the custody of the sheriff and you'll be lodged in jail to await your trial. If only Forney hadn't turned up that payroll. . . . You're sure you've no idea how it got into your house?"

Danny shook his head helplessly. "Just before the sheriff came, Mr. Teel drove up with that fellow, Coffin Creek Charlie, who works for the Clover Cross—but I don't see how he could have put it there."

"Was the money intact—I mean, was any of it missing?"

"I don't know. The sheriff didn't say. In fact, so far as I know, he never opened the sack——"

"Well, we've got to get back to the judge," O'Toole reminded Danny. "I think you'd better keep still and let me do the talking."

The judge looked up as they came into the office. He seemed a little surprised to see the pleased arrangement of the lawyer's features.

Forney surged to his feet with a suspicious scowl. "I think," he muttered, reaching down for his hat, "I better go fetch Teel."

"What for?" the judge asked.

"You're goin' to give this feller a hearin', ain't you?"

"What does Teel have to do with it?"

"You're lettin' Brockett hev a mouthpiece——"

"The boy's entitled to a lawyer."

"Meanin' I ain't?"

Judge Botts eyed him coldly. "Are you expecting to be charged with something, Forney?"

"Course I ain't, but——"

"Then you don't need a lawyer."

"What difference does that make? Mr. Crefts——"

"In what fashion is Crefts concerned with this case?"

Forney gulped, shut his mouth and sat down, looking poisonous.

A sudden feeling of excitement rushed through Danny; and then, as he heard spurred boots come up the steps, he turned his head and saw Congrove Crosby standing in the doorway, taking in the scene with interest.

Crosby, a florid-faced Englishman who looked big enough to go out and hunt bears with a switch, was the express company's agent in this part of the country. His glance went straight to the sack the sheriff had dropped inside the door. Then he nodded to the judge and stepped aside to let Haines enter.

"Come in and find a seat," Judge Botts said, "and we'll get this business over with. The Sheriff informs me he's recovered the payroll. He tells me they found it in the Brockett boy's house. Thus far the Sheriff has not made any accusations. Are you ready to make your charge now, Forney?"

"It ain't my place to go makin' any charges. I went after that payroll an' got it. I told you where I found it. I don't like to fetch in a kid any better than the next man. If there's charges to be preferred, it's up to Crosby here to make 'em."

So they all looked at Crosby. He looked at the judge. "What does the boy say?"

O'Toole took his hip off the edge of the desk. "I'm

speaking for the boy. He doesn't care to discuss the matter."

The judge twirled his mustache.

Crosby asked, "What about you?"

"Same text." O'Toole smiled.

"All right, Sheriff," Judge Botts said. "Produce your evidence."

The sheriff didn't like the way this was going and gave O'Toole a black scowl. "I'll stand pat, too! Time enough to lay down my aces when this young scamp of a horse thief——"

"I object to that statement," Danny's lawyer interrupted, "as incompetent, irrelevant and wholly immaterial. I further object to it as calling for a conclusion on the part of the Sheriff which is not only out of order but is patently based on rumor and hearsay. In addition to being prejudicial to my client's best interests, it is a grossly uncalled-for piece of calculated libel——"

Crosby chuckled.

Judge Botts pounded on the desk. "You may save that oratory for the courtroom, Counsellor." He fixed stern eyes on the sheriff. "Either you've got a case or you haven't. If you have, this is the time to present it—with the proper and sufficient evidence."

Forney flung himself to his feet with a malevolent snarl. He flounced over to the door and grabbed up the loose end of the gunnysack. But, with the sack in his hand, his assurance returned and he stabbed Danny's lawyer with a baleful grin. "We'll *see* whether I've got any evidence or not!"

The neck of the sack was tied with piggin string. One slash of the sheriff's knife cut it open. Then his jaw went slack and his eyes almost rolled off his cheekbones.

Crosby, the express company's agent, moved over and peered into the sack without saying a word.

"Well?" the judge snapped irascibly.

Crosby snorted. "What he's got in that sack is a dead dog."

19

DARK PIT OF NIGHT

JUDGE BOTTS, of course, dismissed the case. After up-braiding Forney in no uncertain terms, he was about to offer his apologies to Danny when O'Toole cut in briskly, "I'm afraid my client's reputation has been materially dam-aged. We are going to file suit against the county and its sheriff for false arrest and defamation of character. We are also charging an employee of the Clover Cross Land and Cattle Company—to wit, one Coffin Creek Charlie—with the wilfull destruction of young Mr. Brockett's property, the dog. I'll have the papers filled out within the half hour and we will expect this character—the said Coffin Creek Charlie—to be removed from the Wagonwheel and taken into custody. I think that's all—for the moment."

He bowed to the judge with formal politeness, waited while Danny sorrowfully gathered up poor old Poncho, and then, still accompanied by the unidentified stranger, herded Danny and Huron Jones from the office.

"Well," he told Danny at the foot of the steps, "you're a free agent now."

"Thanks to you!" Danny sighed. "I don't see how I'll ever repay——"

"Let's not talk about *pay*." O'Toole chuckled. "I was glad of the chance to take a poke at that bunch. But make no mistake," he warned soberly, "you're not out of the woods by a long shot. Crefts and his understrappers won't be turned aside as easily as that. If you have any plans, you had better work fast."

"I aim to," Danny said, gratefully shaking the lawyer's hand.

"Well, I guess I'd better go and take care of those papers," O'Toole murmured. "Thanks for the moral support," he told the stranger, and went hurrying off.

Huron said, "Danny, shake hands with Mr. Creighton. He's the buyer who's takin' the fall shipment from Turkey Track."

"Glad to know you," Danny said. Then he turned to his friend. "If it hadn't been for you roundin' up that lawyer——"

"Don't thank me," Huron rumbled. "It's Snooper you wanta pin the medal on. Mr. Creighton an' me was just ridin' in to get a cashier's check when she come tearin' up like she'd been to a fire an' tells us the Sheriff's out to your place with a posse. She says you got to have a lawyer. So we took care of that. What you goin' to do now?"

"I think we'd better get something to eat," Creighton said and, despite Danny's protests, herded them over to the Lone Star Cafe. Hardly had they taken seats than the door opened and Paula came breezing in.

"Gosh, Snooper!" Danny cried. "Does your Dad——"

172

"Never mind him—it's *you* I want to hear about. Every last thing! Start right in from the time I left you, and don't you dare to leave out one word."

So Danny brought her up to date on his troubles. Then the cattle buyer said, "That lawyer was right about one thing; whatever you do, you're going to have to move fast. I can't think how Forney happened to pull such a boner——"

Paula said, "I can guess. You see, I bumped into him out in those rocks south of Wagonwheel the day the stage was robbed. There's only supposed to be one trail through there, and I was on it when I caught sight of the Sheriff over west of me. He was hurrying down what looked to be another trail. He had a sack tied on behind his saddle—a gunnysack just like the one they found at Danny's. When I saw him a little later, he didn't have the sack."

"You think he left it in the rocks some place?"

"Can you dig up a better answer? I think he hid it and I think he was suspicious I had seen him with it. He made me go back to town with him, probably intending to return and move it. This is all guesswork, but I bet it was the loot from that stage robbery. I'm betting he didn't have a chance to get back there. When he stopped at Wagonwheel today, he was probably just snooping. He got quite a jolt when he found me out there. So, when Haines sang out he had found the payroll and came out of the house lugging that sack, Forney jumped to the conclusion that one of us had found it."

Creighton nodded. "Sounds reasonable."

"We don't know, of course, that Forney robbed the

stage. And, if he did, we don't know whether or not he meant to plant the loot on Danny. If he did the job on his own hook, he probably aimed to keep it, and he may have intended to anyway; they could frame Danny just as well with the slicker and blue bandanna or they could have used Danny's horse," Paula said.

"Well, we could speculate all night," Creighton pointed out. "But I think Miss Herald's right. When the deputy said he'd found the loot, and came out of the house with that gunnysack, Forney decided to pin it on young Brockett here and oblige Crefts by getting him out of the way. If Forney *was* the man who took the payroll off the stage in the first place, he would be pretty sure Danny hadn't much of an alibi."

Huron said, "If I was you, Danny, I think I'd make myself scarce around here for a while. Forney ain't goin' to forget this——"

"Forney," Paula said, "is going to make a bee line for that rock patch!"

Creighton shook his head. "It's a possibility, of course, but I don't believe he will. He's too crafty a coyote to chance being caught out there with the goods."

"He won't be caught with them," Paula said. "He'll go out there with a posse and wait for Danny to find the payroll. Then he'll have him right!"

"You've got a head on your shoulders." Creighton nodded admiringly. "That's pretty sound reasoning. It's probably just what he'll do."

Danny drank the last of his coffee. "It's time you were gettin' back home, Snooper——"

174

"Since when were you appointed my guardian, Danny Brockett?"

"Now don't get your temper up," Danny said hastily. "It's just plain common sense. Your father——"

"Never mind my father. What are you cooking up now?"

"I'm going to have a talk with Mr. Crosby."

"Good! I'll go with you——"

"You'll go along home and keep out of this mess."

"Well, I like that!" Paula flared. "After all I've done——"

"That's just it," acknowledged Danny. "Your father runs the bank. He has to do business with these people. Starl Crefts is one of your Dad's directors and the Clover Cross account is probably the biggest one he's got. What do you think Crefts——"

"I don't care——"

"Of course you do! You want to ruin your father's business? What do you think would happen if Crefts was to hint there was something wrong, maybe pull out all his money? Where would that leave J. Cornelius Herald? You've got to look at this sensibly, Snooper. You run along home now and keep out of trouble. I'll find——"

"But you're so *scatter*brained, Danny! Always slap-dashing around— Look how you let Forney get away with old Rattler! You need——"

"Is that so?" Danny said, flushing, furious. "Maybe I *am* kind of dumb, but I ain't going to be tied to any girl's apronstrings!"

Paula shoved back her chair abruptly and got up.

175

Thanking Mr. Creighton for her supper, she turned away; but not before her eyes slammed Danny a look that was to stay in his thoughts for many a day.

When the door closed behind her Huron said uncomfortably, "Well, what now?"

"Right now," Creighton said, dropping some money on the table, "I've got to get back to Tucson." He slapped them each on the shoulder. "Glad to've met you, Brockett. Good luck—and don't let your gun get stuck in the holster."

"What'd he mean by that?" Danny scowled.

Huron shrugged. "It's probably one of them cityfied sayin's. No kiddin' though, Danny, you wanta watch out for Dode Forney. He ain't goin'——"

"I'm old enough to take care of myself, Huron! You go to talkin' like Snooper and I'm liable to get riled!"

"Well, gosh all hemlock——"

"Get that paint mare I left in front of the sheriff's office and take her over to Fidelio's. Tell him I'm much obliged. Then go over to Stokes' livery and rent yourself a good, tough horse that's got a lot of go in him."

"But I don't need a horse—I got one!"

"You're gettin' this one for me, though you don't have to tell old Stokes that. After you get it, go pick up your own and wait for me back of the stage office. You got that straight?"

"I reckon. What about Poncho?"

Danny's eyes clouded and he clenched his fists. Finally he said in a low, strained voice, "He—he'll have to go with

176

you." He set his jaw with determination. "Now stir up a breeze, Huron. We've got to move lively."

It was twenty-seven minutes after midnight and darker than a black cat's overcoat, when a pair of hard-to-see riders drifted quietly through the slit and stopped tired ponies in the last of the rocks. "This the place?" Huron asked, peering about uneasily.

Danny nodded. Then, remembering his friend couldn't see him, he said, "This is where Forney stopped her and took her on back to town. Over there're the mesquites where the sheriff sat and watched her. I guess maybe we had better light up that lantern."

"I ain't plumb crazy about showin' myself around here."

"I'm not, either, but we're not likely to find that payroll perambulatin' around in the dark. I'd a heap rather wait till morning but I'm afraid by that time it wouldn't be here any more."

"This place sure gives me a funny feelin'. If we bump into that bleach-eyed sheriff——"

"Quit worrying about it. You've got your rifle and I've got this pistol Mr. Crosby loaned me. We've got just as much right to be out here as Forney. I'm a special investigator, hired by the express company to look into that robbery. I've even got a badge——"

"Is it big enough to hide us both?" Huron said, mighty fervently, "I only hope we get out of here before he shows up."

"Say!" exclaimed Danny in sudden excitement. "We're

177

a pair of prize nitwits to go clambering around these rocks in the dark——"

"My notion completely," Huron approved.

"We probably wouldn't manage to locate a thing."

"What I been sayin' right along. If Snooper couldn't see any tracks or find that trail in plain daylight, what chance would we have prowlin' round with a lantern?"

"I've got a better idea. We won't even need the lantern——"

"That's a blessin'," Huron sighed.

"All we've got to do is keep back out of sight. When Forney comes, we'll follow him."

"You sure june up the pleasin'est notions!"

"What's the matter with that?"

"What happens if he hears us?"

"We'll have to be careful about that."

"Best way to be careful is to stay right here. Let him dig up the payroll and grab him comin' back."

"But he might not *come* back," Danny protested. "What if he got out some other way, then where'd we be? Nope, we've sure got to follow him, if we're ever going to get to the bottom of this business."

"Might be better if you followed him and I waited here. That way, we wouldn't have all our eggs in one basket. And if he should happen to get wise or crowd you into a corner——"

"I think we'd better stick together."

"What about the horses? What if one of 'em starts to nicker?"

"Guess we'd better not take any chance on them; I don't

expect we'll be needin' them for awhile yet, anyway. If Snooper's right, Forney cached that sack within a half a mile of here. Tell you what you do. You take these ponies off east a piece and tie them. Take them far enough off so if they make any racket——"

"And how am I supposed to find my way back? By the light of your smile?"

Danny thought a couple of moments. "We could signal with owl calls."

"And after we latch onto Forney, how're you figurin' to turn up the horses? More owl hoots, mebbe?"

That made Danny mad and he came near to telling Huron if he didn't like the setup, he could lope along home; he only barely clamped his jaw in time. For after all, these were important questions. Huron had a right to hunt answers. No good would be accomplished by flying off the handle.

Huron wasn't to be blamed for parading a little reluctance. Danny wasn't deriving much joy from the job himself. In addition to the strain of what he'd been through with the sheriff, he was very well aware that they were courting definite danger. Crosby had pointed out the danger emphatically. "No matter who he is, the man is bound to have the wind up. He may shoot on the least provocation—or without any. Take my advice, young man, and keep clear of this. Just tell me where you think the loot is and, if we recover it, I'll see that you are suitably rewarded."

But Danny wouldn't tell him. Even so, Crosby wouldn't have hired him if he had not realized that Danny was desperate. "I've got to get my hands on four hundred dollars by day after tomorrow or lose my ranch." That was what Danny had told him and that was why Crosby had finally given him the badge.

So it was only plain foolishness for him to fuss with Huron. "We'll have to worry about that when the time comes," he said. "The big thing right now is to be ready to slip after him when he gets here."

"Mebbe he won't come. What if it's all a wild goose chase?"

"He'll come," Danny said with conviction. "He'll come, if it's only to make sure we haven't found it. I think he'll try to move it. He can't be sure how much we know and, whether he's in this thing by himself or with others, he won't want to take any chances. For all we know, he may be in there right now."

"Yeah," murmured Huron, and then on a deep breath, "If you'll climb out of that saddle I'll be easin' off with these nags now."

Left alone with his thoughts, Danny's roundabout glances held little more comfort than Huron's had shown. Not that he was scared, Danny told himself fiercely, but he could sure name a pile of places where he'd just as lief be—if not liefer. The rearing shapes of half seen rocks appeared to shift and writhe out there in the gloom, always to edge just a step or two closer, after the way of redskins, creeping, creeping. The starless night hemmed him round with a monstrous hush that shackled his feet to the ground like roots.

180

He tried to give the call of an owl, but his lips wouldn't respond. Then he summoned all his willpower and moved toward the ink-black blotch of the mesquites, where the sheriff had sat his horse and watched Snooper. Funny thing about that. Coming out of the rocks, she had looked and seen nothing, neither trail, man nor tracks; and then, all of a sudden there he was at the edge of this thicket. Like a jack-in-the-box or a genii.

Very odd, Danny thought. Quite as odd in its way as the fact that he'd been traveling a corridor which hadn't any existence in other folks' experience.

Danny found himself wondering if Paula had imagined it, if she'd made the story up from whole cloth for attention. But that wasn't like Paula, and if she *had* made it up, why had Forney been so sure the sack Haines had found contained the loot from the stage robbery? No, she must have seen him and he must have had a sack.

But how could he have come out of those rocks and not leave tracks? Snooper'd been emphatic about that part. No tracks, she had said, and no sign of a trail. And then she'd looked up and found Forney watching her by the mesquites.

Danny studied them, seeing nothing in this gloom but a heavier patch of shadow, possibly twenty yards across and more than forty feet away from the crouching bulk of the closest rock. Not even a horse could jump that far!

Danny, shaking his head, was about to turn away and go sit on a rock while he waited for Huron when the metallic clank of cold iron against stone jammed the breath in his throat. Half turned, he stood rigid, staring into the murk. The sound had come from the right, off there in the darkness of the trail which had brought Huron and him from town.

But nothing moved out there. The night was quiet as a coffin. A cold shiver chased itself up and down Danny's spine. And then the sound of muffled hoofsteps crept across the hush and Danny, galvanized to action, backed hastily into the fringe of the thicket, oblivious to thorns in his desire for concealment.

He'd wedged into the branches barely in time for now, from the trail, came the unmistakable sounds of an approaching rider—the sand-choked rhythm of a moving horse, the jingle of spur chains, the creaking of leather. Then the shape of this traveler materialized, a solid black in the lesser gloom which enfolded him. The man was bent forward beneath his big hat, with his head half turned as though listening. Now he faced front again and came onward slowly, his thighs cradling the gleam of a rifle, straight toward the thicket where Danny stood petrified.

With a strangled groan, Danny tried to back deeper into the tangled growth. It was like pushing against a hemp mat. The interlacing branches of chaparral released their grip with the greatest reluctance and the thorn-infested foliage of gnarled mesquites slashed across his cheeks and clutched at his clothing till he was in a cold sweat of panic. He forgot the pistol Crosby had loaned him, forgot his brave plans for recovering the payroll. All he had mind for in that moment was flight.

The hoot of an owl softly cried for an answer while the nightmare shape creaked inexorably closer. Danny, with wildly straining eyes, saw the horse's dark nose come thrusting into the foliage.

Danny's knees, turned weak as water, dropped him into a shuddering crouch; but the horseman didn't stop. He didn't swerve or even falter but held steadily to his course, as though the trees that reared up before him existed only in Danny's thoughts. The desperation of terror lent new strength to Danny's struggles and, with chin folded over his kneecaps, he thrust himself frantically backward. He gained an inch, abruptly gained three more and prayerfully dug in his bootheels.

Something, parting, let go behind him and he went through the last of the branches like a bolt suddenly sped from a crossbow. His flailing arms struck nothing but space and his legs went sailing over his head, just as though he were going face first down a well shaft!

20

CAUGHT

DANNY hardly knew whether he had landed on his face or his back and he didn't stay there long enough to find out, either, for he could hear that horse still coming!

Badly shaken, but unhurt, he scrambled to his feet. Then he stared about him wildly. It was the blackest place he had ever been in and he wanted nothing so much as to get right out of it.

His outstretched hand came up against cold rock and, by the deep sand underfoot, he reckoned he was in some kind of cave or cavern. This impression was quickly strengthened when, after staggering several paces, he felt a cold draft push against him.

No wonder Snooper hadn't seen any tracks! Danny understood now why the sheriff had been so insistent about escorting her back to town. He hadn't aimed to leave her alone out here before the wind had had time to rub out his prints. Small wonder this trail had never been discovered with its start in a cavern completely hidden by a thicket that was more than forty feet off the course of general travel.

The slithering rasp of shod hoofs on a slope snatched Danny out of his thinking. This was no place for unraveling riddles. Bending down, he unbuckled his spurs and cached them away in a pocket lest their jingle-jangle betray him. Then his hand found the wall and, with this for guidance, he struggled as fast as he could through the heavy sand, moving away from the rider and toward the source of the draft, trusting that the racket of the horse would cover any sound of his exertions.

It seemed to him as though the wall gradually curved to the left. Before he'd gone forty paces he discerned a blotch of lesser darkness in the gloom ahead. This was probably the other opening, leading into the windy corridor where Snooper had first seen Forney.

He suddenly redoubled his efforts, every thump of his heart crying out for him to hurry lest Forney—or whoever this rider was—catch him silhouetted against the gray shape of that opening. He didn't need to do any guessing about what would happen if Forney discovered him!

When he felt as though he couldn't go another step farther Danny fell down in the sand to catch his breath; and it was then that he discovered there was no sound behind him. At first he couldn't believe it—thought the rasp of his breathing must be covering it up. But when he held his breath he couldn't hear anything either and he jumped to his feet, suddenly remembering what he was here for.

A fine investigator he was!

While he had been running his legs off, spooked by sheer panic, Dode Forney had stopped or taken some other direction—if it *was* Dode Forney.

Danny stood there panting, feeling proud as a lost sheepherder.

He would have to go back, that was all there was to it. The first payment against Starl Creft's forged note was due the day after——

Danny stopped in consternation. Tomorrow was *here!* He had less than thirty hours to rake up four hundred dollars and the only way he could think to do it was by recovering the stolen payroll.

But even as these thoughts went through his mind, his legs were reluctantly taking him back toward the scene of his recent terror. He knew he would never be able to live with himself if he had to acknowledge fright had lost him the ranch.

It seemed to him now that the darkness of the passage was not nearly so black as it had been. He had just reached the place where the wall made its curve when the nicker of a horse pulled him up short. The cavern rang with the sound and Danny, flattening himself against the rough wall, heard a harsh voice growl angrily, "Close your trap, you dang idjit!"

It was Forney's voice, no doubt about that! And it was uncommonly close, certainly not more than a few yards away.

With pounding heart, Danny crouched there unmoving, straining his ears to hear what was happening. But such sounds as he caught did not make sense to him and finally, with a frown, he was about to move forward when the need for stealth made him take off his boots. With bated breath and boots in left hand, once again Danny gingerly started around the bend.

He hadn't crept six paces when he saw the rear quarters of the ground-hitched horse and, simultaneously, saw Forney in the flair of a guttering candle. The sheriff's back was bent above a freshly made hole out of which, with much grunting, he was hoisting a gunnysack.

Danny reached for the pistol Mr. Crosby had loaned him and found nothing at his hip but an empty holster.

He tried to swallow but he couldn't. His mouth felt drier than a barrel with the bung out. The sheriff wasn't more than eight feet away and if he should happen to look up . . .

But he was busy at the moment with the neck of his sack. He plainly meant to make sure he had the right bag this time.

Danny could see the sheriff's rifle but it was too far away. Then he realized the horse was watching him, was winding himself up for another good nicker.

There was just one thing a man could do, and Danny did it. He dived for the sheriff with everything he had in him. He landed on Forney like a she-catawampus and, before the startled sheriff was able to grasp what was happening, had clawed to his feet and backed away with the lawman's pistol.

"Get 'em up!" Danny cried; and the sight of that wobbling muzzle with Danny's trembling shape behind it dumped the starch right out of Forney. He didn't even let go of a cussword, and the alacrity with which he put hands above head would have been a sweet sight for old Wishbone.

"You got any more guns on you?"

"N-n-no!" Forney gasped with his cheeks as white as paper.

"Get the neck of that sack tied up again then——"

"It's the swag that masked devil——"

"I know what it is," Danny snapped at him scornfully. "It's the smelter pay——"

"But you've got this all wrong," the sheriff protested. "I don't know no more about how it got here than you do. I just stumbled——"

"You're apt to stumble again if you're not right careful. Load it onto that horse now——"

"Watch out how you handle that pistol! That gun's set on a hair trigger, boy!"

"Then it'll go off pretty easy if I should squeeze it a little." The sheriff's obvious fright was doing wonders for Danny; he even managed a grin. "They say a kid with a gun's about as risky a mixture as a fellow can bump into. 'Case you want to find out, just keep edging toward that rifle."

Forney jerked back his foot. He hefted up the sack and got it lashed behind his saddle.

Danny waggled his gun. "Go stand over there with your nose to the wall and let's see how high you can get your hands up."

The sheriff scowled but did as ordered and stood there, meek as Mary's lamb, while Danny pulled his boots on and tried to figure out the next step. To get the sheriff outside without losing the drop looked to be as tough a problem as he had ever faced.

He finally thought he saw the answer. He got the lawman's rifle and thrust it in its scabbard. He picked up the grounded reins of the gelding. "Get that candle," he said, "and start hiking."

Forney licked his lips. "You know dang well I never robbed that stage. Cripes, boy," he whined, "a thing like this is liable to ruin me. Let's set down here a minute an' talk this over."

"You can talk to the judge. Now pick up that candle. If you value your health, you'd better see it stays lit."

Forney's eyes glinted balefully but he picked up the flickering dip and started off.

Danny swung into the saddle and followed him. He had no way of knowing where Huron Jones was by now, but as long as Forney led the way with that light, Danny figured he was safe. And, if Huron saw it, he was bound to come running.

"Keep it up where I can see it," Danny cautioned. "My finger's getting slippery. If this horse should happen to stumble, you might never know what hit you."

The sheriff visibly cringed. He went up the slope as carefully as though he were moving through a snake's den. With an even greater care he commenced to sidle through the brush. Then, suddenly, the light was gone and a gun kicked flame through the blackness.

21

"IT NEEDN'T BE THE TRUTH"

WISHBONE'S EYES looked as big around as saucers. It was the cool of the next evening and Danny and Huron, just back from town, had been retailing the news. "An' you mean t' tell me," the old man demanded, "they locked Forney up in his own dang jail an' handed over thet reward money without battin' a eye?"

Huron nodded. "That's right. What else could they do?"

"An' Danny made two payments on thet crooked note?"

"Yep," Huron said, "and got two hundred left over."

"Well, I swan! But didn't Starl Crefts do *anythin'?*"

"Never even showed his face." Huron chuckled. "These crooks is plenty brave long as things goes their way, but when things starts goin' against 'em, they'll pitch in their hands just as quick as the next. I used to figure Forney was brash as a hoof rasp——"

"Well, ain't he?"

"He don't like the smell of powdersmoke much. He

190

didn't know I was around and when he put out that light he reckoned to have clear sailin'. The doggone skunk could of got away if he'd showed a ounce of gumption."

Wishbone's eyes bugged more than ever. "Mean t' tell me he *quit?*"

"Just like a give-out horse. When I let go with my rifle, he went flat on his face and started blubberin' like a baby—it was plumb disgustin'," Huron said. "Been diff'rent if I was another Dave Crockett or a second Big Foot Wallace, but everybody knows I couldn't hit a barn door."

The old man shook his head. He seemed to find it hard to take. And Danny couldn't blame him, going around here shivering and shaking all the years the way he had been. "An' you've got two hundred dollars!" the old man said, still marveling. "Did thet sidewinder admit stickin' the stage up?"

"Not after he got to town," Danny answered. "Said he hadn't nothing to do with it; swore it was all a terrible mistake. Claimed he'd just happened to stumble onto that loot, that I grabbed him right after he'd found it and wouldn't let him explain——"

"And when Crosby told him he'd be glad to hear his story he shut up like a clam," declared Huron. "Said he'd save it for his trial and started howlin' for his lawyer."

"Moses Teel?"

"Who else? That whole crowd's thicker'n splatter—Crefts and Teel and Forney. They always work together."

"Yeah," muttered Wishbone, thoughtfully. "An' don't fergit Crefts' hardcase."

"Is he still around?" growled Danny.

191

"No, he ain't here now. Deputy Haines come out here after him an' showed him some kind of a paper. They went off towards town a couple hours ago—even caught up one of our hosses so the bugger wouldn't hev t' hoof it."

"Never mind about the horse. And you don't need to worry about that Clover Cross hardcase," Danny said, tight of lip. "He's going to find out this tough stuff doesn't pay."

After Huron left for home, Wishbone went and got the shovel and they buried poor old Poncho underneath the scrub oaks on the grassy knoll behind the house where he used to take his bones and the bits of dried hides and hoofs and things he lugged in off the range. They took turns digging, and Wishbone must have worked up quite a sweat to judge by the way he kept sleeving off his face. It was a daunsy chore at best and Danny's eyes felt as though they were filled with dust when the old man allowed it was just like putting away one of the family. "Best help with the stock we ever had," he said. "He could git more outen them than any two hands we ever had on the payroll. I reckon you an' me is goin' t' miss ol' Poncho."

Danny gritted his teeth and when the grave was covered he walked rapidly away without looking back. He didn't feel like talking to anyone. It was an hour and a half later when Wishbone found him soaping leather in the harness shed.

"How're you figgerin' t' make the rest of them payments?"

"I dunno," Danny grunted. Then he said more graciously, "I haven't been able to hit on much yet. Now that

Mr. Lark's got his cattle rounded up, Huron's goin' to ask him if he can take off for a spell. If he can, we're kind of hankering to see if we can run down Paleface——"

"Caliban's colt?" Wishbone rolled his eyes. "Great guns, boy, are ye daft?"

Danny sighed, then moved his shoulders impatiently. Sighing was getting to be too much of a habit around this place, he thought. He blew out his breath and said, "He's getting bolder than ever. Went off with some Gourd and Vine mares the other night—ten or twelve of their tops. According to the talk around town, the Stockmen's Association has raised the bounty——"

"You'll jest be wastin' yer time," declared Wishbone. "Thet confounded hoss'll never be ketched! Great Caesar's ghost—three diff'rent outfits hev a'ready gone broke, tryin' t' lay thet dashblamed stud by the heels! You know yerself ol' Calpurnius Trendle had t' finally give up. How d'ye think you an' Jones——"

"We caught the stage robber, didn't we?"

"Thet Forney!" Wishbone snorted contemptuously. "You'll find ketchin' a wild hoss is somethin' else ag'in. Thet stallion's got *brains!*"

"We figure to try, anyhow."

"Aye, try if ye're bound to, but if I had my heart set on keepin' this ranch, an' had t' scrape up all the money you hev t' do it, danged if I wouldn't find some more likely way than chasin' a dang hoss's tail through the mountains! How much they offerin' t' the feller what nabs him?"

"A thousand dollars."

"Well, you'll sure hev t' earn it, I kin tell you thet. An'

193

say! Speakin' of hosses, thet hoss buyin' stranger was around here ag'in—thet feller we was figgerin' might of been the stage robber. I offered t' show him around, but he allowed he'd come back when he could talk t' you personal."

"We can't sell any horses," Danny reminded him. "You heard what Teel said. We can't sell a thing until we lift that mortgage. Snooper hasn't been out here, has she?"

Wishbone shook his head. "Well, I'll go round up some grub."

"Don't fix any for me," Danny said. "I'm going to bed."

Huron Jones turned up the next morning and got Danny out of bed while Wishbone did up the yard chores. He claimed he'd already had his breakfast but was finally persuaded to have a little more. He even insisted on doing up the dishes while Wishbone and Danny rode out to the trap to see if any of the mares had fetched in their foals.

But Danny didn't see any. He shook out his rope and caught up a gray three-year-old filly that looked as though she had good wind. He chose a filly for the trip because, as Wishbone pointed out, in the Quarter Horse breed fillies were generally fastest and to go after a stallion on a gelding would just be asking for trouble.

"Studhosses," Wishbone told him, "jest nacherly can't abide geldin's. They will kill one ever' time they git a chance—some will even pull a man right outen the saddle, they're that jealous of their rule. Range studs an' wild ones is dang tough actors, an' don't you never think diff'rent." He considered Danny in a worried way. "Why'n't you give up this crazy idea, boy? You ain't a-goin' t' ketch ol' Caliban's colt an' you could easy git yerself stove up an' mebbe kilt."

"I know it's crazy," Danny admitted, "and we probably won't catch him, but there's a thousand dollars on that horse. Added to the couple of hundred I've got now, that'll give me enough to make three more payments. I've just *got* to."

"Then I'll go with you," Wishbone sighed, but Danny shook his head.

"Somebody's got to keep an eye on the ranch and you'll be helping me more if you'll do that, Wishbone."

Danny couldn't be sure, but he thought the old man looked more relieved than anything else. He roped out an older mare that he said would be calm enough and husky enough to make a good pack animal, and then went back to the house.

Huron packed the old mare while Danny put his gear on the eager gray filly. They waved good-by to Wishbone and, with Huron leading the pack mare and Danny leading the horse Huron had borrowed from the livery, they commenced the first lap of their journey.

Danny didn't know how they were going to trap Paleface, but he wasn't worrying too much about that part; they could decide on that when they found the horse and saw what kind of terrain he was in. Danny was a lot more concerned at the moment as to how he was going to scrape up the balance of the money due on the note after paying in the bounty on Paleface. He would still have that whopping sixth payment to make and it called for as much as he would already have paid in.

Danny shook his head stubbornly. He would get it. He didn't quite know how, but he would get it some way. If he was able, on his own, to make the first five payments, perhaps Paula's dad . . . He decided to have a talk with J. Cornelius; and today would be as good a time as any.

Danny and Huron talked about all manner of things as they jogged along the trail, about cattle and local politics and the great need for rain in this region.

"Things is dryin' up somethin' awful," Huron grumbled. "There's talk of buildin' a chain of dams up north of here, accordin' to Mr. Creighton. One at Horse Mesa, one at Mormon Flats, another one at Roosevelt; but I can't see what good it'll do us down here. Cost a pile of dough, Mr. Creighton says. Old Tom don't like it a little bit; says it's a lot of darn foolishness. But Mr. Creighton allows it would let the ranchers in the Salt River Valley put a lot of new land under cultivation."

It was about eleven-thirty, according to their shadows, when they came in sight of town. Huron declared that he was hungry enough to eat a bear with the hide on and said the reason Danny was developing such a puny, peaked look was because he didn't eat enough to chink the ribs of a sand flea. He mopped his double chin and suggested they drop in at the Lone Star Cafe for a steak. "May be several days," he said, "before we catch that stallion."

Danny nodded, squinting ahead at the town. Everything was sweltering in a haze of heat and he reckoned all

196

the rattlers would have taken to their holes. He wished he could feel as sure about the two-legged ones. Starl Crefts hadn't been on hand yesterday when he and Huron had come in with Dode Forney, but it was a cinch he knew all about it by now. Lawyer Teel would have sought him out as soon as Danny'd left his office after making those two payments. No telling what Crefts might be up to, but it was plain as the ears on a mule he wasn't going to let it drop.

Danny suggested as much to Huron, but his fat friend didn't appear to be particularly bothered. "Crefts is probably feelin' touchy as a sore-backed bull, but he's a heap too cagey to show his hand in public. He'll put Teel to work tryin' to get Forney off. Coffin Creek, though, is a diff'rent matter. If he bails Charlie out, we're apt to have trouble."

Then he tossed this off with a shrug and a grin. "Charlie's not much apt to do anythin' as long as we're hangin' round town."

That was probably true enough, but the prospect of a meeting with Coffin Creek later did not greatly improve Danny's appetite.

He gave Huron some money. "You take this rented gelding back to the livery," he said, "and then go on over to the cafe and put in our orders. I'll join you there soon as I get back from the bank. I want to see J. Cornelius a minute."

The bank was situated at the southeast corner of the plaza and, not wishing to attract any more attention than

197

he had to, Danny tied the pack mare and his smart-looking gray filly at the hitchrack flanking the bank's eastern side. It was in this part of the building that Paula's father had his office and, as Danny stepped onto the scuffed plank walk, he could see J. Cornelius Herald at his desk, with his feet comfortably propped against an open bottom drawer and his soft white hands folded across his ample stomach.

Here was luck indeed, catching Snooper's busy dad when he wasn't bogged to the eyebrows in work. Perhaps, Danny thought, his fortune was about to take a turn for the better. He *had* managed to pay off a quarter of his indebtedness; all he wanted from the banker was the simple assurance that, if he was able to take care of the first five payments, the bank would take over the mortgage and refinance that impossible sixth.

Was that asking for the world with a picket fence around it? Danny didn't think so. If Crefts had been willing to risk four thousand on Wagonwheel, the ranch should be worth two thousand to the bank.

Of course, the catch to that was that Crefts hadn't actually risked one cent. But would Herald know this? He'd have nothing to go on but the recorded figures of Crefts' transaction; and the mortgage, according to Teel, was right here in this bank where J. Cornelius could look it over whenever the notion intrigued him.

Encouraged by the logic of these imaginings, Danny hurried into the bank and went straight to the corner where Mrs. Ghent, the great man's secretary, kept an eye on the door to the banker's inner sanctum.

"Just tell him," Danny urged, "that Duke Brockett's son would like to see him for a second."

Mrs. Ghent suddenly smiled. "Aren't you the young man who recovered the smelter payroll?"

Danny managed an embarrassed grin. "Well—one of them," he answered modestly. "My friend, Huron Jones, proved a mighty big help. Please tell Mister Herald I'll not keep him more than five minutes."

She was back in ten seconds with her look turned as bleak as a sleet storm. "I'm sorry," she said crisply, "but Mr. Herald's tied up in a conference and cannot be disturbed."

"But——"

"I'm sorry," she said and turned back to her desk.

Danny stared after her blankly; then he clapped on his hat and made for the door, going past the brass-buttoned flunky as though he couldn't get out of the place quickly enough. He'd been stunned for a moment, but he understood now; and the first thing he did when his feet hit the walk was to take a deep breath to rid himself of the very atmosphere of the banker's duplicity. Then his eyes nearly popped.

A yellow-wheeled buggy was drawn up at the curb, behind a high stepping bay, but it wasn't the elegance of this equipage which caught Danny. It was the vision of loveliness in the taffeta dress being so preposterously helped down by Beau Paul Crefts that stopped Danny cold and left him goggling.

Could this really be *Snooper?* She had the same tawny

199

hair, only it didn't look the same somehow under that bonnet and the little blue parasol she held over her head. Where was the pugnacious face he remembered—the knobby-kneed legs—the cocky tomboy?

No, this could never be Paula with such sparkly teeth and tantalizing red lips. This was a picture jumped out of a lady's book! Snooper couldn't move with such grace. She never would have smiled at Beau Paul Crefts so demurely, nor let him take her arm with such a ravishing sigh.

Danny gulped and stood frozen, rooted in his tracks by shock and sudden envy, achingly recalling the last words he'd swapped with Paula, the swell times they'd had together and which he'd taken for granted for so long. Why, he hadn't ever thought of Paula Herald as a *girl;* she'd been more like a brother, someone to romp and fuss with.

He could have yelled for the change he saw in her. For the grown-up *lady* look she affected. For the show-off dress and the swooning stare she was giving that dope of a smirking Paul Crefts.

It turned Danny's neck red and made him clench his fists. But Paula never noticed him; she had eyes for no one but that dandified dude. Looking into his face with a rapt attention while she hugged his arm as though she might lose it, she swept past the beaming doorman and into the bank with a tinkle of laughter that cut through Danny like the blade of a saw.

He told himself he didn't care, that it was no skin off *his* nose if she wanted to fly round with a guy no right-minded girl would let near her. But the all-gone feeling inside him wouldn't believe it. He guessed the all-gone feeling must be the hole she'd left behind her when she had pulled up her roots and jerked them out of his corral.

"Humph—sissy!" Danny muttered. And with a snort of disgust he stomped around to the hitchrack and got into his saddle.

At the Lone Star Cafe Danny found Huron waiting at a table in the corner. Lawyer O'Toole sat with him and looked about as cheerful as a bloodhound's eye. He poked a chair out with his foot and said: "Get the load off your feet. I've got a parcel of news and you'd better take it sitting."

He chewed the stub of a dead cigar while he waited for Danny to sit down and get settled. "We've already put in your order. I'll get right down to brass tacks. Coffin Creek's out of the cooler. Teel put up bail and the judge had to turn him loose. He's on the prod and looking for blood."

Danny nodded indifferently. Graver things than a Clover Cross bully were bidding for his attention, but he straightened up in his chair quick enough when the lawyer said, "Then there's Miss Herald."

"You mean Snooper?" Danny blinked. "Where does she come into——"

"She'll have nothing whatever to say about Forney."

Danny ran a tired hand through his hair. "I don't get it."

"The situation is this," O'Toole grumbled. "When you

201

fetched in the sheriff with that missing payroll, he was charged with taking it off the stage. Forney won't talk; under Teel's instructions he's saving his defense for the jury. Now his line will probably be that he found the payroll as innocently as you did. Should we prove that the other end of that cavern trail comes out near the vicinity of where the stage was stopped, Forney will presumably try to claim he stumbled onto it while tracking the robber; that he lost the tracks at first but later picked them up and followed them to the cached payroll. Which makes it his word against yours."

O'Toole smiled sourly. "That's the way it stacks up from where I sit. It's been my angle, of course, to hook him up with the loot by means of Miss Herald's adventure in the badlands. We know the robber transferred the payroll to a burlap bag or gunnysack. Miss Herald told you she saw a rider with a burlap sack traveling through the badlands where no trail was supposed to be. She judged the two trails were going to converge. Upon reaching the point where the juncture should have been, she was met by Sheriff Forney who, under the guise of being concerned for her safety, insisted on escorting her back to town. Once the jury is in possession of these facts, your account of surprising Forney in the act of digging up the payroll in that cavern will get him a one-way ticket to Yuma. But—" the lawyer spread his hands with a shrug, "we'll never convict him without the girl's story."

"And you say she refuses to tell it?" Danny asked.

"She simply won't admit having anything to say."

"But she'll *have* to talk if you put her on the stand."

"She'll have to say something. It needn't be the truth."

"Paula Herald wouldn't lie!" Danny cried; and the lawyer looked at him sadly.

"She'll do what her father tells her to do."

22

STARTLING DISCLOSURES

DANNY and Huron were on the trail three weeks before they caught their first glimpse of the notorious yellow stallion. They were to recall these weeks as three of the most arduous, hazardous, heartbreaking ones they had ever put in. Horse hunting, they discovered, was not easy. They were in the saddle for hours on end, searching the rimrocks with burning eyes, making the rounds of the farapart waterholes, trying to stalk down a ghost that refused to appear. They found plenty of tracks—sometimes quite fresh—but sooner or later these always played out. They got hard as nails. They both lost weight; while Huron didn't get down to one chin exactly, his clothes flapped about him like the garb of a scarecrow. He never complained—not even when he found a lady tarantula in his hat. The horses grew gaunt as grayhounds and buzzards began to sail the bright glare.

The hours in the blazing sun were the worst and it blazed every day, a white inferno of heat with the mercury —except at night—seldom falling below 110.

They moved camp twelve times in twenty-one days, encountering all manner of terrain and hardship. At night they dared not trust the safety of their horses to rope corrals or hobbles. Paleface, if he appeared, might have torn a rope corral to pieces and hobbled horses have a habit of drifting, sometimes straying several miles in a night. Men who use hobbles frequently use a bell also, and the sound of a bell would have warned their quarry. To use hobbles without one meant time lost in finding their horses that would be better used in tracking Caliban's colt.

So each night they staked their mounts to picket pins with thick, soft ropes that would not burn their heels. Whenever the boys feared wild stock was near or there was the chance that big game might stampede their mounts, instead of using picket pins, they dug small deep holes in the ground, burying the knotted ends of the stake ropes in these. An excited horse might jerk a picket pin free but it would take him quite a while to jerk a knot from the ground.

They were in the desert east of the Cobble Mountains the day they caught their first sight of the wild yellow stallion. They were tired, hot and hungry and a long way from camp when, climbing the eroded bank of a dry sand wash, they saw two dark buttes before them, less than half a mile away. In a kind of pocket between the base of these buttes a band of mares and colts were browsing. As the boys came scrambling up out of the wash, a palomino stallion swept out of the band with a shrill blast of challenge. Twice more he roared out his rage at this intrusion, spun round on hind legs and drove his mares and their offspring away like the wind. In less than three minutes there was nothing to be seen but a spiral of dust against the fast-dropping sun.

"Gosh!" Danny cried, and Huron nodded.

"That's him, all right, an' gone like a twister. We goin' after him or what?"

Danny looked sorely tempted but common sense won out. "We'd never be able to track him down short of dark. That would give him all night to get away and hole up—besides spookin' him. We'd better let him go. Where would you say he's headed for?"

"Way he was goin' when he took out of here, I'd say straight for the mountains."

Danny turned his gray filly and sat considering a moment. "We'd stand a much better chance of cuttin' him off from water if we could hold him down here on the desert. On the other hand, down here he could probably outrun us; and it's too late anyway to head him off now. We'll move camp tomorrow."

They moved camp twice before they saw Caliban's colt again.

They were well up into the foothills by this time and their supplies were becoming alarmingly short. They had no lack of fresh meat, since there were jackrabbits everywhere and a considerable variety of larger game, but their flour was gone and their store of beans very nearly so.

"I expect," Danny said as they rode along one morning, "you'd better start for town tomorrow——"

He let the rest trail off. Caliban's colt stood watching them from a ridge about a hundred yards due west! With

206

his neck arched, tiny ears pricked forward and long white mane and tail fluffed up by the morning breeze, he was a picture of pride and beauty. His taffy-colored hide threw back the sun in a blaze of glory. His eyes looked them over curiously. He pawed the ground a couple of times and tossed a tentative call, appearing visibly gratified when Danny's gray filly whinnied eagerly.

Striving hard to hold his voice to conversational level, Danny told Huron to ride back a way until he was out of Paleface's sight, to then circle round and try to come up in back of the stallion. "Keep your rope loose and I'll turn him right into you."

Huron grunted and rode off as though departing. The yellow stallion looked after him suspiciously until he passed out of sight, then again turned interested eyes on the filly. He nickered excitingly and the filly answered. Danny, waiting until he reckoned Huron had the stallion cut off, eased the gray toward him.

Paleface appeared quite flattered at this attention at first, but as Danny got closer he began to show signs of increasing uneasiness, finally turning and dropping out of sight behind the ridge.

Danny sent the gray filly ahead a bit faster. When she crossed the ridge he saw the stallion again. He had spotted Huron ahead and to the left of him and was disdainfully angling toward a narrow sweep of windswept land which connected Danny's ridge with a flanking ridge below him. Huron, quick to grasp his intent, spurred his horse forward, forcing Paleface to swerve and, because of a forty-foot drop into timber on the right, come trotting back toward Danny.

Sensing a trap, the stallion stopped. Huron, suddenly standing in his stirrups, came charging licketysplit, rope swinging.

Paleface snorted, wildly rolling his eyes. With ears laid back and squealing with anger, he flashed toward Danny with the speed of a bullet.

Danny shook out his loop, made a lightning calculation and, as the stallion swept past, sent the twirling noose straight at him. It was a good throw—a dandy one. But just as the noose would have fallen snug and true, Paleface tossed aside his head. The rope struck his shoulder, fell away and he was gone, shrilling his defiance, thundering off in a cloud of dust.

Huron came up, pulling in his horse. "We might as well call it quits," he said. "There ain't nobody goin' to catch that horse."

"I will," Danny growled. "I'm goin' to catch that horse if it's the last thing I do!"

"Not this mornin' you won't."

"Not this mornin'," Danny agreed. "But I'll get him, wait and see. That's the finest horse I've ever laid eyes on. Golly! Did you see those legs—that stifle and gaskin? I bet you, by grab, he's the fastest thing in the world!"

"He's pretty fast, all right."

"Tell you what," Danny said, "you go on to town and get some more supplies and rifle shells. We'll leave the camp where it is. I'll try trackin' him around for a spell and see if I can get a line on where he's holin' out. He's

208

got his mares cached out someplace and I'm goin' to see if I can't find where it is. See you at the camp day after tomorrow."

Danny was cooking a meager supper of fried jackrabbit when Huron got back with the pack mare. He knew right away by the look on his friend's face that something had happened.

Huron didn't wait to be asked any questions. He said straight out, "The Squawberry Flats bank was stuck up last week! Right in broad daylight—right after they'd opened up, in fact. Only customer in the place was old Mrs. Ogle and the guy got clean away with it. Stood right in the doorway, bold as brass, with his gun two inches from Mrs. Ogle's nose, and told all and sundry just what he wanted——"

"By grab!" Danny cried. "In broad daylight?"

"Yep—just as cool as you please. I guess they was all scared he would shoot the old lady and mebbe they was right. Anyways, them tellers never moved a muscle. J. Cornelius himself came runnin' with what he asked for and, soon's he'd got it, this guy whirls around and went rammin' head on into Actin' Sheriff Haines, who was just startin' in——"

"Haines grabbed him?"

Huron snorted disgustedly. "All Haines grabbed was a handful of splinters! The sun was in his eyes—claims he couldn't see a thing when he started through them doors. Says the first thing he knew this fellow whales into him, knocks him back across the walk and jumps into his saddle.

He scrambled up quick enough, accordin' to all tellin', and got his gun to workin'—claims he knows he hit him, but the guy got away."

"Didn't they chase him?"

"Sure they chased him. But, time they'd caught up horses, he had too big a start. That fellow wasn't pickin' no daisies! Last they seen of him he was burnin' up the grassroots like heck wouldn't have him, makin' for that malpais up around Dutchman's Butte. And that's where they lost him."

Danny shook his head. "I can't think what this country's comin' to."

"Never mind the country—you ain't heard nothin' yet! This guy was wearin' a yellow oilskin slicker, a Mexican hat and a blue bandanna wrapped across his face."

Danny stared. "Why, that's the rig——"

"It sure as heck is. The very same outfit as that guy that robbed the stage—and Haines is wantin' to see you."

"Me?"

"You."

"Well, why didn't you fetch him out here?"

"I never got within a block of him—I was takin' good care not to. That guy was ridin' Rattler; and guess what he stuck the bank up for? The mortgage Crefts has on your place—that and Duke's note is every last thing he took!"

210

23

ON THE TRAIL

ANOTHER SIX DAYS of horse hunting slipped by without further sign of the elusive yellow stallion. After hearing about the bank robbery, Danny had wanted to go right in and talk with the acting sheriff but, by dint of considerable arguing, Huron had finally worked him out of the notion. "You and me both know you never had a thing to do with it, but Haines don't know it—nor anybody else. Mebbe my word'll be enough to clear you, but it's plain as the hump on a camel Crefts'll use every trick he's got up his sleeve to hang this job right around your neck. Take my advice and keep away from town a while. If they ever get you in that jail, you can say good-by to Wagonwheel."

So Danny had gone on with the search instead. As the Turkey Track puncher had so artfully pointed out, he couldn't be presumed to know the law was looking for him. If Haines had been to Wagonwheel—and obviously he had been—Wishbone would have told him Danny was trying to catch the stallion. O'Toole could have told him also.

"Let him find you," Huron advised. "This whole deal's a frameup anyway. You're the only guy in Folderall County would have any use for that mortgage."

"Gettin' rid of those papers wouldn't do me any good——"

" 'Course not. But it could be argued you might not be bright enough to know that. The thing was either pulled to get you bogged neck deep in trouble or to take some of the heat off Forney—mebbe both." He ticked the counts off on his fingers. "This guy was got up like the stage robber. He was ridin' old Rattler, which you told Forney something happened to. He took nothin' from the bank but the note and that mortgage. That'll spell *you* to most folks; nobody'll bother to look any farther."

"Do you suppose," Danny asked, "Crefts could be a bit worried about those signatures? Could have thought up this stunt to get them out of the way?"

Huron scratched his head. "It's a thought," he agreed. "If that's so, we'll never lay eyes on them again—far as that goes, *we* never have laid eyes on them. But the main thing right now is for you to keep out of jail."

It was on the following evening that Danny decided to cut across the Cobbles and have a good look into the Devil's Hip Pocket. This was a maze of chopped up gulches and canyons giving onto a range that spread north and east of the mountains' eastern flanks. It was a place most ranchers and their cowboys kept away from, a desolate region of great heat and little water which had finally been abandoned to the gophers and rattlesnakes as too unfit for man to bother with.

"I think," Danny said, "we might as well break camp right now. We'll ride until we're tired, then get an early start in the morning. If we don't catch old Paleface soon, we're going to have to let him go. We've got just fourteen days until that next payment's due."

"It's a hard world," Huron decided.

They filled all their canteens and water bags. Huron fetched in the pack mare and Danny got busy. He had long ago learned to be extremely careful never to become entangled in any rope attached to a pack animal. Making sure the lead rope was not underfoot, he shook out the blankets, carefully brushed them free of all twigs, leaves and dirt, folded them as Wishbone had taught him and placed them on the mare in such a way that they extended well down over the mare's sides. This was to prevent rubbing because a horse will get more sore there than from anything packed upon her back.

He was careful, also, to see that all the wrinkles were smoothed out. He used a saddle with a sawbuck tree, believing it the best for all around use; and he set it well back, adjusting the breeching to hold it there. He knew what could happen on a steep mountain trail if the pack saddle got to riding the mare's withers. He knew the breast strap wasn't so important and was careful to leave it loose enough to prevent any chance of choking. He pulled the cinches tight with a foot against the mare's ribs so she couldn't hump up on him.

By this time Huron had their other horses saddled and

the packs made up. When these had been secured, the two boys mounted and started off, Huron leading the pack mare. Normally this wouldn't have been necessary as, by this time, she would have gone anywhere with them. But Danny wasn't taking any chances on her seeing Paleface and bolting.

They rode half the night and made camp on Gray Sentinel's eastern slope. Getting up with the dawn, they made a hasty breakfast of sowbelly and beans and again pushed on. At six-thirty they caught their first full view of the region Danny'd hit on for their final try. The pocket itself was actually one great gash splitting open Red Mountain, starting with its highest peak and finishing in a rock-rimmed lake thousands of feet below. The way the sun was now you could see the canyon's whole length, so narrow in places it seemed as though a wagon could scarcely have squeezed between its perpendicular walls.

They studied its contours and, as best they could, its side canyons and open-faced gulches for nearly twenty minutes without discovering any movement. Then Huron spied a group of dark dots which he declared were browsing horses.

Danny wished he had his spyglass. "If those are horses," he said dubiously, "I don't know what they'd find to browse on. Except for that rock-bound lake, there's not supposed to be any water around here."

"What do you suppose keeps that lake goin'? Run-off water from the winter snows? That might be part of it, but I'll bet you it's fed by a bunch of little creeks. If there's creeks, there's grass. Anyhow, I'm bettin' them dots is horses."

They got into the main canyon a little before noon and found it hot as a furnace. They munched a ration of chipped beef, washed down with some of their precious water, and kept going. The trail dropped so steeply in places it pretty nearly made them giddy, but Danny wouldn't quit. "There's deer sign in here and where a deer can go, we can."

By one o'clock the canyon had widened until its walls were almost a quarter of a mile apart. As Huron had guessed, there were hidden springs here which aided vegetation and formed a tiny creek that sparkled and gurgled as it ran through the rocks toward the lake far below.

Abruptly Huron pulled up with a sudden exclamation. "There!" he cried, pointing. "What did I tell you?"

They were horse tracks, right enough. "By golly, he's here!" Danny nodded. "That's Paleface, all right—I remember noticin' that funny shaped frog in his left hind foot."

He could see the tracks were not more than half an hour old. "We'll have to be careful," he cautioned excitedly. "He may be right around close and if he sees us first, we won't get near him."

They decided to leave the pack mare on a stake rope. There was good browse here and she was smart enough not to tangle up in her rope. Danny lifted off the packs and unsaddled her. Remounting, he hurried after Huron who, some two hundred yards down the trail by this time, suddenly held up his hand for silence. Danny stopped. When the hand beckoned him on he eased the filly up gently in the lee of his friend. "Horses!" Huron whispered. "Hear 'em? Sounds like it might be a stallion fight."

It sounded that way to Danny, too. Just ahead of them the canyon made a sharp left bend and it was from the far side of this that all the racket was coming. Listening to those sounds of battle, Danny knew that they might never have as good a chance again. Save for this fight, it seemed extremely unlikely they ever could have managed to get so close without discovery.

"Quick!" he cried, taking down his rope; and they spurred around the bend.

A lush meadow opened before them. To Danny's excited eyes the place seemed crammed with horses. Mares and colts fanned out like splatter, fleeing in all directions as the two friends tore through the waist-high grass, riding their stirrups with swinging ropes. But so engrossed in battle were the two squealing stallions, it wasn't until Huron, streaking down canyon to block the lower trail, let out a Comanche war cry that Paleface suddenly snorted in alarm. On that instant his antagonist, a blocky blue roan with blood streaming from torn neck and lacerated shoulders, abandoned the fight and fled after the mares.

Paleface stood like a horse hacked from stone, only the roll of his white-rimmed eyes betraying the terror that held him rooted. He made a magnificent picture with the sun glinting off his golden body, with the wind whipping through his white mane and tail. Then his head was flung up and, fiercely trumpeting defiance, he wheeled like a shot, thinking to break down canyon.

Huron cut him off there and he came charging back, cut off this time by Danny before he could get into the upper trail. He stopped again, quivering and snorting. Spinning around on his hind legs with an ear-splitting scream, he went charging full tilt at the rock wall behind him.

Though it was hardly more than eighty yards away, Danny failed to see any thread of trail, any tunnel or cavern for the horse to duck into. Broken rocks lay about the base of the cliff, sections fallen from the rim, but they were packed in solid; there was no way through them. Caliban's colt was trapped, or soon would be!

A quick glance at Huron showed that the Turkey Track puncher had the same thought. They had Paleface dead to rights this time! With happy grins, they closed in for the capture, Danny from the upper side and Huron from the lower, lagging only far enough back to make sure both ropes could snag him should he try to bolt between them in a dash for the other wall.

Never had Danny seen a horse run like this. What grace and action—what a thrilling picture! White mane and tail flying, golden legs flashing with the precision of pistons, the wild horse sped like a shadow on the wind.

"Golly! What a beauty!"

Heart pounding madly, trembling with excitement, Danny spurred the filly forward. Very shortly now the stallion must whirl in one direction or the other. The devil would be to pay for sure if they were to let him get away from them now! Huron appeared to have the same notion and rose up in his stirrups with twirling rope.

Nearer and nearer they came to the pile of jagged rocks

that lay like dumped coal about the base of the cliff. The wall threw back the pounding hoofs like thunder. Another thirty feet, another ten and they would have him. He couldn't turn now. He'd have to stop. He'd have——

Incredibly he showed no intention of stopping. Straight at those jagged rocks he flew, straight into the jaws of certain death! He was crazed by fear! He must be running blind!

Danny saw the sweat on Huron's face. His stomach turned cold and crawled. The rocks were not three seconds away when Huron made his desperate throw.

Danny groaned aloud when the rope fell short. Paleface rose in one magnificent leap, to land on the jagged rocks and keep going, scrambling and clattering onto a shelf which the rocks had concealed from the gaping boys.

They pulled up and sat watching him with breathless attention while he picked his way across that shale-littered shelf, slipping and snorting, yet going steadily upward as though he meant to scale the sheer rock face of the cliff.

"Gosh!" Huron gasped. "A mountain goat couldn't get up that wall——"

"Paleface won't, either!" Danny cried, suddenly pointing. "We've got him! We've *got* him!"

And it looked as though they had; at least it seemed pretty certain that the yellow horse was stumped. He had climbed as far as he was going to on that trail. Forty feet above the meadow the ledge had petered out. There was no place for him to go except back down or into space.

"He's goin' to jump!" Huron groaned.

"No!" Danny yelled. "No, Paleface—*no!*"

Teetering on the very edge, the horse looked down at him nervously.

Coiling his rope, Huron came down off his horse and started forward.

The yellow stallion had backed down a few feet from the edge, but as Huron moved into the rocks he went out to the edge again and stood there trembling. He showed the whites of his eyes and hunkered against the cliff in a kind of half crouch, as though gathering himself; and Danny called Huron back.

"It's no good," he said. "He's scared enough to jump. We'll never get him that way."

Huron looked to be a trifle on the peeved side. "If you know a better stunt, go right ahead, Mr. Brockett. Mebbe you're thinkin' of puttin' salt on his tail?"

Dragging a sleeve across his face, he scowled up at the ledge disgustedly. "I ain't no more anxious to see him jump than you are, but we ought to look at this thing a little practical. If he jumps, we've got him. That reward don't say we've got to bring him in alive——"

"I don't want the reward if we have to kill him to get it."

Huron snorted. "You want to save your ranch, don't you?"

Danny led the gray filly back away from the rocks. "If we leave him alone, he'll come down off of there."

"Not while we're here, he won't."

"I think he will," Danny said. "It's just a question of waiting."

"You mean . . . *starvin'* him down?"

"Hunger or thirst, or both of them together——"

"You may be right, but I doubt it. Why'd he run away in the first place? Because he didn't like *people*."

"He didn't like Crefts' methods. He was shapin' up fine till Crefts put Shag Kelley to workin' him. When he sees we're not goin' to hurt——"

"Storybook stuff!" Huron scoffed. "That horse is a bronc—a dang outlaw. Been runnin' wild for ten years an' he ain't gettin' over it in any five minutes—if ever! Just the smell of a man is enough to stampede him; you seen how he done! Long's we're hangin' round he ain't goin' to move one foot. He'd sooner starve."

Danny considered these things in silence. "We'd better fill the canteens," he said finally, and all the time they were doing it he kept thinking about Paleface and about what Huron had said. The need to save Wagonwheel was very real to Danny. The horse *was* a bronc. At the time when he should have been learning to be useful, at the age when care and kindness would have paid the greatest dividends, he'd been subjected to the tutelage of Clover Cross' Shag Kelley. It wasn't Kelley's way to waste time "gentling" horses; nor had Danny forgotten it was the scream of this yellow horse which had lured old Wishbone into Crefts' trap.

"You're probably right," he told Huron. "But I can't do it. I wouldn't ever feel right about Wagonwheel, knowin' I owed it to the death——"

"That's talkin' foolish!" Huron snapped. "There ain't

no horse worth givin' up your ranch for. I can get that son of a gun. Just let me——"

"You'll scare him off," objected Danny.

"He's had some trainin', ain't he?"

"I doubt if Kelley——"

"Wishbone had him on a stake line, didn't he? All right," Huron said. "Then he knows about a rope. Once I get a rope round his neck——"

"He'd never let you. You saw how he was when you started up before; he'd jump before you could throw it. And, besides, we couldn't get him out of those rocks with a rope on. No," Danny said, "that's out. We'll go cut some poles and throw up a corral——"

"Who's goin' to watch him while we're doin' it?"

"Then I'll go and cut them; you can stay here and watch him."

"We'd have to enclose that whole darn rockpile! It would take us three weeks to do a job like that. We couldn't do it in three weeks. And we ain't got *two!*"

Now that they had moved away from the wall, Paleface had backed down the ledge far enough to turn around and was watching them.

Danny said, "He's goin' to get pretty tired of that place. Apt to get right chilly up there at night and powerfully hot in the daytime. He's goin' to get pretty thirsty. He won't have much to look at but this grass. He'll be lonesome for his mares and this water in the creek is goin' to look more interestin' the longer he stays there. I'll give him three days; if he hasn't come down by then, you can try your methods."

"Fair enough." Huron grinned. "What about the mares?"

"I'd sure like to get them, too," Danny admitted—"especially my own. I've been thinkin' maybe some of these roundabout ranchers might be kidded into partin' with a buck or two for such of their stuff——"

"Ought to be worth five dollars a head, anyway. And registered stuff more. After all, these fellows have lost them. You might make a good——"

"You're in on this deal——"

"I'm enjoyin' myself or I wouldn't be along. Any money we get goes to pay out your ranch. What about me—while you're here watchin' Paleface—driftin' on down the canyon a ways and seein' how many of them mares I can find us?"

"Watch out for that runty blue stud."

"I don't guess he'll be aimin' to make me much trouble after that poundin' he took from the yellow boy. I'm surprised he dared venture in here a-tall. He's the kind of Percheron misfit a lot of these boys think'll sire a good cowhorse. I'll fetch old Dolly over."

Old Dolly was the pack mare, but as he was starting off to get her Huron turned back and said, "That ain't goin' to work—I mean leavin' you here. What'll you do for sleep? You can't——"

"Go ahead. I'll make out."

"While you're catchin' your forty winks is when that critter's most likely to come down off of there. You can't stay awake three nights——"

"I'll have him down off that ledge before tomorrow night."

Huron smiled skeptically. Then he fetched up the mare, rolled enough flour, dried beans and salt in his slicker to keep the wolf away, and set off on the trail of the yellow stud's harem.

FOR SOME TIME after Huron's departure Danny put-
tered about, setting up a new camp by the side of the creek,
a good couple of hundred yards away from Paleface. With
malice aforethought, he staked out old Dolly and the restive gray filly forty feet from the water and anchored their
ropes' knotted ends in the ground. He emptied the water
bags and filled them fresh from the creek, making a considerable ceremony of it, and dug out three buckets from
the duffle he and Huron had brought. He got out their
Dutch oven and set it up on a bed of embers, the way he
had so often seen the roundup cooks do. He had a little
trouble gathering fuel in this vicinity but finally found
enough dried cow flops—called "prairie coal" by most
range hands—to get a fire going. Then he cooked up some
grub and ate it with relish, and all this time he didn't send
one look to see what Paleface was doing.

He was pretty well convinced the horse wouldn't attempt to come down yet. He wanted to get him in the

notion that he wasn't at all important to what was going on, which was quite a bit of fooling to do with a stallion like Paleface; but Danny knew horses. He had his father's flair in that respect and, as the cowboys say, could "talk" with them. Having spent all his life around horses, he understood pretty well what things pleased or worried them; what they were most apt to do under a given set of circumstances. He'd discovered that they were very much like children in their reactions.

By ignoring Paleface, he hoped to quiet his alarm. He'd refilled the waterbags to remind the horse he was thirsty and had staked the mare and filly away from the creek with the same idea in mind, to stimulate his memory by watering them from buckets. He was pretty sure that the stallion wouldn't attempt to leave the ledge before dark, and probably not before morning; but even if he did, Danny reckoned he could cut him off before he could reach the upper trail. This was why he'd made camp in the spot he had chosen. In the weeks they'd spent hunting down the stallion he had schooled the filly to obey without bridle and he could throw the stake rope loose in a twinkling. He wasn't figuring on having to chase Paleface, though. As Huron had reminded him, the stallion had learned about ropes at the Wagonwheel before Starl Crefts had ever got hold of him.

A thing once learned generally stays with a horse and, if he knew about ropes, he would know about buckets—perhaps remember the grain he'd eaten from them as a colt. This was what Danny was banking on; it was on this foundation that he had laid all his plans.

225

So, after washing up his supper things, he picked up two of the buckets, filled them at the creek and took them over to the mare and the filly, still ignoring Paleface. The stallion gave a faint whinny as he stood watching them drink, but Danny paid no attention.

Huron had fetched a sack of grain back from town, thinking to keep their horses from giving out on them. Danny, though laughing at any such foolishness, had been giving them a measure each evening. There was still a little left, quite enough for his purpose. When the gray filly had finished drinking, he emptied out her bucket, put a little grain in the bottom of it and then did the same for the mare, taking care that the stallion could see what he was doing. After they were finished he took the buckets back to camp.

Dusk had fallen now. Danny spread his blankets and lay down as though to sleep. He kept one ear against the ground and rested with his face where he could watch the stallion when the moon came up. He was a lot too excited to worry about falling asleep; nor did he. It was the longest night he had ever put in. Three or four times, near morning, the yellow stallion came down to the bottom of the ledge, sniffed and pawed a few times, looked around and retreated. Most of the time he watched Danny.

With the first crack of dawn Danny got up and fixed breakfast. He took his good-natured time about it, dawdling over his coffee while the stallion fidgeted. After a night spent in such cramped quarters, Danny reckoned old Paleface might be ready to do business but he paid no attention to the fellow at all.

Whistling cheerfully, he filled his buckets at the creek and watered the gray filly and the pack mare. Then he staked them out on fresh grass and, picking up the buckets, went and fetched them a little grain. Paleface, moving up and down his narrow ledge, snorted and pawed and finally nickered impatiently. Catching up the third bucket, Danny scooped some grain into it and headed for the rock-pile. The yellow horse came halfway down the ledge in his excitement but, when the man smell reached him, suddenly snorted and went back.

Danny didn't even look at him. His heart was beating hard enough to break through his ribs, but he kept his pace unhurried and his movements wholly casual. Still not looking at the horse, he climbed up into the rocks, placed his bucket at the bottom of the ledge, climbed down and returned to his camp.

The sun was five hours high before the horse would approach the formidable receptacle. Even then he wouldn't touch it. Danny lost count of the false starts he made before he conquered his fear enough to come up and sniff it. He jerked his head back then as though a scorpion had stung him and went scrambling back to safety.

A quarter hour passed before he came down again. This time he actually touched the bucket. He backed nervously away, thrust his nose up into the air and made a horrible grimace. He flapped his upper lip like an old woman shaking out a rug.

But he couldn't keep away now. The bucket drew him like a magnet. Hunger and curiosity both had hold of him. With ludicrous caution and very obvious suspicion, he finally lowered his muzzle and felt around in the bucket's bottom.

Again his head came up with curled-back lip and he waggled it very comically. But he appeared to fancy the taste of the grain, after all, and soon had his nose back into it. He didn't lift his head again until the last of the food was gone. Then he nudged the bucket with an experimental hoof and sent it clattering into the rocks.

Danny went out and retrieved it and sat there a while, softly talking to the stallion and, that evening, he repeated the process and fetched Paleface a drink after he'd eaten his grain. When he returned for the bucket he talked to him again. He couldn't tell how much this business with the bucket brought back his days as a colt to the stallion, but he felt very much encouraged. He hadn't coaxed Paleface off the ledge before sunset but he thought, with luck, he might succeed tomorrow.

When he rolled up in his blankets he put his lass rope underneath him so the dampness wouldn't kink it all up before morning. He might get only one chance to put his loop around Paleface and he didn't mean to gamble any more than he had to.

Paula came stealing into his thought unbidden, as she had done so often of late. She was all fixed up in her grown lady's dress as she'd been that day in front of the bank, lovely as a barn ablaze and just about as hateful. It was a dreadful vision, her on the arm of that smirking Paul Crefts! But, Danny thought, he had no one to blame but his own durn self for telling her off like he had in front of Creighton. And to make everything a thousand times

228

worse, he'd let her birthday go by without giving her a present. No wonder she'd refused to open up about Forney! She would never tell it now.

It was odd how sad and deep-down miserable the thought of a girl could make a fellow; but that was how it was. He might as well admit it. He had never thought about love and Paula Herald, but he considered it now, with his thinking going down a long and lonely spiral to a flock of dread tomorrows. Paul and Paula. Just like corned beef and cabbage. She would probably marry that low-down fellow now and go out to live at the Clover— Why, they might even live at the Wagonwheel, if Crefts got the place away from him!

It hadn't entered Danny's calculations that he might fall asleep, yet the next thing he knew he found his eyes wide open, staring in consternation at an empty ledge. The yellow stallion was gone!

On the edge of panic, starting up in dismay, he heard the gray filly nicker. At once, so swiftly as to seem almost an echo, the call repeated itself from the direction of the wall. Across the dark meadow a cloppety-clop of hoofs came sweeping in crescendo.

A chaos of emotions held Danny rigid in his blankets. The stallion hadn't gone yet—he was coming after the filly! Scarcely daring to breathe lest some telltale movement catch the stallion's eagle eye, Danny slid his hand beneath him, fingers closing on the rope.

Careful, careful, an inner voice cautioned. Let him get up closer.

It was fearfully hard to remain there in the shadows of

that moon-bathed wall with the racketing pound of hoofs rolling over the meadow; hard to hold yourself still when every nerve and tortured muscle howled in agony for action. What if Paleface didn't come for the filly? What if, even now, he were speeding like the wind to cut into the upper trail?

Danny's hand grew damp around the coils of his rope, but he made himself lie still, knowing a wrong move now would lose him Caliban's colt forever. The gray filly was staked barely forty feet away; the farthest point of any circle she might make was twenty feet more. Danny's rope was a thirty-foot one, so the only possible chance he had was to let his quarry become engrossed with the filly.

Danny prayed desperately that the stallion would and that the filly's rope would hold her. He could see her now against the moon-silvered ledge, all attention with excitement.

Now he saw the stallion—he was wheeling to stop in front of her. He could hear the filly squeal. Now they were touching noses.

Not yet—not yet, Danny told himself. Give him a little longer and he might forget the wary caution this wild, free life had bred in him; at least forget enough so that——

The filly whirled away. She paced a circle, running the full, clear sweep of her rope, whinnying at him. Now she was coming around again, this time the stallion circling with her, showing off.

Danny was hard pressed then to stay quiet; but even when they were nearest him he knew his rope couldn't reach them. He would have to slip up closer and this was no time to try it.

They'd stopped again now. They wheeled and faced the moonlit ledge.

Like a wraith, Danny stole from his blankets, tiptoed across thirty feet of grassy earth, flattening into the deeper shadows barely in time to escape their notice as the filly whirled once more and kicked up her heels. Paleface appeared to go into a fury. He reared, his hind feet shaking the ground, his shape sharply limned against the bright cliff.

Danny flung his loop.

Paleface heard it coming and tried to throw himself aside—too late! He screamed with rage and Danny braced himself, half expecting the stallion to tear the rope from his hands.

But Paleface remembered. Angry, bewildered and frightened, he stood quivering in his tracks, knowing better than to fight the hateful thing about his neck.

25

"LET'S SEE THE COLOR OF YOUR MONEY"

THEIR DUST must have been seen from a good way off because when Danny, leading Paleface, with Huron herding his harem behind him, turned into the Squawberry Flats stockyards, half the town was assembled to find out what was happening.

As Huron said later, with a deal of pleased chuckling, "Looked like everybody and his grandmaw was out there. I never seen so many bugged eyes and gawpin' faces since Jim Woofter chased his pig across the plaza with two guns blazing! Sure done me good. I reckon folks know now who the horse hunters are around *this* hunk of prairie!"

There wasn't much doubt that folks recognized Paleface. His name was passed around with considerable excitement, and both Danny and Huron were asked a million questions, to which they had neither the time nor patience to return adequate answers.

"Let 'em stew," called Huron. "If they can't see what we've got, they better get themselves fitted for spectacles."

When they had the mares and their progeny safely closed into the biggest corral and Paleface shut into a smaller one next to it, Huron heaved a great sigh of relief. "There's been times, I don't mind tellin' you private, when I wasn't even sure we could fetch our *selves* in."

Danny, squinting through the dust, pushed up his bandanna and mopped off his face. "We aren't done with this yet," he answered, watching the yellow stallion running nickering and snorting up and down the heavy fence. "Teel was here a while ago; I wouldn't be surprised if someone tried to turn this——"

"Oh-oh!" Huron said, looking nervous.

The words were hardly out of his mouth when a harsh voice rasped, "*I wanta see you!*" And a rough hand, catching Danny by the shoulder, spun him around.

It was Acting-Sheriff Haines. He had a gun in his fist and a grinning Coffin Creek Charlie hulking just behind his elbow.

"Well," Danny said, "I guess you're seeing me, Mr. Haines."

"An' I don't want none of your lip. Go on—get movin' now. Step lively."

"Would you mind telling me what this is all about?"

"You'll find out what it's about before I get done with you," the officer promised. "Never mind them horses. We're goin' over to my of——"

"What's going on here?" a new voice demanded, and Danny felt a mighty gladness to see O'Toole come pushing through the crowd. "What do you think you're doing, Haines?"

"I'm takin' this feller——"

"I can see that much. Laying the foundation for another false arrest?"

"You keep your dang trap outa this! All's I'm doin' is taking him over to my office for questionin'——"

"What's the gun for, then? Afraid he'll get away from you? That why you've got this jailbird helping you?" O'Toole flicked a contemptuous thumb at Coffin Creek Charlie. "It sure beats all, the kind of clowns that get elected in this county for public office."

The star-packer's scarlet cheeks looked poisonous. But while he stood fuming and spluttering the Clover Cross hardcase, with a savage snarl, caught the lawyer by the shirtfront and hoisted him clear of the ground. "Fer two cents, you dang little shyster, I would pop you right in the kisser!"

O'Toole, though shaken, wasn't taken back a bit. "Give him the two cents, somebody. If I'm going to get smacked, I want everyone to see it."

"Ahr," Coffin Creek grated, "I wouldn't dirty my hands on you!" And he set O'Toole back on the ground very carefully.

The lawyer straightened his celluloid collar. He said briskly to Haines, "Are you questioning my client or aren't you?"

"You're dang right I am——"

"Then let's get over to your office and cut out this gab."

The first thing Haines said when they got to his office was, "I'm goin' to get to the bottom of this an' I'll get there quicker if you keep quiet, O'Toole." Then he waggled a finger under Danny's nose. "Where was you on the mornin' of the eighteenth? Now don't give me no run-around. I want the truth—understand?"

"I was about eight miles east of Shadow Creek Basin, huntin' horses."

"Got any proof of that?"

"Huron Jones was with me."

"Humph! Jones! I wouldn't take his word on a——"

"Well, I would," O'Toole said coolly, "and so will most everybody else."

"Who's packin' this star?" the acting-sheriff rasped, glowering.

"You may be packing the star, at the moment," O'Toole answered, "but that gives you no right to asperse a man's character. When you decry a man's word you're maligning his reputation, and that's slander and actionable. I think perhaps Mr. Jones may wish to institute a libel——"

"I'll take back the remark. Mebbe I spoke a bit hasty. You got any other proof, Brockett?"

"When a fellow's minding his own business," cut in O'Toole, "he doesn't expect to have to furnish——"

"Your name Brockett? Then let him answer his own questions."

"No, sir," Danny said.

"Ain't it true Starl Crefts holds a mortgage on your place?"

"Yes, sir."

"Oh. So you admit it. What'd you stick up the bank for?"

"I didn't."

235

"Are you denyin' you took a note signed by your father *and* the papers of this mortgage from the Squawberry Flats bank on the mornin' of——"

"Yes, sir. I told you where I was that mornin'."

"Then how does it happen," Haines said grimly, "we found this jigger on the ground where the bandit jumped onto his horse?" He pulled a brass telescope out of his desk. "It's yours, ain't it?"

Danny looked at it blankly and could do nothing but nod.

"And how does it happen he was riding your horse?"

"You mean Rattler?"

"I don't know what his name is. Bay geldin'. Your brand."

Danny looked at O'Toole. The lawyer said, "Better tell him——"

"Just a minute," Haines rasped. "When's the last time you was out to your ranch?"

"A little over six weeks. I haven't been home since we went huntin'——"

"Then how did this Rattler get back to your place the day after the hold-up? I suppose the robber took him back?"

"Either that or turned him loose and the horse went back himself," O'Toole said. "Tell him about the horse, Danny." And when Danny had explained about the stage-robber taking it, the lawyer said, "It's very evident someone's trying to get my client in bad with the law——"

"They don't have to try. He's doin' all right without any help. That's as hairbrained a tale as I ever heard yet!"

"I agree," O'Toole smiled. "Makes the truth pretty apparent. If he'd been making it up, he could have done a lot better——"

"A kid in three-cornered pants could do better," Haines grumbled, but he didn't look nearly as sure as he had looked. A thin edge of doubt had crept into his stare and he scrinched up his lips and glared at Danny reproachfully. "When you fetched in the payroll you claimed Forney robbed the stage. Now you're claimin' the stage robber stole your geldin'. By that line of reasonin' Forney stuck up the bank an'——"

"I didn't say so."

"The guy was ridin' your horse! If he wasn't the one that took off with it, where'd he get it? If he *was* the original grabber, then Forney sure as heck never stuck up that stage——"

"Nothing to prevent Forney having some helpers," O'Toole said, "or, for that matter, being a helper himself. Let's try to clear that up. Here's a fellow trying to pay off a ruinous note secured by a mortgage. He's got six monthly payments, failure to make any one of which entails immediate foreclosure. Not having any means, the fellow takes any work he can find which might help him to meet these payments. Now—who gains the most if this fellow's put in jail?"

Haines gulped, almost swallowing his cud in his excitement. "You talk about libel! Starl Crefts is liable to——"

"It was you put the name to him, not I." O'Toole chuckled. "That's an admission of knowledge you can't

237

very well duck. You going to side with the buzzards or are you turning Danny loose?"

"Drat it! Stake out your lip an' let me think fer a minute——"

"Thinking won't help you. You've got to make up your mind which you're going to be, St. George or a polecat."

The acting sheriff went striding about the room like a hen on a hot griddle. He came back to his desk, put the flats of his hands on its burn-scarred top and said, "Durn you, O'Toole! It could be like Danny here tells it, I reckon—but hellsfire, man, I got a family to think about! I got to *live* in this town," he went on, scowling blackly. Then abruptly he shrugged. "Go on, boy. Get out of here. But watch your step!"

"Now, what are you going to do with those mares and colts?" the little Irishman asked as he and Danny came out in the sun.

Danny explained his plan, ending with the anxious question, "Would that be all right?"

"Yes, you ought to be entitled to some form of remuneration for all the work you put in. The thing poses a lot of knotty legal problems though. Almost anything you like could be argued about it; it could even be argued they were yours to dispose of in any manner that pleased you. We have to remember that a lot of this stock has been out of the hands of its owners for years. Then there's the branded and unbranded angle, and the matter of increase. If the people owning the branded stock could prove to a court they had not abandoned it, you might be made to return it; though in such case, of course, the court would probably name a fixed fee per head which you could charge for your labor."

"Gosh!" Danny muttered uneasily. "I sure didn't count on winding up in court——"

"No reason why you should. Your idea's all right. I'll have some handbills printed up. We'll warn all interested parties to come in and claim all the horses with their brand on and whatever's left over is yours free and clear."

Thanking the lawyer for all his fine help and insisting he be billed for services rendered, Danny struck off to hunt up the stock growers' secretary in order to put in his claim for the reward on Paleface. But, halfway across the plaza, he saw Paula's horse, Plumb Duff, hitched to the rail in front of Kemper's Emporium. Hoping to make things up with her, he cut over.

While he was still thirty yards from the horse she came out in a saucy skirt of blue denim, tied a parcel on her saddle and climbed up.

"Hey, Snooper!" he called. "Wait a minute! I want to——"

But she rode off at a lope without turning her head.

Danny gulped. For weeks he'd been telling himself that pride wasn't worth it, that a man should admit he'd done wrong and apologize. Now, when he'd tried to, she wouldn't even talk to him.

His cheeks turned hot when he heard someone laugh. He squirmed uncomfortably, standing there in the sun, but he wasn't really mad. He felt too sad for anger, longing mightily for something which, without his knowing, had slipped beyond his grasp.

At last, with a sigh, he turned around and went on. Twenty paces later, the sound of horses approaching pulled up his head and he saw the man he was looking for, Christian Fletcher, riding toward him across the plaza at the side of the great Starl Crefts. He didn't have to flag them down. They had already spied him and were quickening their travel, as though they more than half expected he might try to get away.

The cattle baron boss of Folderall County was a tall, gaunt man with hunched, meatless shoulders and an egg-shaped head that was bald as a baby's underneath his black hat. All the hair he had on him was on the backs of his hands and his pale, sly, secretive, frightening eyes were the color of tobacco juice.

"Hold on, boy!" Crefts hailed. "What you figurin' to do with that big bunch of mares you turned into the stock-yards?"

A white edge of fear dug its spur into Danny and he said, with sudden caution, "I'm not quite sure. It de-pends——"

"Well, you can't leave 'em there! I'm goin' to use them pens the first thing in the mornin'. Is that clear?"

"Yes, sir." Danny nodded and, before they could ride on, "Mr. Fletcher," he said, "I'd like to claim the bounty the Association put up for the capture of that wild stal-lion—Paleface."

Fletcher looked at Starl Crefts.

240

"I've got him right here; got him over at the stockyards. I've heard you would pay a thousand dollars——"

"That's correct," Crefts said, "and we'd just as lief pay you as anybody else. Chris will make you out a check soon's you turn the stallion over."

"Turn—" Disbelief rooted Danny in his tracks like paralysis. "T-turn him over?"

Crefts hawked loudly and spat. "Nothin' wrong with your hearin'. Fill out a quitclaim, fetch the horse over and pick up your money. Just as easy as that."

Danny's neck got red. He glared at them angrily. "I never heard anythin' before about *that* part——"

"You're hearin' about it now." The hooded eyes of the cattle baron boss glinted balefully. "What do you take us for? Think we're payin' out good money without we get somethin' for it?"

Danny clenched his fists. "Then you can keep your darn money!"

Crefts showed his snaggly teeth in a grin. He kicked his horse with a spur and rode off, Fletcher following.

Danny, panting for breath, hurried around to O'Toole's. It didn't take him long to give the tale to the lawyer. "And he won't pay a nickel unless I give him the horse!"

O'Toole clucked around like a broody hen. But, as he pointed out, "They can make any kind of conditions they want. I don't see how we can do anything about it. You'll have to give him the horse——"

"I won't do it!"

241

"Well, but what about your ranch? How'll you pay off the note?"

"Gosh!" Danny moaned with his jaw coming down. But as they stood looking at each other, miserable gray eyes peering into blue, the lawyer's expression began to lighten up gradually. He started to nod, but then he suddenly shook his head. "It might work," he muttered, "but we haven't got the time."

"What might work? Gee whiz, Mister O'Toole—couldn't we give it a try anyway?"

" 'Fraid not," O'Toole said, regretfully. "I was thinking we might sell off those mares and that young stuff. . . . We can do it anyway; but, even if we get enough to make the payment, it will be too late to save your ranch. That next payment's due, cash down on the barrelhead, three days from now."

"But it won't take three days——"

"You're forgetting the way these brands are scattered round. Most of these ranchers pay their hands on the first. The hands generally come in that night for a spree. They wouldn't buy enough horses to do you any good and by the time the word gets back to their bosses your Wagonwheel Ranch will belong to Starl Crefts. Besides," O'Toole said disconsolately, "there's a law in this county that strayed stock can't be sold until the recorded owners have been publicly notified and given ten days to put in their claims."

"If we get out those handbills . . ."

"Oh, we'll do that anyway. We would have to do that. I suppose you could sell the increase all right—I mean you

242

wouldn't get in trouble with the law about that; but I can't see any way for you to profit on those mares in time to make your payment." He picked up his hat. "Let's go over and take a look. . . . Here, wait till I get some paper. We'll catalog the bunch and then I'll take the list to the printer."

The sun, fiercely cooking the unshaded plaza, was broiling up heat like a fiery furnace but Danny, scuffing along beside the frock-coated lawyer, was in such a daze he could hardly have told melted tallow from stiff water. Yet he did think of something, and he asked O'Toole, "Have you heard anything about Paula's new saddle?"

The lawyer looked at him curiously. "Didn't even know she had one. What about it?"

"Oh . . . nothin', I guess." But he still wasn't sure and so he told O'Toole about the one he couldn't afford and of how he had allowed Fidelio to sell it to Paul Crefts, who had been in such a swivet because his own hadn't been ready. "It was just before Snooper's birthday and I reckoned Beau Paul wanted the saddle for her. But the funny thing is I saw her not a half hour ago and she wasn't using it. And I saw her right afterwards—right after her birthday, I mean—and she was usin' her old one then, too. What I was wonderin', did he give it to her or didn't he? And if he didn't, then why the tearin' rush and all the fireworks at Fidelio's?"

O'Toole looked thoughtful, but he only shook his head. They turned to the left when they came to the stage depot and took a short cut through back lots to the stockyards.

"I've been thinking," O'Toole said, just before Huron

spied them; "that in a couple of months from now this town will be holding its annual Old Timers' Stompede—the twenty-eighth of September. Having it at the time of the County Fair, of course, there'll be all kinds of contests—calf roping, bulldogging, steer wrestling, wild cow milking. But the thing I was thinking of, there'll be some ripsnorting races. Ed Stokes—he's on the committee this year—says the Stallion Stakes will have a purse of twenty-five hundred dollars. That's an awful lot of money. If only you didn't have to lose your place, I was thinking you might train one of the Wagonwheel——"

"It wouldn't do any good," Danny said, though rather wistfully. "The Wagonwheel horses are all Quarter stock. We've had good blood, but it's kind of played out, my dad bein' sick so long and—. Besides, the Stallion Stakes is a full half mile. We haven't got a horse that would stand any chance against the class of top sprinters that'll go after *that* money."

He looked away for a minute and blinked his eyes hard. "Anyhow," he muttered, squaring his jaw on a gulp, "if we've got to keep this stock for another eleven days, I won't have any ranch. Or much of anything else."

Tugging on his lip, O'Toole considered him covertly. "You might if you'd give up that stallion——"

"Aw, heck," Danny groaned, and stumbled away from him blindly.

"Your name Brockett?" a man asked, catching hold of his elbow.

He was a wrinkle-faced codger in a narrow-brimmed hat

and a loud striped shirt, over which pink galluses kept his wide-waisted, baggy-kneed pants from falling off.

Danny nodded, not knowing him from Adam's off ox.

"Been out to your place a couple times," the fellow said. "Name of Garrity— I buy horses. Understand you raise——"

"I can't sell them," Danny broke in. "Wagonwheel's mortgaged."

"What about this stuff? Your partner over there—" Garrity jabbed a thumb in the direction of Huron, who was standing just behind him, "sort of seemed to think you'd sell it."

"Well, that unbranded stuff," Danny answered, looking hopeful. "I——"

"Too young," Garrity said, "and not my kind of hides. I'm lookin' for polo prospects. Got to have a full mouth. Don't want nothin' under five. Now, those Wagonwheels . . ." he hinted, and looked at Danny shrewdly. "Seven of them I could go for—that one, that one and that one, the dun, those two bays and that brown. Give you a hundred bucks apiece for the seven."

"Done!" Danny cried, and O'Toole slapped his thigh.

Garrity looked at him doubtfully. "Thought you couldn't sell 'em?"

O'Toole chuckled. "What he can't sell are the ones on the ranch. Let's see the color of your money."

26

GREAT CAESAR'S GHOST!

THE LITTLE MAN in the big pants whipped out a roll of bills that was big around enough to choke a hippopotamus and he shed the top seven bills into Danny's shaking hand. Dropping the balance back into his pocket, he said, "Cut 'em over there into that Number 7 pen," and turned a bland look on the lawyer. "Got a bill o' sale form handy? Kind I want don't bounce."

"If this one does," O'Toole said, grinning, "it'll be the first one I ever fixed up——"

"And the last." Garrity laughed, spitting on his fist. "You can find me when you want me over at the Longhorn Hotel."

After the boys had cut out the seven Wagonwheel horses, O'Toole said, "We'll go and get a bite to eat, then I think you had better latch onto your wild horse and strike out for home."

"I've got to make that next payment——"

"You just give me that money. *I*'ll make your payment.

The sooner you get out of this town, the better I'll like it," O'Toole said soberly. "We've had enough luck for one day. Let's not crowd it too far."

"Well, but," Danny protested. "I've got to move those horses. Mr. Crefts wants to use those pens in the mornin'——"

"I'll take care of all that. If I'm to act as your agent, you've got to give me something to do. Now how about money? Got enough left out of that two hundred dollars to piece out two payments, if I put it with this seven?"

"Yes, sir. We had to spend some for a grubstake, but here's a hundred and ten."

"Keep the ten," O'Toole said, picking up the rest of it and tucking it away with the seven centuries from Garrity. "I'll get out the handbills, take care of your payments as they come due and try to get enough from those mares and colts to keep you going for a while. But I want you to get right out of town and *stay* out. If there's anything you need, send Wishbone after it. Get your horse and hide out any time you see Haines coming. Teel will put the pressure on him. They figured he'd arrest you on account of Herald's bank; since he hasn't, they might get Herald to push the matter. Right now's the time to play careful. Crefts is going to be hotter than a biscuit. And don't forget about Coffin Creek Charlie. I want you out of here right away, and take along that stallion before something happens to him."

Danny asked in quick alarm, "Could Mr. Crefts take Paleface away from me?"

"I don't think he could legally, but he might have him

247

stolen or impounded while he goes to law about it. He
may try that with Garrity's mares. When Crefts finds out
about those Wagonwheel mares, he'll probably pry hell up
and put a chunk under it; that's why I want you out of
here. After he cools off, I think he'll put his brain to work,
but right now anything could happen. You hit for home
and lie low till you hear from me."

Danny did as the lawyer had bidden him, spending his
time during the next three weeks in gentling and riding the
big yellow stallion. Huron went back to the Turkey
Track to help old Tom Lark with the early fall work and
Wishbone and Danny spent about all their time with Paleface. He was pretty nervous and excitable at first but he
took to Danny right from the start. Danny broke him
with a hackamore and he learned so fast that in no time at
all Danny was using a bit and riding him with confidence
all over the ranch. He seemed to enjoy these rides fully as
much as Danny and, although Wishbone grumbled and
predicted dire consequences from trusting a "studhoss"
any farther than you could throw him, the two became
inseparable. The stallion's hoofs were hard as flint and
Wishbone said there was no use shoeing him, although he
did take a rasp and even them up some.

Preoccupied as Danny was with the horse, he did not
forget the things O'Toole had told him and kept a sharp
lookout for a visit from Haines. One of the first things
Danny had done when he got home was to repair the
stoutest corral and build it up three rails higher, so there'd
be no chance of Paleface getting away. Not satisfied with

this, he spent his nights outside, too, curled up in his blankets in the shadow of the stallion's pen, just in case Coffin Creek Charlie should come snooping around.

But nothing happened. At the end of the third week O'Toole came out bright and early one morning in a rented buggy, and the first thing he said was, "Well, how's that stallion?"

Danny grinned. "Fine as silk."

"You been able to get on him yet?"

"Git on him!" Wishbone snorted. "I kin hardly git him off'n him long enough t' eat!"

"Shaping up all right, is he?"

Danny answered enthusiastically, "He's the smartest horse that ever peeked through a bridle. I tell you, Mr. O'Toole, you can turn him on a dime and throw nine cents of it away!" After a moment's hesitation, "Care to try him?" he asked politely.

There was no hesitation on the part of O'Toole. "Not today," he said firmly. "A great honor and a privilege, but wild stallions and lions——"

"Aw, he ain't wild—not really."

The lawyer grinned but shook his head. "Let's get out of this sun and I'll give you my report. I've got to be getting back."

If Danny appeared reluctant to leave the yellow horse, this impression was no more obvious than the stallion's plain aversion to having Danny go. Crowding the rails, getting as close to his young master as the bars of the fence would let him, he kept tossing his head and whinnying softly until Danny, unable longer to resist him, said, "You all go on up to the porch—I'll be right along," and turned back to the corral. At once a joyous nicker rent the morning quiet asunder, a sound of such pure happiness that Wishbone shook his head in envy.

"Doesn't he ever seem to want to get back into the hills?"

"Well," Wishbone reflected, "he kinda' did at first. But you see how they are? I don't think he would go if we turned him loose—be a heap more apt t' come traipsin' into the house. Never seen such a hand with a hoss as this Danny. I swear thet boy kin talk to 'em! Never bucked a jump, by grab!"

O'Toole's eyes really opened wide when Danny came riding up to the porch. He was sitting Paleface without any saddle, riding that big yellow devil without reins, putting him through figure eights, making him wheel, walk and canter with nothing but knees and his own shifting posture.

It was incredible. The lawyer said so. Danny just laughed, rubbing the big fellow's shoulder, but in his eyes was the look of eagles, as proud and flashing as the eyes of Paleface himself. He chuckled. "Told you he wasn't wild."

Wishbone nodded. "You kin stake him to a hairpin he's thet gentle. With Danny," he added significantly. "I tell you, I never seen nothin' like it. We cleared a little track——"

"Speaking of tracks," O'Toole said, "have you been keeping in mind what I suggested in town? About the Old Timers' Stompede?"

Danny sighed. "I've looked over every horse on the place. We've got one pretty fair sorrel and there's old Rattler, of course, but we haven't a thing that could run in that company."

"Keep looking. Winning that race is the only chance I can see for you to make that last payment."

He cleared his throat, consulted some papers, chewed his lip and looked at Danny. "Crefts was considerably put out when he was told you were able to meet that last payment. Guess he figured that business with the stallion was going to put you right out of the running. Teel got hold of him right away and they snooped around till they found out about Garrity. That blew the lid off. They went tearing after Haines, but couldn't get hold of him. So they went to the judge. Judge said he couldn't see anything criminal about it; they were horses you'd recovered. Told Crefts to file suit if he wanted to, but advised it might be better to let well enough alone. Garrity, by that time, had departed with the mares and Haines hadn't shown up. Crefts said something about going after them himself, but the judge talked him out of it and he went along home."

"Humph," Wishbone grunted. "We better watch out fer dirty work."

"Yes." O'Toole nodded. "I think we'd better watch out. If he's smart, he'll play it close to the vest. He doesn't have to do anything. He may suspect you can make your fifth payment but that still leaves you faced with paying two thousand dollars by the first of October or losing the ranch and everything you've put into it. He doesn't think you can do it. I don't believe you can either, unless you ready a horse that can win that race."

"However," he continued, "to get down to the mares. Thirty were claimed at five dollars each. Six were bought up at ten. That left twenty-two mares we couldn't get rid of; Ed Stokes finally took them at two dollars a head. Sixteen mixed colts, fillies and sucklings were bid in for a lump sum of forty dollars by the Horseshoe Star. Jed Hoskins, who handled the sale, got sixty-four dollars for his time and bother. The stockyards— Crefts didn't use the pens, after all—charged you thirty-five dollars for feed, care and handling. What was left," said O'Toole, passing up the money, "comes to exactly one hundred and eighty-five dollars."

"You done purty good," Wishbone told him.

"And I certainly appreciate all you've done for me," Danny said. "If you'll just send me your bill or tell me what it comes to——"

"Let's not worry about my bill." O'Toole smiled. "I'll get it out of Crefts when Coffin Creek comes up for trial. Both trials, his and Forney's, are set for the week following the Stompede."

"Crefts won't pay——"

"I think he will. We're going to win that suit against Coffin Creek. The man hasn't any money. But he's working for Crefts. If Crefts doesn't take care of him, he'll lose his tough crew. He's got where he has in this country because his gun-slingers know he'll take care of them, and Coffin Creek's the brass-collar dog of the bunch. Crefts will pay anything we get out of that monkey, and we're

252

going to get plenty. Just wait till I get up in front of that jury."

He chuckled, then said seriously, "You keep that money, son. You'll have expenses to meet, groceries to buy and what not. Besides, you'll need fifty dollars to get into that race."

"Jest be throwin' good money after bad," Wishbone sniffed. "We ain't got a young hoss on the place thet could go a half milé an' do any good."

"Have you seen anything of Coffin Creek?" O'Toole asked, tactfully endeavoring to change the subject. "He hasn't been around town for a couple of weeks. Thought maybe he'd be snooping around here."

"If he is," Danny said, "we haven't seen him."

"He's the one you want to watch out for. If there's any skullduggery afoot, he'll be into it. By the way, I had a talk with your Mexican friend. He sold that saddle to young Crefts, all right. Something odd about that. Miss Paula's been in town half a dozen times lately, but always riding with Crefts or in the same old saddle. And young Crefts, himself, seems to have given up riding. Well, I guess——"

"Uh . . . about that race," Danny questioned. "Any special rules about weights or riders?"

"No, it's wide open. They're riding catch weight and you can put anyone you want to in the stirrups. I wish you'd think about it, son. You've got to scrape up two thousand——"

"I've been thinking about it. . . . You got an entry blank with you?"

"Got one right here." O'Toole shuffled through his papers.

"You fill it out for me, and here's the fifty dollars. Put my name there where it says 'owner.' Where it asks for the breeder, put Wagonwheel Ranch. Where it calls for the name of the entry, put Paleface."

Wishbone threw up his hands. "The boy's teched," he growled. "Runnin' a wild broomie ag'in' a field of real bangtails!"

With flushed cheeks, Danny said: "He was bred to run, wasn't he? Didn't you say he was by old Barlow out of Caliban by——"

"Oh, he's bred good enough, no question about thet. But what's he know of racin'? Ain't never been near a track in his life. You can't jest pull a hoss outen the brush——"

"He can run like the wind. You said so yourself!"

"Sure he kin run—so kin a gopher; but you wouldn't match a gopher at a bunch of grayhounds, would you? Great Caesar's ghost, boy! Thet dadburned hoss is twelve year old!"

27

THE LAST HALF MILE

THERE ARE THOSE who will tell you it takes a pile of work to get a short horse ready. There are several schools of thought on the subject but almost everyone agrees that the very first requisite is to have your horse near a race track. This was where Danny ignored the rules. He kept the yellow stallion hidden out at the ranch and didn't even bother to rig up a makeshift track.

He had thirty-five days to get Paleface in shape, to teach him to behave and to run with other horses. At the end of the fourth day Wishbone quit cold. "I dunno where you got all these crazy idears, but you never latched onto them around no racetrack! No leg liniment! No bandages! No workouts! How do you figger this hoss is goin' t' learn—larrupin' aroun' through the brush in the moonlight? Or was you figgerin' t' git him a book on the subjeck?"

"I don't have to teach him to run," Danny said.

The old man knocked out his pipe in disgust. "Well, live an' learn, I allus say. No twelve-year-old hoss has got any business in the Stallion Stakes anyhow. Only thing, I thought since you put up the money——"

"Do you suppose," Danny asked, "that Beau Paul Crefts robbed that stage?"

Wishbone's mouth flopped open in amazement. "What in the world ever give you thet notion?"

"I keep thinking about that saddle—" He broke off abruptly. "There! There it is again! Don't whirl around quick, but when you get a chance, kind of let your eye wander up through that mesquite thicket on the ridge behind the barn."

A moment later Wishbone turned, as though to adjust the girth of Danny's postage-stamp saddle, and when he straightened up he nodded. "Someone up there, all right. I seen the flash of glasses. Wait'll I git my rifle——"

"No," Danny said. "It might be Coffin Creek Charlie. Let him snoop. He won't find out enough to do us any harm and while he's busy doin' that, he'll be kept out of mischief. I had a feelin' all day yesterday someone was doin' some spyin' around here."

"But he'll carry it right back t' Crefts!"

"Fine!" Danny grinned. "That's just what I want. Go saddle up Rattler and I'll give you a race. Warm him up a little and I'll run you from the barn to that dead cottonwood down yonder—go on! Shake it up! I want to give him somethin' to look at."

When Wishbone was ready, Danny said, "Now don't hold him in. Give him everythin' you've got."

The distance was roughly about three furlongs and Paleface held the lead to the quarter, piling up six lengths of daylight; but from the quarter on out he began to lose ground rapidly, barely leading by a nose as they went pounding past the tree. Rattler wanted to keep going but Paleface was plainly willing to quit any time and Danny had no trouble pulling him up at all. Danny's face wore a worried look when Wishbone rejoined him.

The old man looked at him sourly. "So you don't hev t' learn him t' run, eh?" He shoved back his hat and glared at Paleface disgustedly. "Boy, you've throwed fifty bucks plumb away."

"What's the matter with him, Wishbone?"

"In the first place, he ain't no distance runner. In the second place, he's a heap too old t' git put in a race ag'in' younger hosses——"

"But he isn't even puffin'."

"By gollies!" Wishbone scratched his head. He looked at the stallion perplexedly. "Walk him ahead a little. Yeah. Keep goin'. Hmm," he said, fetching Rattler abreast again. "Seems inclined t' favor his left front some. Hold him still a minute."

He got down and lifted the stallion's foot. "A dad-burned stone no bigger'n a pea." He worked the pebble loose and got back in his saddle. "We'll work on his feet a little after grub."

That Wishbone should be willing to bother at all Danny took for a pretty encouraging sign. His hopes bounded up, and rose still higher when the old man suggested getting Huron over with a couple of Tom Lark's punchers the following week and trying Paleface out with four other horses. "Thet way," he said, "we'll hev a better idear; but

I don't cotton t' the notion of puttin' on no show in front of whatever skunk's up there back of them glasses."

"We could run him off with the Turkey Track crew by pepperin' that ridge with four or five rifles. Let's try him out tomorrow."

"A dang good idear! By grab, we'll do it, too!"

Wishbone rode over to Lark's that night and came back the next morning with Huron, two of the Turkey Track punchers and the three fastest horses in Tom Lark's outfit. But, though they combed the ridge and found plenty of "sign," they caught no sight of the unknown skulker. "I reckon," Huron said, "that coyote has sloped." They rode back to the house and got ready for the workout.

"You givin' that horse any exercise?" asked Huron.

"Rides him a coupla hours every night," Wishbone answered, "an' fiddles him round on a rope half the mornin'. I try t' tell him what he needs is more workouts. He ort t' hev thet hoss in a stable at the Fairgrounds an' run him over thet track every day."

But Danny only smiled. He was basing his entire strategy on something his dad had told him away back. Duke Brockett had known horses well and out of the wealth of his experience had arrived at the conviction which was guiding Danny now. "When a man makes up his mind he's got a racehorse, Son, the less foolin' around he does with him the better. Get him hard and keep him hard," Duke Brockett had said. "Regular exercise will do it. You don't have to work him on a track every whipstitch. More races have been lost in workouts than have been won in the whole durn history of the game."

What was good enough for Duke was plenty good enough for Danny.

Two weeks later, in the middle of a morning, Clancy O'Toole again drove out from town.

"How's that stud horse coming along?" he asked.

"I reckon he'll run the first quarter," Danny answered with a grin.

"What will he do in the second?"

"Thet's what *I* wanta know!" growled Wishbone. "I keep tellin' him you got t' stretch the hoss out, but he don't want my advice. Alls he'll let me do is whittle around on his *feet!*"

"Break all right, does he?"

"Oh, he gits away," the old man admitted. "But it takes more'n break——"

"How *are* his feet?"

"Feet is my business. Before I enlisted with Roosevelt's Rough Riders I was the best dang hoof shaper west of the Hudson. This critter's feet is all right. I've got 'em honed down t' where they'll do him fer wings."

"He's going to need wings," the lawyer said pretty grimly. "Something's leaked out. He must have shown a lot better than you fellows are letting on because Starl Crefts has entered the race. He's fetched in an outside horse and, from all I can hear, he's got hold of a second Hindoo. A horse named Falcon Knight that's been running in Oklahoma and never lost a race."

"Any chanct of gittin' our entry fee back?" Wishbone questioned dourly.

O'Toole shook his head. "Forty-three stallions on the entry list last week—before Starl Crefts made his entry. Now there's only five and you'll owe another fifty dollars the night before the race. That's what I really came out for, Danny, to find out if you were still set on running."

"Sure we'll run," Danny said; and O'Toole heaved a sigh.

"You've got a lot of grit, youngster."

"Not a question of grit. I can't see that I've got any choice," Danny said. "I've got to win that race or say good-by to this ranch."

The next afternoon, while Danny was rubbing down Paleface and Wishbone was soaping the racing tack they'd resurrected from the dust of the harness shed, a visitor dropped by and pulled up near the barn. The old man spotted her first. He grinned widely. "Look what's blew in with the tumbleweeds."

Nobody else said anything. Wishbone seemed happy to knock off work but Danny kept right on rubbing.

After a while Paula, tucking some hair up under her riding cap, asked, "Boss around any place?"

"Tell her," Danny said, "that she could put her hand out and touch him."

Wishbone goggled. Color rushed into the visitor's pale cheeks. Then her chin came up and her look hit the old man like a pair of blue mallets. "Ask him if he minds if I get out of this saddle."

Danny turned around then. "I thought you had a *new* one."

"I *have* got a new one, if it's any of your business. Paul Crefts gave me one for my birthday. I liked your present, too."

"I didn't know whether you'd welcome any presents from me."

"I don't know whether I would. Is that your horse?" she asked coolly. "Do you think he'll stand any chance next Saturday? They're saying around town he won't last the first quarter; you can get almost any kind of odds you want on him—even thirty to one."

Danny picked up his swipe and started rubbing again. "So you came out here to see what you could see and tell Paul Crefts, eh?"

If he'd been looking at her then, he'd have seen her chin start wobbling. But, since he wasn't looking, all he had to go on was what she actually put into words. "I hope your horse *does* get beaten!" she cried, and wheeled away.

The Fairgrounds Track was a half mile oval gouged from the earth, four blocks north of town. At some forgotten date in the community's early history a Fair Committee with more civic pride than sense about money had equipped the place with a sun-bleached, roofless bank of benches and five unplastered adobe horse barns, each barn divided into twelve double rows of back-to-back stalls. Once each year, for three hectic days, this ancient plant put on a fresh coat of whitewash and awakened to a very frenzy of life.

Danny and Wishbone, with the excitable Paleface, arrived on the grounds late in the evening of the twenty-seventh, the day before the Fair's racing calendar was to culminate in the supreme spectacle billed as the annual Stallion Stakes. O'Toole was on hand and conducted them at once to the stall he had reserved in the name of the Wagonwheel entry. This was in the fifth barn, at the extreme northern edge of the Fair's sprawling grounds; there was nothing beyond it but wide open prairie.

"I can get you odds of thirty-five to one," O'Toole confided, but Danny shook his head.

"I hope you know what you're doing," the lawyer said. "I've sunk fifty bucks of my own in this race and it would sure be hard to see it go down the spout. You'd better stay right here at the stables tonight and keep your eyes open. There's a rough crowd in town and Haines is short of deputies."

After O'Toole departed Wishbone happened to recall a chore of his own that needed tending to and went hurrying off into the gathering dusk, promising to fetch back some grub from the Lone Star. Left alone, Danny gave the yellow stallion a very slim block of alfalfa and, when he'd finished half of it, his ration of grain.

It was right after this that a blurred figure materialized out of the gloom, looked about a little wildly, and then sped straight as an arrow to the dark blotch of tack, hay and sacked grain piled before the door of Paleface's stall.

With a queer, prickly feeling Danny recognized Paula. She didn't wait for any greeting. "Quick!" she panted. "Get over to the Clover Cross stalls in Barn 3— I don't know the numbers—they're the last three stalls at the southeast end; but hurry! Don't stand there like a goon! Get——"

"Now, wait a minute, Snooper——"

"You want to win that race, don't you? Then don't stand there scowling—get over there! And be careful they don't catch you—go on, *go on!* I'll watch your horse!"

She gave him a push and Danny started running.

It was really getting dark now but, by straining his eyes, he was able to avoid the mounds of stacked paraphernalia and rounded the corner of the end barn going strong—so strong, in fact, that he caromed head-on into a group of idling gabbers who went down before his impact like a bunch of out-sized ninepins. Clawing up from the tangle, ignoring the yelps and curses, he dashed around the end of the next barn and paused to get his bearings. Barn 3's broad bulk was before him and the southeast corner was down at the farther end.

There were eight or ten lanterns sending out sickly gleams into the thickening darkness between the wooden awnings of barns 3 and 4. One or two were hung from the awnings (against all regulations); the rest were set on cleared ground between the manure pile in the center and the doors of their owners' stalls. There were no lanterns burning near the southeast end of Barn 3.

Danny, cutting to the left of the manure pile, made his way down the side of the third barn, passing stall after stall at a leisurely stroll, intended to convey the impression he belonged here. He passed a couple of fellows who were walking a horse while they argued which race they should put him in, passed another gent eating his supper off a packing crate; and it came over him suddenly that perhaps he'd been a fool. Snooper and he had moved a long way apart—were hardly on speaking terms. Was it reasonable to suppose she'd put him next to something which might prove disadvantageous to the father of her particular friend, Paul Crefts? Wasn't it much more likely that this was something they'd put her up to?

With a smothered growl, he was about to turn back when somebody rounded the corner up ahead and slipped through the open door of a box stall. A mutter of guarded voices filtered out and Danny, ashamed of his recent suspicions, catfooted forward.

The man had gone into the second stall from the end. There was a nail keg in front of the door to the third stall and Danny lost no time in easing himself onto it. By straining his ears he could catch quite a bit.

Coffin Creek's bull rumble was giving someone a scorching.

"But dangblast and blow it," this fellow said aggrievedly, "I told you I had a date——"

"Yeah. A date! You got no time fer yer ol' man's business. All you got time fer is chasin' these skirts! 'Fyou was any kin of mine——"

"Okay—*okay!* Get on with it. I'm here now, ain't I?" Danny recognized the voice of Beau Paul.

"An' you better be here tomorrer when it's time to ride Falcon; yer ol' man's got twenty grand on that hide an' he's figgerin' this race to cut that Brockett kid loose of the Wagonwheel. He don't wanta be disappointed."

"So I'll be around," Beau Paul snarled testily. "I took

care of that other job, didn't I? Let's cut the gab and get down to cases. What's the deal?"

"Simple as stubbin' yer toe," Coffin Creek answered. "Sticks Gainor is gonna ride the Three Bells' entry, Billy Blue. Sticks is with us. He's gonna set the pace an' wear this yeller hide to a nubbin'. When they hit the stretch turn, he'll give you the rail an' let the Falcon take over——"

That was all Danny heard. Just then something gave his head a terrific nudge and it was all that he could do to keep from falling all a-spraddle. He grabbed wildly for his hat; but something else grabbed for it, too, and the other grabber got it.

A tremendous relief surged through Danny when he discovered his assailant to be nothing more baleful than the horse whose stall he'd been leaning against. But fright came crowding back when this old reprobate, with Danny's hat in his teeth, began flapping his head. He wouldn't let go of the hat for anything, and each downswing of his powerful jaw slammed against the door with a louder thump.

Cold sweat enveloped Danny. He began trembling like an aspen. The stall next door had gone quiet as a tomb and he could picture Coffin Creek Charlie with his hand closing around a gun butt.

It was more than Danny could endure. He abandoned the hat and bolted.

When he reached Barn 5 there was no sign of Snooper, and that was when he really got rattled. All manner of thoughts whammed through his head and none of them likely to brighten his outlook. All his earlier suspicions came back to unnerve him and he flew to the stallion's door in a fever. But the horse was still there. His eager whinny was the sweetest music in the universe; and Danny clung to the door, too weak to move.

Yet only for an instant. Then the thought of Paula's defection was back at him, worrying him worse than ever. If the whole thing wasn't some kind of raw deal, where had she gone and why had she left, after promising to stay here and watch out for his horse? What if one of that Clover Cross outfit had sneaked in here?

In a lather of torment, Danny lighted his lantern. He was just picking it up to go inside and look at Paleface, when Wishbone came back with coffee and steak sandwiches.

Danny waved them away. "No time to eat now. Here—catch hold of this lantern." Ignoring the old man's spluttered protests, he unbolted the door, snapped a halter on Paleface and led the horse out. "Watch close now. See if he limps," Danny growled, leading him around. "Find anything? Does he act at all peculiar?"

"He don't ack no diff'rent than he allus does. What's eatin' you, boy?"

Danny told him about leaving the horse with Paula, of later coming back to find Paula gone. "If those blamed——"

"If they'd been around, the hoss wouldn't be here. You're a-makin' a mountain out of a molehill."

Wishbone seemed to have the straight of it. A half hour's inspection, going over Paleface by inches, failed to disclose anything wrong with the stallion and Danny finally put him back in his stall, worriedly watered him and locked the door. "I'm going to sleep in here with him. You sleep right outside and don't you dare to go away for a minute."

The day of the race dawned a little overcast but a breeze off the prairie soon whipped away the clouds and gave promise of cooler weather. Danny was up at the first crack of dawn, leading Paleface around while once again the old man went over him as carefully as a mother cat looking over a strayed kitten. As before, they found nothing. Wishbone scoffed at Danny's fears. "If that dang bunch of polecats had done anythin' to him, it would of showed up by now."

"Go over his hoofs again. Look for thorns, nails or bruises."

So the old man looked again and found nothing. Satisfied at last, Danny put him back in his stall and gave him his grain. After he'd finished he gave him a swallow of water and led him around while Wishbone shoveled out the bedding. Then they put him back in and muzzled him to make sure that, in his hunger, he didn't chew up the door. Wishbone headed up town to hunt a hash house. Left alone, Danny went over what he'd learned last night. The Clover Cross strategy was clear enough. But knowing about it was no proof that he could beat it. And the chances were that, having discovered his hat, they would change their plans and cook up some new stunt. They didn't have to be sure the hat was his. The fact that *any-one* might have overheard their talk would be sufficiently good reason for not going on with what they had intended. But there was nothing he could do.

When noon rolled around Danny unmuzzled Paleface, gave him his ration of grain and muzzled him up again. The stallion looked outraged but Danny left him alone until it was time to clean his feet. Wishbone went over them, weighing them in his hand and using the rasp again for a little touch·here and there. Then Danny put some vaseline away up in his nostrils, wiped them out and gave him a swallow of water. Just as he set the bucket down he heard the blast of a bugle—the call to the paddock. It was time to go out there and saddle up.

When Wishbone and O'Toole scrambled into the bleachers that served the Squawberry Flats track for a grandstand the first thing they saw was the upturned face of Paula Herald. She was sitting just in front of them and hastily squirmed around and climbed into their row, squeezing herself in between the two men.

"Just like sardines." She grinned. "Never saw such a crowd in my life—they've all come to bet their last shirt on the Falcon."

Wishbone scowled. "You bettin' on him?"

"What do *you* think?"

"How does it happen you're not down in the paddock with young Crefts?" asked the lawyer. "From what I've heard around town——"

"You shouldn't listen to gossip." Paula laughed. "Gee, I'm excited! I hope Danny wasn't mad about my leaving last night; I really had to. Anyway, I knew they wouldn't bother the horse—they don't think he's got a chance. Do you think he has, Wishbone?"

"He better," Wishbone growled. "I bet my——"

"They're lining up!" Paula cried.

And they were, sure enough.

"Horses now lining up for the event of the season, the annual half mile Stallion Stakes—once around the track, folks—for a guaranteed purse of twenty-five hundred dollars!" roared Megaphone Mike from the judges' stand. "Two thousand of it goes to the winner, four hundred to place and a C-note to show.

"We've got just about time for another quick run-down. On the rail it's *Billy Blue* from Three Bells, Sticks Gainor in the irons. Number Two horse is the inimitable *Falcon Knight*, one of the greatest sprinters ever to put foot west of the Pecos. The Falcon's running today under the colors of his new owner, that great sportsman and long-time patron of the turf, Mr. Starl V. Crefts—young Paul Crefts up. In the third position we have Jim Faigan's *Asterisk*, ridden by the owner. Number Four is that veteran of the short tracks, *Keelbone*, property of Mr. Hiram Falkner— J. Boule in the saddle. Lastly we have the fabled King of the Hills, the wild stallion known as Paleface, captured and ridden by the young owner of Wagonwheel, Daniel Brockett.

"Horses are all in line now. The man is lifting his— Nope, he don't like the look of 'em. He's going to bring 'em back again."

"That Falcon's a neat piece of baggage," O'Toole said. Sixteen hands, with a rather plain head but standing very alert, the Falcon looked every inch a race horse. Stout neck, well inclined shoulders, a shade long in the back but with a good middle and great depth through the heart, good hips, quarters and stifles and an action that appeared easy and frictionless. "Be a hard hide to beat," the man next O'Toole said. "Got this race pretty well in his pocket, I'd guess."

Wishbone handed the man a dirty look and then the horses were brought up again and sent back. At the fourth attempt the starter brought his flag down and the five got away in no great style. *"And it's Billy Blue on top by a nose!"* roared Megaphone Mike above the shouts of the crowd.

"He won't be long," Wishbone muttered to Paula. "Thet yeller bronc breaks like a bolt of forked lightnin' but he never puts all his eggs in one basket. Last time we run him out t' the ranch we had a field of five an' he come in first by more'n a little. Watch now. Jest watch 'im."

Paula *was* watching and Paleface was forging ahead, sure enough, but she wished she knew what the Falcon was up to. He was running easily now in fourth place under wraps. Keelbone was fifth and Asterisk third by a length and a half.

"Going into the turn it's Paleface first by half a length, Billy Blue second and Asterisk," came the gusty shout through the end of Mike's tube.

The yellow horse was still first as they came out of the turn, a good length ahead and still gaining, Falcon running easily in fourth place, five lengths behind. But now, on the rail, Sticks Gainor was giving Billy Blue his head. It was almost as though he'd been running in hobbles, the way he suddenly rocketed forward. Wishbone, glaring, started up excitedly. "Go on, Paleface—don't let 'im ketch you!" In his absorption the Wagonwheel foreman disturbed the cant of the stovepipe hat on the man next in front of him. "Sorry!" he growled as he bumped it again. "Mebbe you better hold it in yer lap— *Come on, Paleface!*" he bellowed. "*Git out there!*"

But Billy Blue was still gaining, still creeping up on the white-maned stallion. Now he had his nose at Paleface's middle, now it was at his shoulder. Asterisk began to fade like a cut flower left too long without water. For a moment Billy Blue and the Wagonwheel entry ran neck and neck, then Gainor went to the bat and the Three Bells' entry opened up.

Wishbone's face grew black as a thundercloud and O'Toole half rose from his seat, plainly worried. So did the man in the stovepipe hat, and Paula seized O'Toole's arm.

"What's the matter with Danny? Can't he go any faster? Oh, hurry, Danny, hurry!" she cried.

"I can see the game now," the lawyer said grimly. "The guy on that Three Bells roan has been fixed. No horse can keep that up and last to the wire——"

"An' who wants him t' last!" wailed Wishbone. "I bet on the broomtail an' lookit the critter—shufflin' along like a creepin' palsy! I could git out there an' run better'n thet myself!"

"I rather doubt that," O'Toole said. "The boy's using his head——"

"Why doesn't he try using the bat for a change?" growled the irate gentleman in the flossy silk tile. "Wouldn't hurt our investment if he'd get off and start pushing——"

"Father," Paula pleaded, "he's doing the best he knows how——"

"Danged if he is!" Wishbone exploded.

J. Cornelius twisted around on his seat like a porpoise and the look he gave Wishbone would have chilled Spanish rice. "I'll thank you," he snapped, "to be a little careful of my hat."

"*Down the backstretch*," roared Megaphone Mike, "*it's Billy Blue leading by nine open lengths, Paleface second and the Falcon Knight!*"

Even Paula could see that Asterisk and Keelbone were off the pace and hopelessly outdistanced. But the big roan was tiring. Paul Crefts had loosened the wrap on the Falcon and the bay was coming up. Gainor's roan was swinging its head now. Nine lengths behind, the yellow horse held his own.

No longer running under a pull, Crefts on the Falcon was coming up fast. The bay's free-swinging stride was gobbling the ground up and he looked solid as an iron bar. But he was still two lengths behind the Wagonwheel entry and a bit over eleven behind Billy Blue, with the start of the turn less than forty yards away.

Gainor twisted his head, didn't like what he saw and commenced urging the reeling roan with the bat. Simultaneously, Paleface began closing. Foot by foot he crept up on the leader, while, apparently running wide open, without shrinking an inch of the two lengths between them, the touted bay Falcon thundered, with his backers howling their lungs out for action.

"And going into the turn it's Billy Blue still on top by three open lengths. Coming up very fast on the outside, it's Paleface second by two and the Falcon. It's beginning to look as though the great Oklahoman might have to fetch his race track with him."

The Falcon's backers roared like a flash flood gutting a canyon. At this taste of their tempers, implemented by Crefts' bat, the Oklahoman began to hunt for the shortest way home. He shut his mouth in a sullen rage and lunged for the rail like a rutting bull. Five lengths ahead, Gainor took a final look, found the Falcon in position and yanked the staggering roan's head sharp around to the right.

For one awful instant the crowd watched spellbound, then rose en masse, with three women fainting, as the exhausted Billy Blue, in a tangle of crossed legs, went down in the path of the extended wild stallion. A scream sheared the silence like the gash of a razor. Through a curtain of dust, Paula, rigid, saw Danny lift the wide-open Paleface in a magnificent leap that cleared down horse and rider as a hunter clears fences and go thundering on, yawing wide in the curve but still keeping his feet and, incredibly, still running.

The crowd was too shocked, too stunned to applaud. And Megaphone Mike, his paid act forgotten, stood ludicrously gawping with his mouth wide open. But the Falcon and Paleface, attending strictly to business, swept into the stretch running neck and neck.

Crefts, desperate, was riding for all he was worth, with his right arm flashing up and down like a flail. The Falcon's nose crept forward, he got his head out front, but none of Crefts' devices could needle it farther.

A quick jerk of Crefts' head showed him Danny, hand riding, doggedly keeping the wild one coming. Then the yellow nose commenced to come forward and Megaphone Mike, suddenly aroused to his job, cried: *"Down the stretch it's the Falcon and Paleface neck and neck!"*

"Come on, Paleface!" chanted Wishbone and Paula; "Come on, Paleface!" shouted Clancy O'Toole—and Paleface came. Foretop flying, flaring nostrils showing their ruby glow, his nose inched out in front and stayed there. Half crazed, Beau Paul swung around in his stirrups, viciously slashing at the game yellow horse whose great heart and courage had withstood every treachery attempted. But good blood paid out. Duke Brockett's judgment was vindicated. The yellow horse would not swerve, his tireless stride never faltered; and this was the way they crossed the line, with the Wagonwheel stallion's nose still in front.

The crowd was delirious.

"Paleface! Paleface!" A thousand throats hoarsely took up the cry. Old Wishbone jumped up and down like a gopher, banging his fists on J. Cornelius' silk hat; and the banker, with the wreck of it over his ears, was shouting so lustily he never even noticed. "Oh, you Paleface! Golly, what a race!"

But O'Toole, more practical or perhaps less hysterical, was anxiously hustling toward that part of the track where,

274

just beyond the judges' stand, two furious youngsters were doing their best to beat each other insensible.

"Now," demanded Haines when a pair of his deputies had finally succeeded in dragging the two apart, "what's goin' on here, anyway?"

"First," young Crefts snarled, "he slams my horse across the head with his bat! Then, soon's I slide off, he jumps me before I even know he's around and——"

"Lies!" Danny panted. "A bunch of lies!"

Blood from a split lip was running down Beau Paul's chin and he fished in his hip pocket for something to staunch it. He pulled out a blue bandanna, without noticing, and was putting it to his mouth when Danny, leaping free, snatched it out of his hand.

"Look at this!" he exclaimed, holding it up in front of the astonished acting sheriff. "Eye holes and everythin'!"

Haines took it, looked it over. "You want to make a statement?" he asked Beau Paul.

Starl Crefts' son sneered. "You're not serious, are you? I never saw the thing before. He must have stuck it in my pocket while we were wrestling around——"

"I don't think so," Paula said, pushing up to look at him scornfully. "That looks just like the one you showed me the night you were bragging about holding up my father's bank."

"So you're trying to frame me, too, eh?" Crefts snarled. "Well, it won't work, see? I got an alibi for where I was when Brockett was sticking up that joint. I was playing penny ante with Lawyer Teel and Coffin Creek Charlie in Teel's office—and how do you like that?"

"I'm afraid you're in for a disappointment, if you're counting on Coffin Creek and Teel to back you up. Teel took the stage for Nogales this noon and I don't think, judging by the amount of his baggage, he plans on coming back."

"Coffin Creek——"

"I saw that gun fighter clearing out of town ten minutes ago," Haines said. "In fact, I helped him leave. I guess you had better——"

J. Cornelius, hot and puffing, pushed his bulk through the crowd. "I'm prepared to state in court," he declared, "that Paul Crefts is the one who held up my bank. I am prepared to go further and admit that I have known it all the time."

"But—but—" Haines couldn't seem to collect his wits.

"I am thoroughly ashamed of not telling you this before. I've been intending to— I simply couldn't get up the courage. Starl Crefts, as you know, is our biggest depositor. I was afraid— But, no matter. The holdup man had on a blue bandanna, like the stage robber, but the hand that held the gun that day wore a turquoise ring on its longest finger. The ring belonged to young Crefts and I notice he's still wearing it."

"Okay," sneered Beau Paul. "So I stuck up the bank to get a laugh on Shrimp Brockett. The old man wanted to throw a scare into him, figuring he might beat it and let his payments lapse. It was Coffin Creek's job, but he didn't have the nerve——"

276

"And you did. Well," Haines said, "I hope you've had your laugh——"

"Aw, what're you howlin' about? Nobody was hurt. I didn't take any——"

"You took Brockett's note and that Wagonwheel mortgage!"

"Are you kidding? All I took was a sealed envelope marked 'Wagonwheel Ranch.' There wasn't anything in it but some folded-up pieces of butcher paper——"

"Why, you goldarn fool!" came Starl Crefts' angry yelp. "I'll——"

"Grab him, boys!" cried the sheriff, and deputies had the cattle baron handcuffed before Paula Herald could say "Gee whiz!"

It didn't take long to get at the truth. Beau Paul, in his excitement, had let the cat right out of the bag. There never had been any note or any mortgage. It was all a villainous hoax, cooked up by Crefts and his lawyer to get hold of Wagonwheel with its long-time reputation for breeding top horses. Crefts was after the ranch and brand and Teel, for his connivance, was to get whatever money they could squeeze out of Danny before they closed him out.

"You're going to get that money back," Haines told Danny. "O'Toole will file suit and the court will award you such damages as can be levied from the assets of Clover Cross. With these and the purse which your horse won today, you will be pretty well fixed——"

"What about Forney?"

"Forney's confessed to robbing that stage both times on

277

his own hook. It was a real break for him when he saw you up there the second time and was able to involve you by riding off on Rattler. He got to thinking if he could palm it off on you, he'd have a wedge to use with Crefts for furthering his own ends. That's the way it is with these crooks—dog eat dog and no more honor amongst 'em than you'd find in a pack of coyotes.

"Forney will get his just deserts. While you went off to look after your horse, Paula Herald told me she'd be at his trial to tell how she saw him in the badlands with that sack. You've got nothing more to worry about. Truth and honesty always prevail. The right wins out every time, in the end."

He shook Danny's hand and J. Cornelius did, too. And a lot of other folks wished him well, quite a number of them making arrangements then and there to breed their mares to Paleface.

Then, while Danny was waiting for Wishbone, who'd gone hurrying off to collect his bets, Paula came up and shook his hand shyly. "You'll be building the old ranch up again now. I'm so glad for you, Danny!"

"I'm pretty tickled myself," Danny answered. "You come over some time, Paula—you come over and I'll let you ride Caliban's colt."